THE BIGGER PICTURE

A Novel By

Minda Budzinak

This book is a work of fiction, inspired by the lives of the many people the author had encountered in her life.

Publisher: Minda Budzinak (August 31, 2019)

Published on Amazon

For inquiries, contact the author at mindabud@bresnan.net

ISBN-10: 0578441233
ISBN-13: 978-0578441238

ACKNOWLEDGEMENTS

First and foremost, I'd like to thank my niece, Virginia Gaces. If it weren't for her, this novel would have never been started. She introduced me, a long time ago, to the world of blogging, and encouraged me to write. When I told her I didn't have anything to write about, she said, "Write anything." She kept insisting, "Write short stories, novels, poems, or any type of articles. Then post them in your blog."

I also want to thank my husband, Michael, who puts up with my constant badgering about my writing issues and questions. He also helped edit my blog posts.

In addition, I want to thank my daughter, Nicole, for helping me finish my book's spine and back cover. She did a wonderful job at incorporating the colors of the front cover into the spine and back cover . She's also my harshest critic. Because of her honest, sharp criticism and positive input, my novel has evolved from a weak novel into a strong, solid one.

I'd like to thank my son, Derek, who is often a source of spiritual inspiration as I read his thought-provoking and philosophical words and musings. He's my spiritual buddy.

Thank you to my friend, Sarah Rodemaker, for designing my book's front cover. And, also a big shout out for my friend, Tim Bjorseth, for reading and critiquing my novel before I sent it to my editor.

Finally, I'd like to thank Marvin Wilson, my editor and friend, for taking me under his wings, not only as my editor, but as my personal writing mentor. Marvin taught me the art of writing. He definitely helped me transform my simple and ordinary novel into a more professional and sophisticated one.

CHAPTER 1

O n Monday, April 12, 1999, Sandy and her husband, Steve, were having lunch at the officers' club at Minot Air Force Base, North Dakota. Sandy looked outside through the glass window, while she sipped some sweetened iced tea. She noticed how perfect and ideal the weather appeared—sunny, clear blue skies, and a gentle breeze rustling the leaves of the trees outside. Inside where she was; however, she thought the atmosphere was cold, gloomy, and stormy.

Even though there was plenty of activity around them—people walking past, others talking at their tables, silverware and plates clanking together—neither of them was talking. There was a palpable tension between them. Not even the delicious aroma of the different dishes mingling in the air could soothe nor defuse the tension.

After a major argument a month ago, Sandy was determined to spend more time with Steve. She hoped that joining him for lunch, at least once a month, would help get them better connected again.

At the moment, the painful, prolonged silence between them was just too much for Sandy to bear. So, she started talking. "Our lab's new chemistry analyzers were delivered at work today." She was forcing a smile and infusing some enthusiasm in her voice, trying to engage Steve in some form of conversation. "They look more streamlined than the ones we have now. They can do BMPs in fifteen minutes and CMPs in twenty-two minutes, which the ER doctors will definitely like."

Sandy thought the topic would interest him, since he was a doctor. "The best thing about them is that they require very little maintenance," she continued, all the while observing him for any signs of being the least bit receptive. What Sandy saw, instead, were Steve's openly unresponsive and expressionless face and a general stiffness in his overall posture. He grudgingly uttered the absolute minimum of words in response to her statements, until they had finished with their lunch and were getting up to leave the club.

"By the way," he said, "I'll be a little late coming home today. The hospital commander has scheduled a meeting at seventeen hundred hours."

"Why?"

"Don't know. It's probably our usual monthly meeting, except that we're doing it today rather than on Friday."

Sandy was suspicious, but she brushed it off. She was all too familiar with the unpredictable nature of military life.

Since Steve was going to be getting home a bit late, Sandy and the children went ahead and ate their dinner. It was almost 7 p.m. when she recognized the sound of Steve's Toyota SR5 pickup in the carport outside, followed by the sudden silence of the engine. She heard the vehicle's door open and close. As she looked toward the kitchen door, she saw the door knob turn. The door opened slowly and Steve walked in.

"How did the meeting go?" Sandy said as she met him at the door. Steve didn't answer right away. *He looks distraught.* She hugged him. Steve didn't hug her back, but he gave her his usual casual peck on the lips. She had to be satisfied with those nowadays. It seemed to Sandy that Steve was only going through the motions with her lately. Gone were the warm hugs and wet kisses he used to give her in the past. *Oh, how I miss those loving and passionate moments we used to share with each other.*

Steve went to their bedroom without saying anything. Sandy followed him. Still waiting for his response, she faced him with a questioning look and demanded, "Well, are you just gonna ignore me?"

Steve heaved a sigh—the kind of sigh that told her he'd like to say something, but was finding it difficult to get it out. "You're not gonna like what I'm gonna say," he finally said, and then paused. More pause created a rigid pressure in the air. He removed his shoes and socks, and tossed his socks in the hamper. Sandy's feelings changed from questioning to worrisome. "I hate to tell you this," he said, and then stopped talking while making a swift change out of his uniform into his shorts and t-shirt.

Sandy's heart jumped to her throat. She wasn't sure she wanted to hear the rest of it. With the way Steve had been acting toward her within the last three years—becoming more aloof, unloving, and less caring, she was afraid the day had finally arrived for him to say they were through. She tried to prepare herself for the worst, but it wasn't helping.

"But I've got orders to go to Kosovo this Saturday. That's what the meeting was about. It's not all a secret, but it's not something we want to be advertising or necessarily be telling people about, either. NATO has agreed to get involved in Kosovo. My group and I'll be assigned there for medical support."

"*What?*" Sandy clasped her heart—even though she was relieved to know Steve wasn't asking for a divorce. Panic soon followed with the realization Steve was going off to another country and would be leaving her and the children behind. She would die if something bad were to happen to him in Kosovo—or anywhere else in the world. "How long will you be gone," she asked, when her nerves finally settled a bit.

"Don't know for sure. I was told to get all my personal affairs in order before shipping out. One thing they assured me was that this deployment would be for at least twelve months."

Hearing the news, Sandy didn't know if she could survive without Steve that long. It would mean she had to do everything while he was away. They'd been married almost ten years and had never been apart for any length of time. After dinner, she cleared the table and started the dishwasher.

She took a shower, then sat on the sofa next to Steve and started massaging his neck and back. It was a routine she was always glad to do. Steve was more talkative and social this time, which made her elated. They talked and wondered how the kids would handle the news and whether she could manage work and the whole household by herself. She'd never asked her family for help before, but she decided to ask her sister, Carrie, and her mom for help this time.

"I'm sure Carrie doesn't mind moving from the dorm to come live with us for a while until you come back," Sandy said. "I'll call her tonight, and also call Mom to see if she could come over to stay with us until Carrie comes back from Florida."

"What's Carrie doing in Florida again?" Steve said.

"She and her class went to attend a two-week study of the Florida Everglades' ecosystem." After the massage, she scratched Steve's back. His pleasant groaning expressed his appreciation to her.

"Oh, yeah, I remember now ... thanks for the massage and scratch."

"You're welcome."

She said goodnight to him and then to the children who were playing with their toys in Sheyenne's bedroom. In bed, after she set her alarm clock, she made her calls to Carrie and to her mom. The news earlier had been as stunning and devastating as stepping on a land mine. She had a difficult time falling asleep, so she tossed and turned. Sleep finally came, but it was seemingly just in time for the alarm clock to sound off.

Taking her lunch break that night, she ordered a Philly Cheese Steak sandwich with a large-sized Coke. No matter what time of day or night it was, all shift workers at the hospital called their meal in the middle of their shifts, 'lunch'. She took a seat and started to eat. Besides her, there were only two other people sitting and eating in the entire cafeteria. The three of them were seated alone, each to their own table. The other two were busy reading paperback books while they ate.

Sandy wished the lighting there was brighter. She didn't like it being so dim. There was a spooky, ghostly feeling she experienced each time she ate there, but tonight she didn't feel it. Her mind was preoccupied with thoughts of Steve going to Kosovo and about her and the kids getting by without him.

She was thankful Carrie had agreed to move in with them until Steve returned, and for her Mom to go over to be with them for a short while. Otherwise, she thought, she didn't know what she would do.

CHAPTER 2

Sandy had Tuesday night off. She and Steve went back to the Officers Club to celebrate their 10th Wedding Anniversary. The night didn't turn out the way she'd expected it to be. She'd felt rejected and frustrated—again. Feelings so strong, they had kept her awake. She was in a bad mood before she left home to go to work on Wednesday night. Her lack of sleep compounded it.

"Sandy, have you met the new temp?" Celia said when she arrived in the lab at Trinity Medical Center in Minot, North Dakota.

"*No*. And I don't even care *who* that person is," Sandy said as she was donning her lab coat. She knew her face lacked the usual friendly smile. Mostly, she went to work in good spirits, saying hello to everybody on her way to the time clock.

"I'm sorry, I asked," Celia said. Her face turned solemn.

Sandy noticed it right away. "Oh, Celia, I'm so sorry. I didn't mean to snap at you," she said with a shake of her head. "I'm just not myself tonight, and I can't seem to shake off this mood I'm in. I'm wrong to bring it to work."

"No worries."

She sensed the curtness in Celia's voice, but she still said, "Thank you." She started to walk away to go to her department, but glanced back and said, "Celia, may I come talk to you later?"

"Sure. What's it about?"

"I'll tell you later."

"*Orighty* then," Celia said. Sandy was happy with Celia's lighthearted response.

"Hi Joe," Sandy said as she passed him by on her way to the blood bank department. Joe waved his right hand in acknowledgement. Sandy was glad Joe was in her team in the nightshift. Joe was one of the few medical technologists who was able to tolerate the nightshift with her and Celia.

Sandy inherited several complicated issues from the evening shift that were time-consuming to resolve. So, she went to work right off the bat and was busy for a solid two hours.

"*Whew*. It's been a nightmare in blood bank," Sandy said when she went to Joe's department. She was standing by Joe and leaning against the counter.

"Why?" Joe said. He was sitting on a chair in front of his computer, reviewing and finalizing hematology test results.

"Well, first off, there were three patients with positive antibody screens that I had to ID. Then there was a transfusion reaction I had to work on, too."

Joe swiveled his chair to face her. "I'm sorry," he said, furrowing his eyebrows.

"Oh, well. At least I'm finished now," Sandy said with a feeling of relief.

"That's good. When would you like to go to lunch?"

"Later, if that's okay."

"In that case, I'll go now before I do my maintenance."

"Okiedoke. I'll cover for you."

* * *

"Celia, how are you doing," Sandy asked. Celia was loading QCs on the designated *number two* analyzer when she went to the chemistry department.

Celia stood straighter from her hunched over stance. "Good so far. Things are running smoothly tonight. What about you?"

Sandy relayed to her the same things she'd said to Joe. Celia also expressed her sympathy.

"Celia, I apologize again about earlier."

"Oh, don't worry about it. I've recovered," she said, giggling. "Something the matter?"

Sandy looked down before she looked up again to face her. "I'm upset with my husband."

"Oh … why?" Her face showed her concern.

"Well, last night was our Tenth Wedding Anniversary."

"Congratulations!" Celia gave her a hug.

"Thank you." She felt loved.

"So, why are you upset about that?" Celia sat on the swiveling chair in front of her computer. She talked facing Sandy, who was then leaning her elbows on the end of the counter.

Sandy straightened herself up before she spoke. "Well … you know … before we went out, I spent considerable time prepping myself for the occasion. I styled my hair, put some make-up on, wore my low-cut, black evening dress, and put on my favorite pair of black heels."

"I bet you looked very pretty." Celia beamed.

"Thanks. I thought so, too, when I checked myself in the mirror. I even thought I was *sexy*." She giggled. "Anyway, my husband rarely compliments me, but I was hopeful he would at least say something, right? But, *no,* not a word. Not even after I made a point to compliment him on how handsome he looked. He didn't take notice of my new dress with its plunging neckline as we ate dinner seated across from each other. You know?"

"Hmph. That's disappointing." Celia pursed her lips.

"My point, exactly," Sandy said with elevated intensity. "I'm glad you see why I'm upset with him."

"I sure do," Celia said, giving Sandy a sympathetic look.

Sandy felt a sense of validation from Celia's show of empathy toward her. However, she didn't have the heart to share with Celia the rest of her disappointments.

As let down as she was at the club Tuesday night, Sandy

had still hung onto hope for the rest of the night. When they arrived home, she had eagerly anticipated a romantic night together in bed. That hadn't happened, either. Instead, Steve turned his back on her and went to sleep. She'd cried silently, wondering, *does he still love me ... at all?*

"I didn't see Joe in Hematology," Carmen, the phlebotomist, said. "Want to let somebody know that I brought some STAT specimens there."

"Joe's at lunch. I'm covering for him," Sandy said. "So, I'll take care of them. Thanks, Carmen." At that, Sandy went to attend to the STAT specimens.

When she went back to Celia's department, she said, "Anyway, I haven't met the new temp, but have you?"

"I caught a glimpse of him yesterday morning as I was leaving, but I haven't met him yet, either. I hope he's more help than Janet was."

"Oh, so it's a guy this time?" Sandy had been on the night shift for six years, the longest of any of the current night shift staff. Celia had been on it for four years now, and Joe for three. Since Sandy had started on the shift, she had seen many faces come and go to fill the different slots, especially the 4th slot in her shift. Aside from her, only Celia and Joe had been able to handle working the night shift. All the others had left within a year of their hiring.

CHAPTER 3

Today, Sandy noticed a stranger standing in front of a computer when she came out of the blood bank department. She walked toward him. "Hi there."

The man made a snappy left turn to face her. "Oh, *hello*."

"Sorry, didn't mean to startle you."

"No problem. I was so caught up with my reading, I didn't notice you walk up to me."

She half-smiled then said, "I'm Sandy. And you are ...?"

He grinned back. "Rob, your traveling tech."

After exchanging pleasantries with each other, Sandy said, "By the way, that's Celia and that's Joe over there." She pointed her index finger toward the two. Rob's eyes followed it. Joe and Celia were busy chatting with the day crew, so they didn't see Sandy pointing to them. "We all work the night shift. You'll like them. They're both easy to get along with."

"Good to know," he said and gave her a warm smile.

In such a short encounter, Sandy found him to be congenial. She had a good feeling about working with him. "Well, I must be going now and leave you to your reading. Good luck reading all those boring procedures."

"Thanks," he said, again flashing that nice smile.

❊ ❊ ❊

"Hi, Sandy, how was your night?" Rob ask the next morning.

"ER kept us very busy. I'm glad I get to go home soon," she said. She glanced at him a second time. She noticed his well-groomed and abundant wavy, dark-brown hair—almost black —especially his ruggedly handsome face, with deep-set eyes of midnight-blue. It's not that she didn't observe all of those yesterday; she just seemed to notice them more today.

When she left work, she went to pick up Sheyenne and Taurea from the babysitter's house.

"*Mommy*," Sheyenne and Taurea exclaimed when they saw her.

"Are you ready to go to school?" She squatted to meet them.

"Yes, Mommy," they said and then hugged her.

"See you later, Doreen," she said to the babysitter.

"See you." Doreen saw them to the door.

"Okay, get in the car and get strapped in."

"Okay, Mommy." The children almost always answered her in unison.

"Mommy," Taurea said with anxiety in her voice, as Sandy pulled out onto the street, "Megan scratched me again." She pointed to her arm.

"She tried to scratch me, too, but I ran away," Sheyenne said.

Sandy was furious, but what could she do to a two-and-a-half-year-old girl who didn't know any better. Sandy wished she could tell Sheyenne and Taurea to retaliate the next time Megan scratched or bit them. But that would be teaching her six-year old and her five-year old daughters a poor lesson in dealing with violence. Instead, she assured them she would call and talk to Doreen when she arrived home.

After dropping off Sheyenne and Taurea at school, Sandy went home. She pulled her cell phone out of her purse, flipped it open, and called Doreen.

"Doreen, Taurea showed me more scratches from Megan today. I know you can't be one hundred percent watching *all* the kids *all* the time, but can you at least ask her mother to trim Megan's fingernails? And, if you see her scratching or biting the kids, to somehow discipline her?"

Doreen said she would try to do what she could.

Sandy decided that was all she could do about the situation for now, and went to bed. While she lay in bed, her mind wandered through a myriad of thoughts.

If I want to continue pursuing my career while the kids are still young, I have to make this work somehow. I'm thankful Steve is supportive of me by agreeing to dropping the kiddos off at the sitter's before going to work in the morning. I know the girls hate going to the sitter's house. But they're only there for one hour. Even then, to hear them talk about it, it's one hour of misery, every weekday.

CHAPTER 4

F riday arrived too soon for Sandy. She had asked for the night off to spend some time with Steve. Steve, though, was busy throughout the day and into the evening at work. It was 9:05 p.m. when he arrived home. The girls were already in bed.

"Sorry, I'm so late," Steve said when Sandy went to meet him at the door. They gave each other a peck on the lips.

Sandy felt a little perturbed that he hadn't called to let her know. "You could have called me. I started to wonder and worry. So, what happened?"

Steve went to change his clothes while she stayed behind in the living room. When Steve came back, he said, "I wasn't able to call because I was on the go ... pretty much the whole day. I attended four different briefings. Did my final out-processing. Had to brief Doctor Levi who is, temporarily, taking over my place at the hospital. Yes, I could've called you before doing my dictations. But I just wanted to get everything done, so I could get outta there to come home. Then, of course, I had to pack everything up and clean my desk."

Sandy felt bad for feeling miffed with him. She went to hug and kiss him. "I made some spaghetti. Would you like to have some?"

"Oh, sure. Please. Haven't had any chance to eat either, so, I'm pretty hungry right now."

Sandy heaped a pile of refrigerated spaghetti on a plate and warmed it in the microwave oven before serving it to Steve. She delivered it to him in the family room and he began to shovel the spaghetti into his mouth. They sat there and discussed family matters and some last-minute details about his deployment while they watched TV. After that, Sandy helped him get his bags packed. She announced the compiled checklist to him.

"Shot records."

"Check."

"Dog tags."

"Check."

"Passport"

"Check."

This exchange went on until Sandy reached the last item on the list.

"Funeral arrangements ..." *What?* Sandy came unglued. She looked at him, incredulous. "F-fu-funeral arrangements?"

"Um ... yeah, well ... you need to designate where you want my body to be shipped to and buried at."

"No, I don't want to do that!" She grabbed her head with both hands and winced.

"But you must, Sandy." He held out his arms, palms up. "The military needs to know in case I die in Kosovo."

"You're not going to die, so why should I be making funeral arrangements?" She flopped onto the couch, sobbing.

"I don't expect to die, either. But, we have to be practical about that possibility anyway. After all, I'm going off to a war zone."

Sandy couldn't help herself. She was inconsolable. She wept for at least half an hour. Her face turned red, her eyes became swollen, and her nose got stuffed up from all the crying.

"Did you get ahold of Mom?" Steve said, when Sandy had regained a modicum of composure.

"Yes, she arrives tomorrow afternoon at five." She sniffled in between sentences. "Carrie also agreed to stay with us until you come back." She sniffled again.

"Good. Thank Mom and Carrie for me. I'll call them once

I'm settled in Kosovo," Steve said while packing his things into his duffle bag.

It had been three months since they last made love. Sandy was depressed when Steve didn't show interest in having sex with her. *His hectic schedule and lots of things on his mind right now surely must be the reasons.* They cuddled until both of them fell asleep.

Sandy was awakened by the alarm clock when it went off at exactly 4 a.m. She put her left arm around Steve, who had also wakened. He rolled over to face her, and they cuddled, but it was short-lived. Steve reminded her he needed to get up to get ready to go.

* * *

At the Base airport, Steve lifted the girls to him—one in each arm. "Behave yourselves and listen to your mommy, okay?" Steve said as he pulled them both into a tight embrace. He kissed them, and they kissed him back. He eased them both down and shifted his attention to Sandy. "I'll try to get ahold of you as soon as I can. Don't really know how things are set up over there. I'm sorry you're left alone with all these responsibilities at home." He gathered her into his arms while she cried.

Why can't he be more like this with me all the time? Why does it take an event like this for him to show me his tender and caring side?

"I love you," Steve said.

Lo and behold! Did I hear him right, or am I delusional? It was one of those rare occasions since they'd been married that Steve was the one to say those words before she did.

"I love you, too … I'm going to miss you … take care," She said in between sniffles. Sandy and the girls stayed and watched until Steve's plane, a C-130, lifted safely off the ground and disappeared from sight.

* * *

At 5 p.m., Sandy and the girls were at the Minot International Airport, located just outside of the city of Minot. They were there to pick up Sandy's mom, Christina.

"Hi, Mom. It's really good to see you," Sandy exclaimed when she and the girls saw her emerge from the terminal gate.

"It's good to see you, too, Punkin," Christina said. At Sandy's age, her mom still called her Punkin, replacing the letters "m" and "p" with the letter "n". Sandy and the girls gathered around her, and they had a long and happy group hug.

"Thanks again, Mom, for coming over."

"I'm glad you need me for a change," she said in her sweet, but sarcastic tone.

Sandy knew where her mother was coming from. Sandy had never asked her parents for anything after she'd gotten married—until now. Even when she had her babies, she'd never asked her to come to help, but her mother volunteered each time. For each child Sandy delivered, her mother went to stay with them for two weeks.

"Steve wants me to tell you 'thank you'. He said he'll call you and Dad once he gets all settled in."

"Oh, bless his heart," Christina said.

CHAPTER 5

Within three weeks of his arrival in the lab, Rob had gone through all the different departments, familiarizing himself with chemistry, hematology, coagulation, urinalysis, blood bank, and microbiology procedures and protocols.

In his third week, Sandy asked him when he would start working the night shift.

"I'll start next Monday. Then I'll be off Friday, and then work the weekend," he said. He expressed his words with a lot of hand gestures and different facial expressions. It appeared to Sandy as if Rob was searching his brain for the information to accurately verbalize his schedule.

"Then you and I will be working together that weekend," Sandy said. "You better enjoy the lax time you have right now, because you might not get many opportunities for a break once you're on the night shift."

"I like being busy, so I don't mind not taking breaks. I'm really looking forward to actually be doing what I've been hired to do, rather than being in this training mode."

"That's the kind of attitude we like from people coming onto our shift. It really makes a big difference when people are enthusiastic about the work. The night shift can be rough, especially when you can't get enough sleep before coming to work."

* * *

The Friday evening before Rob was to begin working the night shift, he went to eat dinner at the local Red Lobster restaurant. A few minutes after he was seated, a waitress came to ask if he wanted anything to drink before making his order. She soon came back with his drink and some hot, freshly baked biscuits.

"Are you ready to order?"

"Yes, I am." Looking at the menu, he said, "I'd like the sixteen-ounce prime rib with the ten-ounce lobster tail, mashed potatoes and gravy, and some mixed vegetables, please."

"Got it," the waitress said, and scampered off to the kitchen. He relished eating the hot buttered biscuits while he waited for the rest of his food.

Since he would be working nights and mostly weekends after this week, he planned to go to the Starlight Club one more time. The Starlight Club was a local club he'd been frequenting every Friday and Saturday night since his arrival. They had a live band performing on those two nights.

It was 9:00 on a Friday night when he'd first visited the place three weekends ago. A female singer had caught his immediate attention and interest.

She's definitely a beauty. He liked everything about her. He liked her gorgeous, long, dark-brown hair that cascaded in different layers down to her waist. He was always partial to women with beautiful long hair. He liked how the woman looked in her dark-blue, tight-fitting jeans along with her almost see-through blouse with its two top buttons undone, exposing a bit of her cleavage. He also enjoyed the way she sang and moved on stage as she tapped her pair of black western-style cowgirl boots on the floor.

Even though he wasn't planning on pursuing a romantic relationship with the woman, he couldn't resist checking out her ring finger. From where he sat, he could clearly see a large shiny diamond.

Rob had enjoyed the night, listening to her soothing, but somewhat gritty voice, singing the songs of Patsy Cline, Patty

Loveless, and Tammy Wynette. The songs seemed to connect with him. They touched his wounded, lonely heart. Time had gone by all too fast. Before he'd known it, the band was playing its last piece and was giving its acknowledgments. It was already two in the morning—closing time.

"Please give Dee a big hand," the bandleader had said. Rob made a mental note of the woman's name. The remaining crowd, including Rob, clapped thunderously. After Dee acknowledged the crowd, she grabbed her purse from the stage floor, behind the drummer. She came down the stage steps, made a goodbye sign to the band, and then took off alone through the back door.

* * *

The next night, Saturday, Rob had gone back to the club to watch the band. The bar was already half full. Cigarette smoke and its discomforting odor filled the room. Loud conversations, over the band's instruments being tuned and adjusted, also filled the room. Finally, the band was ready.

When Dee took the stage, Rob had made note of everything about her. Instead of blue, this night she'd worn a pair of black tight-fitting jeans. Instead of a loose-fitting white top, she wore a thin, black, stretchable top with three-quarter sleeves and a low neckline, decorated with delicate black lace. Her clothes accentuated her exquisite curves. Matching silver jewelry with touches of tiny diamonds throughout was also complimentary. She was wearing the same black boots. If he'd thought Dee looked beautiful on Friday night, on Saturday night he concluded she was elegant, stunning and seductive.

"How're y'all doin'?" Dee shouted out to the crowd. "Are ya ready for some entertainment?" Her twang was not quite like a redneck's, but she didn't seem to care. Rob had assessed that she was a city girl and, that taken into consideration, her attempt at it was impressive. Besides, he could tell, in her heart she was all country.

"Yeah!" The crowd chanted. Dee sang the same songs as the previous night while couples got up to dance. Rob, of course, just sat at his table, drinking Bud Lite and watching her perform. He was completely taken in and seduced by Dee's singing and the way she appeared. His heart was gushing warm sensations all over his body. It was the same kind of feeling he felt each time he had fallen in love with a new woman.

For Rob, the next Friday could not have come soon enough. When it finally arrived, he went to the club, but was disappointed to find a different female singer performing. He went again on Saturday but, still, Dee was not there. His level of interest wasn't the same without her there, so he had left the club around 10:00 p.m. each night.

* * *

Tonight, Rob was feeling optimistic. He checked his watch after he paid for his meal. It was only 7:35. *Too early. The band wouldn't start playing until 9:00. No matter, I think I'll still go there now. Besides, I have nothing better to do back in my apartment.*

Rob ordered his usual Bud Lite when he arrived at the club. Before he sat on a chair by the bar, he walked toward the jukebox. The jukebox was standing against the wall, next to the dance floor. He fed two dollars in and then picked out a few songs to be played. Michael Montgomery's song, *I Swear,* came on first. It was one of his all-time favorite tunes.

Since there were hardly any customers when he arrived, Angela, the waitress who served him, took the time to chat with him.

"New in town?" She said in her casual way. She was standing behind the bar, across from him. Her left arm was resting on top of the counter, while her right hand was holding a cigarette, from which she often took a puff.

"Three weeks," Rob said. He appreciated her direct, but

friendly approach.

"Are ya with the Air Force?" She took a puff of her Marlboro menthol cigarette and blew the smoke upward, away from her face.

He appreciated that she didn't exhale her cigarette smoke toward his direction. "No," he said, and took a drink of his beer. He relished its satisfying cold and smooth taste as it travelled down his throat.

"Hope I didn't offend ya," she said, shifting her weight to her left side, taking another puff. After exhaling, she said with a smile, "Just that most folks who come to Minot are military, stationed up at the base. And, you look like one, too." She tapped her cigarette on the ashtray.

Rob was amused by her analysis, so he smiled back. "Actually, I was one of them, but not anymore." *Working for the Weekend* by Loverboy came on the jukebox. He moved his right leg up and down to the beat of the song. "I came here for a job at the hospital in town."

Through the mirror behind the counter, he could see the reflection of the band gathering up on the stage as he took another drink of his beer.

Angela mashed her cigarette in the ashtray. She pulled a cloth napkin underneath the counter to wipe the moisture where Rob's beer was. "Trinity or Saint Joseph?"

Rob set his beer on the new napkin Angela placed on the counter. "Trinity ... seems like a nice hospital. The lab is short of med techs right now. That's why they hired me."

"That's what you'll be doing, then?"

"For six months," he said, nodding his head.

"Well, it's been nice talkin' to ya. Looks like I gotta get my butt back to work now. Customers are startin' to pour in. Enjoy the rest of the night."

He took note of her name tag. "Likewise, Angela, and thanks for your time." He was glad the jukebox played *Stairway to Heaven* before the band started.

The band had warmed up and it was, at last, time for them

to start playing, but … there was no sign of Dee. Rob left after a few songs with a heavy heart.

For the past two years, he had successfully stayed away from getting romantically involved. But now, Dee, this mystery woman, had captured his attention and was driving him mad. Thoughts and mental images of Dee occupied his every waking moment. They had kept him awake and restless at night, for three weeks now.

Since he'd been burned before, all he'd thought he wanted to do was to admire her from a distance. Even with this in mind, he knew somehow this was different, and there was nothing he could do to change it. He couldn't help but feel that he just had to meet her. But now, she might already be gone. Life seemed so unfair.

CHAPTER 6

I t was Rob's first work day on the night shift. Joe gave him a run through on how things were done during the shift. Fortunately, this night was not as busy as most nights as far as patient testing was concerned, which allowed for more "show and tell" session time.

Joe's primary job was with the Air Force. He worked weekdays for the Air Force and nights for Trinity Medical Center, getting by on three or four hours of sleep. Sandy was amazed at how he could function so well with so little sleep. That would definitely not work for her. She had to have at least six to eight hours of sleep every day. Joe had told her his reasons for his maniacal daily schedule, with which Sandy couldn't completely agree.

Sandy emerged from the blood bank department for the first time since shift change. "Hi, Joe. Hi, Rob. Sorry, I wasn't able to come help you out here. The condition of our heart patient deteriorated today. They took him back to surgery. I would have been done sooner, but he has two different antibodies. I had to crossmatch eighteen units to find six compatible ones that they need."

"We have everything under control here, so don't worry. Just take care of what you have to do in blood bank," Joe said.

"And here I was thinking you just didn't want our company," Rob said.

"Moi? Not wanting your company? You must be joking."

Sandy knew her dimples were showing more prominently as she smiled in a teasing way. "Actually, I'm finally finished in there now."

"In that case, I think I'm going to lunch," Joe said.

"Go for it while you can. You might as well go, too, Rob, if you want."

He shrugged his shoulders. "That's okay. I'll wait and go last."

"How are things going for you?" Sandy asked Rob after Joe had left.

"In terms of?"

"About tonight. Your first night of work." She sat on one of the chairs with rollers.

Rob sat on another next to her. "Good. Joe's been showing me a bunch of stuff, and I'm learning the ropes. How 'bout you? Did you enjoy your weekend off?"

"I did. I cleaned the house and did some laundry."

"Sounds real exciting."

Sandy sensed his sarcasm and shrugged her shoulders. "What can I say? I lead a pretty boring life." She noticed Rob had his eyes fixed on hers.

He took his eyes off of her, but he still kept on glancing at her as he spoke. "I shouldn't talk. My life is just as boring."

"You call your life boring? Traveling all over the place? Seeing beautiful places … and meeting interesting people?"

"In some ways it is, but it's not as exciting and adventurous as you might think."

Sandy wanted to discuss the topic further, but she still had things to do. She decided to save it for another time. "I'm going to leave you alone for a bit. I still have to take care of the chemistry analyzers. If you get busy and need help, come get me."

In between running STAT and routine specimens, Sandy performed the daily maintenance and then ran the quality control—QC—specimens on the designated Number One analyzer. After she finished with the Number One analyzer, she did the same on the designated Number Two analyzer. At last, she loaded the QC specimens on the Number Two analyzer and pushed the RUN button.

CHAPTER 7

T he next night, Joe showed Rob how to do the maintenance and QCs on the two chemistry analyzers. After that, Joe went to lunch.

Rob noticed that Sandy was busy, so he went to help her.

"Thank you," Sandy said.

"You're welcome."

When they got caught up with work, they sat on the two rolling chairs. They talked face to face and occasionally looked into each other's eyes. Rob was studying and observing Sandy with keen eyes. He felt they hit it off right away, laughing at the jokes he was telling her, or some of the things he was discussing with her.

As he spoke, he intentionally made use of a range of different facial expressions, hand gestures, and other body language to get his point across.

On closer inspection, he noticed Sandy's smooth skin. He felt the urge to touch and feel the softness of her face. He, of course, controlled that urge. For all he knew, he might have gotten slapped if he had touched her face right then and there. As he watched her speak, he became mesmerized by her emerald eyes. So unusual, he thought, for someone of her skin color to have those eyes.

That explains her exotic, stunning beauty and natural tanned skin color, Rob concluded after Sandy told him that her mother was from Bolivia. And that her mother was crowned Miss Bolivia, representing her country in the Miss Universe

Pageant in 1965. He also learned that her father was from New Zealand with Scottish ancestry.

He took delight in the fact that Sandy appeared to be truly entertained and was enjoying herself around him. His thoughts of Dee were now gone. He'd become almost entranced with Sandy's attention and verbal playfulness.

Specimens were coming down the chute again, now at a faster pace, and the phones were starting to ring more often to where their conversation was being frequently interrupted.

"I see it's getting busy," Rob said, "so I better get back to my department."

Sandy acknowledged him with a nod. "I'm all caught up with patient runs," Sandy said to Joe when he arrived back from lunch. "I suppose it's my turn to go to lunch since Rob is not yet ready. There are no patient specimens running right now. Analyzers are good to go."

When Sandy retuned thirty minutes later, Joe said, "Now that you're back, I'm going to Micro for a bit to set up some positive blood cultures."

"Rob, I'll cover for you if you're ready to take your lunch break." Rob agreed and left, but he came back after only ten minutes.

Sandy was making a blood smear when Rob joined her. "You're back so *soon*."

"I eat fast. Usually don't sit down for long."

Sandy finished making the slide before she faced him. "I don't want you cheating yourself out of your lunch time."

"I'm not. I'm perfectly okay with it."

"Well. I'm glad anyway, because the morning draws have started coming down the chute in rapid succession now."

The chute was sounding again. "I'll get that while you finish what you're doing," he said.

"Thanks," she said. When she finished, she went to help Rob in receiving the samples into their computer system. Soon, Joe joined them. They were all busy with receiving, centrifuging, and running tests until their shift ended.

CHAPTER 8

After a few days of working together on the same shift, Sandy ran into Rob at the commissary. She had to take another look to make sure it was Rob.

"Rob?"

"*Sandy?*"

"Yes, it's me."

Rob approached her with arms wide open. He bent to give her a hug. She hugged him back. After they released each other, Rob said, "Sorry I didn't recognize you right away without your baggy lab coat and baggy scrubs."

"Same here," she said, chuckling.

Rob gazed at her and said, "By the way, you look fabulous."

Sandy saw his eyes twinkled as he spoke. She took her eyes off him, gushing at his compliment. "Thank you." *You're very handsome, too.*

"You're welcome," he said.

Sandy was perplexed to see him there. "Did you come here with somebody?"

He looked around. "Does it look like I need a chaperone?"

"No—I don't mean it that way. How'd you get in, then?"

With his eyes glinting, he grinned mischievously. "Well, let me see. I entered through that door over there, which I think is where I was supposed to come in?"

"Will you stop?" Sandy said, clapping him on the arm.

Still confused, she frowned and then gave him a side glance. "You're not in the military, are you?"

"Retired."

"*No way* ... I'm not believing that. You look too young to be retired."

He stopped walking—then looked around.

"What?" Sandy looked around too.

"Making sure no one is around," he said. Then he did a Superman pose with his fists punched onto his sides. He also narrowed his waist by puffing his chest out. "How old do you think I am?"

Sandy broke into a fit of giggles at his silliness. She forced to control herself, then pretended to study him. She rubbed her chin with her left fingers as she eyed him up and down. "I don't know ... thirty-five?" She noticed him blushing a bit while undoing his pose.

"Thanks. I'll take that as a compliment. I'm forty-six, and retired almost six years ago."

"Really?" Sandy took a step back, eyed him up and down again ... this time, with seriousness.

"Really. Here's my military ID." He showed his card to her.

She looked closely at it, studying it. "Wow. You retired as a Major at age forty? How did you manage that?"

"Are you familiar with the SERB program?"

"I've heard of it, but don't remember what it stands for or what it is."

"Well, after the first Gulf War, there were a lot of pilots with nothing much to do. To resolve this over-staffing, the military instituted the Selective Early Retirement Board—SERB —program. Under the program, pilots, like me, and people in certain over-filled military career fields, were offered an early retirement with full benefits. I was one of those who took advantage of their offer. After only fifteen years in the military, I retired."

"Lucky you. So, you were a pilot?"

"Yep."

"So, what are you doing working in a medical field?" She gave him a questioning look.

"That's a very good question. Make a long story short, after I got out of the military, I flew commercial airplanes for Frontier Airlines out of Denver. Unfortunately, I started losing my right peripheral vision. When it was time to re-certify, I failed the vision test. The FAA board informed me I couldn't fly anymore." He took a box of Cap'n Crunch cereal off the shelf.

"That's too bad. So, any idea what caused your peripheral vision to deteriorate?"

"You certainly have an inquiring mind," Rob said in a teasing way.

"It's my nature, unfortunately, which many times has placed me in awkward situations," she said, grinning.

"Nobody knew. After blood tests, and MRIs, the doctors didn't find anything. They couldn't determine what caused it."

They continued their discussion as they walked through the aisles, dodging the few patrons along their way, occasionally stopping and picking items that were on their shopping lists. Sandy liked going to the commissary in the mornings after dropping off the kids at school, because it was never busy during that time of day.

"When you stopped flying, you went back to school to get a degree in Medical Technology?"

"Actually, I was a med tech before I joined the military … and long before I became a pilot."

"Hmm."

"My first job as a med tech was working at the Hershey Chocolate Factory in Pennsylvania—in the quality control department. A couple of weekends a month, I worked at the Hershey Medical Center laborat—"

"I *love* Hershey's Kisses. My all-time favorite. Sorry, I didn't mean to interrupt."

"No problem. They're mine, too. Hey, what do you know? We're in the candy aisle. Here, have a bag of Hershey's Kisses. It's on me, so I'll give it to you after we checkout."

"No, don't do that." She tried to snatch the bag from him, but Rob kept it out of her reach.

"Hah, I won." He gave her a sly grin while he placed the bag into his cart.

Sandy looked at him, smiling and shaking her head. "Okay, if you insist. Don't forget to tell me the rest of your story, though."

"Yes, ma'am, um ... where was I?"

"You worked at Hershey Medical Hospital..."

"Oh, yes. Anyway, I didn't want to completely retire three years ago when I was informed I couldn't fly anymore. So, I tried my luck at the Hershey Company and the Hershey Medical Center. Hershey Company didn't hire me back, but Hershey Medical Center did. I really didn't think Hershey Medical Center would hire me, since I'd been out of the field for so long. I had to retest, though, to renew my ASCP certification."

"May I help you, ma'am?" Rob asked an elderly woman who was eyeing an item well above her reach.

"Yes, please. Kindly get a bottle of cooking sherry for me."

"Certainly."

Sandy could see that Rob didn't have any problem reaching the bottle. She was gauging his height to be at least six-foot one to six-foot two inches, basing it on her own height of five-foot nine inches.

"Here you go, ma'am."

"Thank you so much."

"You're welcome."

"You're so nice for helping her," Sandy said once the woman was out of their sight. Rob thanked Sandy for her compliment, but downplayed his act of chivalry.

They continued their shopping. "How come you're doing the traveling job if you were already hired by Hershey Medical Center?"

Rob chuckled. "Do you really want to know the whole story?"

"Sure. Your life story, so far, sounds fascinating."

"To you, maybe, but *not to me*." He laughed again. He stopped walking and Sandy followed suit. His face turned somber. She couldn't help but notice the change. "It's another long story, so, perhaps, some other time?"

She hesitated. "Okay, I'll wait. But the suspense is killing me." She smiled. He smiled back.

"I can smell fresh ground coffee," Sandy said, and took a deep breath to smell more of the aroma.

"Yeah, me, too."

Sure enough, when they turned to the next aisle, a man was grinding some roasted coffee. "Do you drink coffee?" Rob said.

"No, but I love the smell. And, you?"

"I don't, either. And, like you, I also love the smell."

By the time they finished working their way through the last aisle, Sandy had ended up with one heaping cartful of groceries.

"Is someone going to help you unload your groceries at home?"

"No, but I can manage."

"I'd be glad to help … and would like to if you don't mind."

Sandy eyed her groceries and gauged the size of the cart's load. A short hesitation followed before she spoke. "Sure, if you truly don't mind. Thanks."

"My pleasure," he said, and made a funny mock bow of servitude.

Rob followed Sandy to her home in base housing. When he brought in the last bag of groceries, he commented on a framed picture that hung on the wall.

"That's Steve and his crew in Kosovo. Just got that from him the other day. I thought it would look good up on the wall."

"It does look good." He stepped closer to check it out. "When you say you've just received this photo, does that mean he's in Kosovo now?"

"Uh huh." Even though she wasn't supposed to tell anyone, she couldn't lie about it when asked.

Rob moved to the next picture on the wall. "Your daughters?"

"Yes. That's Sheyenne on the left and Taurea on the right."

"They look just as beautiful as their mother," he said, without looking at her.

Sandy felt her face become tepid. She was glad Rob didn't see her blush. "Do you have children, Rob?"

He turned to face her. "No. No children. Can't have children without a wife, right?"

She sensed his cynicism and bitterness. "I'm sorry, I didn't mean to intrude." She was going to add that there are many who are not married, yet have children. But with Rob's initial reaction to her question, she chose to not go that route. She didn't know him well enough to push it any further. She also knew that, perhaps, today was not the right time to be asking him any more personal questions.

"No reason to apologize."

Sandy now felt sorry for him. For the second time in the span of an hour, he looked solemn and melancholic. She wondered why the subject of children and wife affected him that way. His reaction increased her intrigue.

When they finished talking, Rob said it was time for him to get his own groceries home. Sandy thanked him again for his help as he made his way out to his vehicle and drove away.

CHAPTER 9

S aturday night started off with a bang for Rob and Sandy. They were slammed with all kinds of STATs. And then ... "Trauma respond, ETA five minutes, trauma respond, ETA five minutes," was announced in the overhead speaker system.

Sandy went to the chemistry department. "Rob, I'm going to be in blood bank for a while."

"Okay, I'll keep an eye on things out here."

"Thanks. Sorry, I can't answer the tube system right now, either."

"Don't worry about it. Just do what you have to do in blood bank."

Sandy rushed to get there. She took four units of uncross-matched O Negative packed red blood cells from the refrigerator and tagged each one with an emergency release form, along with an assigned tracking number. After logging them on the log sheet, she attached a temperature indicator on each unit of blood, which would monitor the 2 to 8 degrees Celsius temperature needed to be maintained while they were in transport. She packed them in a small red cooler with some ice packs around the open container that held the units of blood inside the cooler.

"Rob," she shouted across the room, "I'm going to deliver this cooler to the ER. Be right back."

"What's the trauma about," Rob asked when Sandy got back to the lab.

"A guy on a motorcycle got hit by a semi. He looks pretty

messed up. The sight of him made me gag; I had to leave. Carmen is drawing his blood right now. ER's waiting room is packed. Even the hallway is full."

"Great," he said, with a roll of his eyes. "Is it this way every weekend?"

"Not all the time, but a lot of the time."

"Trauma specimens ... type and cross four units," announced Carmen while delivering them. Sandy went to work on the type and cross right away.

For standard trauma tests, Rob performed a complete blood count—CBC—complete metabolic panel—CMP—alcohol level, and Pro-Thrombin Time—PT—as well as an Activated Partial Thrombin Time—APTT.

"What's the trauma patient's H and H," Sandy asked Rob when she came out of the blood bank department.

"They're both critically low. Hemoglobin is six-point-nine and hematocrit is eighteen-point-three. Looks like he already lost a lot of blood."

"At least the patient is O Pos, antibody screen negative. We still have ten units of O Pos left after the four I just cross-matched."

The phone rang. Rob picked it up. "Sandy, ER is putting additional order for cross-match two units of packed cells. The patient is now in the OR. So, take the blood to the OR when you're done with them."

"Okay ... thanks. It looks like I'll be in blood bank for a while."

Carmen was still in the ER, drawing other patients, while Ralee, the other phlebotomist, was drawing blood in other departments of the hospital. Sandy came out to help Rob in between specimen incubations. "How're you doing?"

"Well, I'm behind with my maintenance and QCs in Chemistry. The tube system is non-stop. I'd process four to five tubes, then, when I'm done with them, *four more* are waiting to be processed."

He rubbed at his temples, grimaced and said in a near-shout, "And, the loud buzzing sound of that tube system is just driving me nuts. On top of that, the phones are ringing off the hook. The ER doctors and nurses are calling for results *every freaking five minutes*." His face was red and serious.

"I'm so sorry," Sandy said in a soft and sympathetic voice.

He blew out air, flapping his lips, with a slow wag of his head. "Hey, not your fault. I guess, I didn't expect this at all." He gave her a faint smile. "Answering the tube system, receiving all those specimens into our system, and answering those phone calls really put me behind in chemistry."

"Yeah, I'm behind in hematology, too, because of blood bank issues. That's the bad thing about weekends. We don't have specimen processors and no lab assistants. When the phlebotomists are not here, that normally means they're busy. When they're busy, we're busy too."

"That's for sure."

The timer sounded inside the blood bank department. Sandy went in there to finish her cross-matchings and then packed the units of blood into a cooler. "Rob, I'm going to deliver this cooler to the OR now!"

"Okay!"

When Sandy returned, she hurried to do the daily maintenance and run quality controls in the hematology and coagulation analyzers. She went over to read some urine microscopies.

"Lab, Rob speaking," Rob said, with the phone that had just rang again nestled between his shoulder and cheek.

"Doctor Smith here. Any lab results yet on Aranda Lotus?"

"Hi doctor Smith. Just released the CBC results. The urine microscopic is now being read, and the CMP is still running."

"Kindly tell doctor Smith that I'm about to release the urine microscopic results in the computer," Sandy said to Rob. After relaying Sandy's message to Dr. Smith, Rob hung up. Sandy was grateful that she and Rob made a great team.

"Sandy, I'm going to Micro to set up a STAT sputum culture and gram stain."

"Okay, thanks."

Work finally slowed down, but there were still some slides for manual WBC differential counts to be done. Still looking into the microscope, Sandy felt Rob's presence nearby after he came back from the microbiology department. Feeling somewhat stiff from the work-related stress tension and from looking into the microscope for too long, she lifted her head and then rotated it. She lifted her shoulders and rotated them forward and backward to relax.

"Here," Rob said, "Let me massage you."

"Nah, that's okay."

"You've been working non-stop and so intently that you definitely could use it."

Sandy thought about it and then assessed her level of comfort with the idea of him massaging her. After having worked together for over a month now, she thought she was comfortable enough and found nothing wrong about a massage.

"You sure you don't mind?"

"Don't mind it at all."

"Okay then. Thanks."

Rob started on her shoulders, massaging them gently, but with the right amount of pressure—not too hard and not too soft—just the way Sandy liked it. She felt his hands moving a little lower toward her shoulder blades and toward her middle back. She felt a sensual sensation pass through her body. Hmm, that feels good, she said inwardly.

"How's that feel now?"

Sandy moved her neck and shoulders to evaluate her discomfort. She felt relieved and relaxed. "Feels much better now. Thanks."

After the massage, she and Rob checked all the lab departments and made sure all the work was done. When they finished, Sandy decided to reciprocate Rob's thoughtfulness.

"Rob, let me massage you to return the favor."

"Sure," he said, and then gave a big smile. "I'm sure not gonna pass up a massage." He sat on a chair and turned his chair to face the opposite direction. Sandy sat on another chair and moved closer to him. She went to work on his neck and shoulders. She moved her hands down his spine and down to his lower back muscles. Rob's body shivered.

"You okay?" She peered around to observe his face.

"Yes," he said, but something in his body language and voice tone made Sandy sense there was a little more going on inside him than a simple 'yes' could represent.

Sandy kept kneading his neck and shoulders, but she was aware of some kind of struggle happening within Rob. He squirmed and shivered again. "Are you sure you're okay? Do you want me to stop?"

"No, don't stop. It feels really good."

Sandy smiled. "Okay...if you say so."

"I hope if I ever find the right woman for myself that she can give me a massage like you can."

Sandy felt heartened by his compliment. After she withdrew her hands, Rob let out a moan of satisfaction and thanked her. Sandy thanked him also for massaging her earlier.

She walked away to answer the beeping call of the pneumatic tube system. Morning draws had started coming down the chute. They were now starting into the second segment of this busy night's work before their shift would come to an end.

Even though work had picked up again, Sandy couldn't shake off the arousing sensation she felt earlier. It stayed with her even after she and Rob said goodbye for the day.

CHAPTER 10

The next night, after they got caught up with work, Sandy and Rob had time to chat again. They both sat on the two rolling chairs in the hematology department. "You mentioned before that your mother is from Bolivia and your father is from New Zealand?"

"That's right."

"How'd they meet?"

"They met at the University of Minnesota in the twin cities. My dad was pursuing his master's degree in business under the Fulbright Scholarship Program. My mom, on the other hand, was pursuing her master's degree in social work under the Miss Bolivia Pageant Scholarship Program."

"That was very impressive of them."

"Why are you staring at me like that?" She crinkled her face.

"Because you're gorgeous. And, your deep green eyes are mesmerizing."

"You're embarrassing me," she said, blushing.

"I'm sorry. Didn't mean to. I'll try not to embarrass you anymore. But, want you to know that I meant every word."

"Don't get me wrong, I'm very appreciative. I'm just not used to these types of compliments."

"But you *deserve* such compliments."

Sandy could feel her face getting warmer, still. "Thanks again."

"You're welcome. So, after earning their master's degrees, your parents stayed in the U.S.?"

"Uh huh. They got married three months before they finished school. Then Dad was recruited and hired by Sears after he interned at one of their stores in Minneapolis. What about you? Can you share some things about you and your family?"

"Well," Rob rubbed his chin, "I have an older brother."

After a long, silent pause, Sandy said, "Yeah?"

"Tom and I used to work the barges up and down the Missouri River in Saint Louis through the summer months during our college days. I played soccer as a youngster and all through high school. I also took ballet lessons."

"Really? You took ballet lessons?" She couldn't picture him in tight-fitting leotards.

"In ballet, I learned control, balance, and flexibility, which translated well into my soccer skills and performance." He took the samples that Carmen dropped off and loaded them onto the CBC analyzer.

The centrifuge stopped and Sandy fished out three blue tubes to load onto the coagulation analyzer. "Does your family still live in Illinois?"

"Not anymore." He shook his head. "Both my parents have passed away. My Mom … only a year ago. And, my brother and his family now live in Sedona, Arizona." Ralee delivered more specimens. Rob loaded the specimens onto the CBC analyzer. "What about yours?"

"Hold that thought," Sandy said when she heard the chemistry centrifuge stop. "Need to go load the chemistry specimens."

"Okay."

Sandy unloaded the samples from the centrifuge. After making sure the specimens were not hemolyzed, lipemic, or short, she loaded them onto the chemistry analyzers.

"Mom and Dad still live in Minnesota," she said when she went back to join Rob. "Both retired now. After my sister, Carrie, finished high school and moved here to attend college, my parents joined the many snowbirds who go south for the winter. They go to Dallas and stay there from October to March."

"Dallas is nice. If I were to choose a place to live in Texas, Dallas would be it," he said with a wink and an upright forefinger.

"Haven't been there, so I wouldn't know. But my Mom loves it there. She's been trying to convince my dad to move there permanently."

The other chemistry centrifuge stopped; Sandy had to leave to load more specimens onto the analyzers.

"What were your parents like and what did they do," she asked when she joined him again.

Rob swiveled his chair. "They were great people. Dad was in the Air Force for thirty years. I was a military brat, as people might say. We went everywhere until my dad got stationed at Scott Air Force Base in Illinois as the base commander. He retired there as a full bird colonel. Mom was a singer in a band in Hawaii, where they met."

"Hm …was she Hawaiian?"

"No. Actually, she was born and raised in Chicago."

Sandy was intrigued. "Is that right?"

"Yep. Her ancestry was Greek. She was just in Hawaii for a singing gig. After she and Dad got married, she went back to school and earned her degree in accounting. She worked in the accounting office of whatever air force base they happened to be stationed at."

"I'm impressed. That's neat. Was your dad from Illinois also?"

"Philadelphia. He was a first generation American in his family. Both his parents were full blooded Irish—came straight from Ireland by boat." He picked up the stack of hematology results from the printer. He checked the integrity of the results before releasing them in the computer. "So, what brought you here to Minot?"

"Steve, my husband, as you know, is in the Air Force."

"Yes, of course. Anyway, what does he do?"

"He's a flight surgeon at the base. Of course, not at present because he's now in Kosovo. He's originally from Colorado. He moved with his best friend and his best friend's family to Minneapolis when he was sixteen years old. He didn't get along at all with his Aunt Millie and his aunt's husband, Rick."

"Did he live with them?"

"Yes. They were his guardians after his mother died from a car accident. Steve was twelve at the time."

"Ah." Rob nodded.

Their conversation for the moment had to end. Batches of specimens from the morning draws had started arriving through the pneumatic tube system—one after another. More would arrive from the phlebotomists until all hospital patients with doctors' orders were drawn.

"Talk to you later," Sandy said as she headed to the chemistry department. She knew they would have more opportunities to chat and to learn more about each other before his contract was finished.

CHAPTER 11

S andy and Rob had been working together for two months when Sandy found the courage to ask him what had been on her mind for some time now. Rob never brought up the subject, and she'd been itching to find out.

"May I ask you a personal question?" She said, as they were walking out the door after work.

"I'm an open book. Fire away."

"Do you remember when we ran into each other at the commissary?"

"I sure do. How could I not? It was the most fun I'd had in two long years. Chatting pleasantly with you, while walking up and down the aisles, was pure pleasure for me. Was it for you, too?" He smiled at her.

Sandy felt herself turn pink. "Aww ... thanks. Yes, it was for me, too."

"You were gonna ask me something?"

"Oh, yeah." Sandy was still trying to absorb what Rob said to her just a bit ago, so she was somewhat distracted. "I'm still dying to know the reason why you're doing the traveling job."

"Ah ... yes. I did say that I'd tell you about it some other time, didn't I?"

"Yes, you did." She crinkled her nose.

"I'll tell you, on one condition." He gave her a side glance.

"What?"

"Say 'yes' to having breakfast with me."

"Right now?"

"Sure."

"Where?"

"Would Denny's do?"

She pursed her lips as she looked at her watch. "Today is Saturday, so, I suppose, I can do that. My kids and sister normally sleep in on weekends anyway."

They walked down the four flights of stairs and then out to their own cars in the open parking lot. When they arrived at Denny's and got seated, a waitress approached, and Rob was first to order.

"I'd like an omelet with sausage, green peppers, onions, mushrooms, diced tomatoes, and shredded cheddar cheese." He grinned at the waitress; his white teeth gleamed from his firm lips.

"May I have two sausage links, two scrambled eggs, and some hash browns, please?" Sandy said.

When their food arrived, Rob consumed his breakfast as if he wouldn't live long enough to finish it. "Anyway, the reason behind this traveling job is a difficult thing for me to talk about," he said.

"Oh ... would you rather not go into it, then?" She took time eating her food.

"It's okay, especially now that I was able to bribe you to have breakfast with me. Besides, you said you're dying to know. Well, can't let you go home without you knowing it now, can I? Just can't bear the thought of you dying of curiosity." He gave her a mischievous look, his eyes sparkling in the morning sun shining through the window.

She feigned a cute little blush, one hand over her heart. "So thoughtful of you."

"I'd feel most responsible for it. Definitely." His tone was pleasant and playful.

"Glad you feel that way," Sandy said, maintaining a smile.

"It's a long story. So, be prepared to be bored."

"I'm all ears." She emphasized it by craning her neck, showing him both of her ears.

Rob chuckled at her silliness. "When I was stationed at Homestead Air Force Base, I went TDY to MacDill Air Force Base. You do know what TDY means?"

"Temporary duty? It'd be embarrassing if I didn't know that, being married to a military man. And those bases you've just mentioned, they're both in Florida, correct?"

"Yes, Ma'am."

"But, of course, MacDill is the only one that still exists because Hurricane Andrew wiped out most of Homestead Air Force Base."

"Correct again. I'm impressed." Rob tapped the table with his right forefinger twice.

"Well, I'm not all-brunette for nothing," she teased.

"And a very attractive brunette, I must say."

"Aww, thanks." She felt her face get warm. She guessed she must really be blushing by now. *Oh, Sandy, stop gushing like that. Surely, you're not the only one he's said that to before.*

"I met Barb, a surgical nurse, while working out at the base gym at MacDill. We went out on dates a few times."

Sandy listened intently as Rob continued his interesting revelation.

"When I was deployed to Saudi Arabia during the Gulf War, I didn't think she would wait for me. But she did. When Hurricane Andrew wiped out Homestead in nineteen ninety-two, my Wing, the Four Hundred Eighty-Second Fighter Wing, and I moved to MacDill Air Force Base."

"You were a fighter pilot?"

"Oh, I thought you knew that."

"I knew you were a pilot, but didn't know you were a fighter pilot."

"Yes, I was," he said, his eyes cast downward, forehead creased.

"You don't seem to be cocky and arrogant like the other fighter pilots I've met."

"You didn't know me in my younger days, either. I think age has mellowed me quite a lot."

"Sorry, I got you off track again."

He shrugged. "Anyway, Barb moved in with me, shortly after I moved to MacDill. We got married a year later. She didn't want to have children, though. Unfortunately, I didn't find that out until after we were married. When I got the job at Hershey Medical Center, she got a job there also. After a year, she got pregnant. I was ecstatic, especially when I found out the baby was a boy. I had visions of playing ball with him and talking about flying with him. Those visions and fantasies were all taken away from me in an instant."

Sandy's back straightened. "What happened?"

"Barb ran off with her lover—the hospital's chief surgeon —a few months after the baby was born. She insisted the baby wasn't mine." Sandy noticed his face turn crimson. She observed him taking a deep breath and then exhaling long and hard to settle himself.

"How did you know for sure?"

"When she let me know I wasn't the father, I demanded that we all have genetic testing done. Didn't wanna be denied of my parental rights in my child's life after the divorce. I was totally devastated when I received the results. I don't understand why she waited for me to come back from the war. She said she loved me, yet," his voice elevated and his face muscles tightened, "she didn't want to have children with me. Then …," his voice became raspy and impassioned, "… then she was only too happy to have *another man's baby*. What kind of love is that?"

Sandy felt for him, seeing how hard he was trying to control his voice and emotions. He's getting all choked up in trying to recant all these details. It's all my fault, she blamed herself.

Rob was shaking his head, looking down at his glass of orange juice. He swirled it with his straw and then drank what was left. When he looked at her again, Sandy saw heartache and sadness mirrored on his face and in his eyes.

"Oh, that is so sad," she said, moisture forming in her eyes. "No wonder why it's a difficult topic for you to talk about. I'm so sorry I asked." She lifted her Cat-Woman-like eyeglasses to dab the corners of her eyes. *Yes, I would have done the traveling job also if I were in his place. His life story is deeply touching. I wish I could stop tears from forming.*

"Hey," Rob said softly, "it's okay. It's not your fault. I should be the one apologizing for making you cry. May I?" Sandy nodded.

He reached out to wipe the tear that was about to run down her left cheek. Guided by the delicate contour of her jaw, he traced his fingertips on the side of her cheek down to her chin.

Sandy closed her eyes to better feel her face being caressed. The touch electrified her in an erotic way; she felt embarrassed by it. She opened her eyes to stop the feeling, only to be met by Rob's tantalizing eyes. She melted as her soul floated out into space somewhere beyond Neptune.

Sandy was wondering if Rob was feeling the electricity, too. The current passing through her was making her head and heart seem like they were in agonizing conflict. Her heart was telling her not to let it end. But her head was telling her to stop it. Being rational was not what she wanted right now. Rob took her hands in his and she felt the magnetism intensify.

At some point in her dreamy state, she was able to break the magic spell she was under. She pulled her hands away from Rob's. She scrambled and fumbled to take control of her emotions and of herself.

"Thanks for sharing that painful part of your life with me," Sandy managed to say. She gazed into his eyes once again. "I think my kids and sister are awake by now, so I suppose I should go home." *I'm acting like a fool.*

Rob cleared his throat and blinked his eyes. "Yes. Yes, of course. I'm sorry. I've kept you here too long."

CHAPTER 12

As more months went by, Rob and Sandy's relationship at work developed into an intimate friendship. The delightful conversations continued. Not every day, but whenever the right moments arose. However, after five months of working together, some bold changes had been taking place. Rob showered Sandy with compliments like "you look gorgeous" or "you look stunning." He would gaze into her eyes as he expressed his words of adoration, making Sandy feel weak and unstable in the knees. Inevitably, it made her act clumsily around him.

He had been recording love songs by different artists with lyrics of professing one's love and had given the cassettes to her afterward.

Sandy started questioning these changes and possible motives. One evening, when Rob was off for the night, she approached Joe. "Hey, Joe, I need a man's perspective. Would you come and listen to these tapes and tell me what you think?" He agreed, and listened as she played the tracks.

Dance with me; I want you to be my partner can't you see ... Starry eyes and love is all around us ... I can take you where you want to go ...

Just remember I love you and it'll be alright. Just remember I love you more than I can say ...

You are the woman that I've always dreamed of, I knew it from the start, I saw your face and that's the last I've seen of my heart.

Sandy ejected the tape and inserted another one, it played, *Come fly with me* and *I got you under my skin.*

"What do you think about these songs," Sandy asked Joe.

"They're all love songs to me."

She gave him a *'duh'* look. "*Joseph.* I know they're love songs."

He hunched his shoulders. "What're you gettin' at?"

"Rob gave them to me. Do you think it means anything?"

"He did?" Joe said, his eyes widened. Sandy nodded. "I'd say that he's sending you some not-so-subtle messages, considering that the tapes are that way throughout."

Sandy considered what he just said. "Perhaps we're both interpreting this all wrong. But, then again, I've noticed how he would come stand next to me and then put an arm around my waist then he'd slowly move his hand onto my lower back, lightly running his fingers up and down ..."

She stopped voicing her words, but kept thinking them. *...in a way that sends shivers through my spine and throughout my body, arousing my womanly desires. I've liked the feeling a lot. I've had to quickly step aside each time to put a stop to the wicked, arousing feelings building inside me.*

"I think he's got the hots for you." Joe clucked his tongue and punched her shoulder in play.

She folded her arms under her breasts and snorted. "*Yeah, right.*"

Joe repeated his opinion, this time with much more sincerity. "Seriously, I think he's got the *hots* for you."

"But," she was getting flustered, and she could tell her voice showed it, "I'm a *married woman*, Joe."

"That's not gonna stop him. But, yeah, that's a huge problem."

If she wasn't married, she thought, she'd take all the attention, compliments, and mostly the affection Rob had been giving and showing her. After all, those were all the things she'd been wishing to hear and feel from Steve for a long time. She'd allow the emotions and feelings to continue if the circumstances were different. She would have liked for him to take her into his arms and continue touching her and eventually kiss her. Of course, she'd respond with unbridled passion, surrendering herself to him completely. Or would she? Would she really have the nerve to go through with those fantasies?

She scolded herself. *You fool! You shouldn't be feeling any of this. How dare you to even remotely entertain such thoughts. Or in any way consider the thought of loving another man other than your husband. You should be ashamed of yourself. At thirty-one, you should know better than to entertain such temptations.*

"Just remember," Joe said, his face looking pained and rubbing his chin, "your husband is my flight surgeon at the base." He placed his hands over his ears and shook his head. "I don't want to know anything more than this."

She gasped. "*Oh, my gosh.* How could I have forgotten that?" She clasped her hands together in a praying form. Her imploring eyes directed straight at his. "Please keep this between you and me. Besides, nothing has happened between me and Rob anyway."

He stepped back and raised a palm in a 'stop' signal. "I know. But, please, if it goes anything beyond those songs, just make sure you don't get burned in the process. Just sayin'." He bunched his lips, popped them, gave a few quick nods of assurance at her, then spun around and walked away.

"Thanks Joe," she yelled over as he was leaving. Joe gave her an over-the-shoulder thumbs-up.

After a few weeks, Sandy knew for sure she had fallen hopelessly in love with Rob. How else could she explain why, lately, she found herself missing him on her days off, or on his days off? She yearned for his touch, even though she always pulled herself away from him to stop those building sensual feelings. She tried to ignore her romantic feelings for him.

She was partially successful, only because she was keeping busy at work. As much as she wanted to stay close to him while working, she was relieved their heavy workload had kept them apart. Staying busy also kept her mental focus on her work. She couldn't afford to get off track. Laboratory mistakes are not something to be taken lightly.

Only two more weeks and he'll be gone. Certainly, things would go back to normal, right? No more of these confusing and complicated emotions to deal with anymore?

CHAPTER 13

It was already the middle of October - the last week of Rob's contract with the hospital.

"Call me when you wake up," Rob said to Sandy before they left work in the morning.

"Why?" Sandy's eyebrows lifted.

"I'd like to take you out to lunch."

"Oh, okay. Thanks."

When Sandy woke up at 11:45 in the morning, she phoned Rob. Rob offered to let her choose the place where they'd go to eat lunch. "How does Sorensen's Family Restaurant sound to you?"

"Never been there, but that sounds good."

"Sweet," she said, and gave him directions to get there.

"How 'bout we meet there at one o'clock? Would that give you enough time?"

"Perfect."

After showering, Sandy put on a pair of blue baggy jeans and a nondescript white sweatshirt. Her fashion-conscious mother would have had a fit if she had seen her dressed like that in public. Her hair was still wet when she had gathered and clipped it on the back of her head, away from her face. Her naturally tight curls added volume to her hair. There was no time to put any make-up on, except for some lip-gloss. She took her eyeglasses and handbag from the top of her dresser, before dashing out the door.

In her haste, she was driving ten miles over the speed limit. A police car coming from the opposite direction switched its siren lights on.

Great, just what I need right now. She pulled her car off the road and onto the right shoulder. She was feeling nervous and impatient while she waited for the police. She waited and waited, but the police officer never came. Peering into her rearview mirror, she saw that the officer had pulled over a semi on the other side of the road. *Thank you, Lord.* She let out a big sigh of relief as she put the vehicle back in gear and slowly pulled away.

When she arrived, Rob was already seated at the restaurant, sipping some tea.

"Hi. Sorry, I'm late. Have you been waiting long?" She felt breathless.

"Only five minutes."

The waitress came to ask what Sandy wanted to drink. After the waitress promptly delivered Sandy's iced tea, she took their orders. Sandy ordered the chicken parmigiana, and Rob ordered the seafood Alfredo.

As Sandy sat across from Rob, she noticed the faded blue jeans and the dark-blue knitted sweater he was wearing. *Wow —his sweater almost matches the color of his gorgeous eyes.* "You look nice," she said. *What I really want to say is that you look very handsome. Just don't want you to think that I'm flirting with you. Try to act casually,* she told herself. But she still couldn't help from feeling nervous and excited at the same time. *It's only a lunch date,* she reminded herself. Sure, she had breakfast with him in the past, but she didn't have any romantic feelings for him back then. For some reason her romantic feelings for him now changed all that.

"Thank you. You look gorgeous, as always."

Sandy's cheeks flushed. "Thank you." She tried not to gaze back into his eyes each time he looked into hers. She didn't want him to know she had fallen in love with him. She desperately hoped it didn't show.

In between bites and sips, they discussed many topics. But, mainly, they talked about what he would be doing after he was finished with his current contract.

"I'm going to travel abroad. I have a book to write and need to do some important investigative research. After that, with me not having a family waiting for me," he put his palms upward while his elbows were resting on the table, "who knows where I'll be?"

As they talked about his plans and projects, it hit her. *In just a matter of a few days, he will leave and I will never see him again.* The realization saddened her immensely. She felt her chest tighten.

CHAPTER 14

T hree days after the lunch date, Sandy was awakened by the ringing of the phone, disrupting her sound sleep.

"Hi, Sandy, Rob here. You awake?"

"Barely," she said. She heard her own voice sounding scratchy.

"Sorry, I rudely woke you up."

Sandy perked up. "What's up? Are you okay? You've never called me at this hour before, so I'm concerned."

"Yeah, I'm fine ... I'm fine."

Sandy was still waiting. "Rob? Are you still there?"

"Um ... yeah. But just forget I called. Go back to sleep. I'm sorry to wake you up."

"Wait, Rob. There had to be a reason you called me. What was it?"

"Nah, just forget about it. Was silly of me, really. I think I already know the answer.

Sandy could hear sounds—like he was pacing back and forth. "Answer to what?" She rolled over to her stomach, lifting her upper body, using both elbows as props.

"Oh, nothing."

There was a pause, then she heard him sigh.

"Please, Rob, tell me."

"Don't want you to feel pressured."

Huh? Sandy's heart banged against her rib cage. *Oh, my gosh. What is he going to tell me?* She flopped back onto her back and became silent.

"Do you still want me to tell you?"

"Is there a reason I wouldn't want you to?"

"I don't know."

More sounds. Soft footsteps, scratching ... *what is he doing, and why?*

She disrupted the long pause, saying, "Okay, tell me then." She waited with great anticipation.

"Would you like to come over to my place?"

She didn't reply. In the short span of time before this, she thought of every possible thing that he might be wanting to tell her—but never *this*. What does it mean?

"See? I told you I know the answer." He sounded nonchalant.

"No, you don't know the answer. I didn't give you one, yet.

"I sense your reticence, so I best clarify the intent of my invitation. I remembered you telling me you've always wanted to see *Mission Impossible*, the movie—the latest one, with Tom Cruise. But that you've never had the chance. Anyway, I bought it today and was wondering if you'd like to come over to watch it with me."

Sandy was relieved. At least it wasn't something she would have a dilemma with. "Sure, I'll come over. Just give me time to get showered and dressed."

"How'd you like some pizza for lunch?"

"Hmmm. Yummy."

"I'll take that as a 'yes'?"

"Yes, thank you." She sat up in bed.

"I'll order it in about an hour, so it'll get here by the time you arrive ... any special toppings you'd like?"

"Anything, except ham, mushrooms, or anchovies."

Before hanging up, Rob gave her his address and directions on how to get there.

CHAPTER 15

S andy didn't have a problem finding Rob's apartment complex. It was located on top of a hill on the northwest part of the city. What was confusing, was trying to figure out which entrance to take to get to the upper levels of the building. Looking around, she saw Rob wave at her from his balcony.

"I'm glad you were keeping an eye out for me," she shouted. "Or, I'd still be looking for your apartment."

"Go through the east entrance and take the elevator to the third floor," he shouted back, leaning over the guard rail. "Uh, never mind, wait for me there and I'll come get you."

Once inside Rob's apartment, Sandy was impressed at how impeccably neat and tidy his place was. She felt ashamed of her own house cleaning habits. After Rob showed her the inside of his apartment, he led her outside to the balcony.

"Wow. This is a fantastic view." She placed a hand over her heart.

He nodded, his arm in a wide sweep of the horizon. "It's even more spectacular at night when the city is all lit up."

"I bet. I'm envious." From the balcony, she could see the western side of the city of Minot. The vibrant colors of the autumn leaves of trees and shrubs throughout the landscape added rich character, depth, and beauty to the scenery. Sandy was astounded at the grandeur of the view.

Unfortunately, she thought, the sound of cars and other trucks running in the streets, along with the smell of diesel fumes, given off by the trucks, are ruining some of that. She turned her gaze toward Rob. "Thanks for inviting me over."

Rob shifted his weight, dipped his head. "My pleasure."

Sandy was still inhaling and drinking in the beauty of the scenery when the doorbell rang.

"That's gotta be our pizza," Rob said. They went inside.

Sure enough, it was. "Hmmm ... smells good," Sandy said when Rob opened the box. They served themselves some pizza and something to drink before sitting on the sofa, across from the TV. Rob got up to close the curtains and dimmed the lights. He then loaded the *Mission Impossible* DVD into the player.

They finished eating lunch, one-third into the movie. Rob sat closer to Sandy on the sofa and then put his right arm over her shoulder.

Sandy didn't know how to react to the situation. She felt uncomfortable, yet she didn't want to object to it, either. In fact, she liked him snuggling with her. She liked it even more after she got a whiff of his Brut cologne. It pleased her nose. When Rob caressed the side of her neck, her heart thumped faster, making her lose all attention on the movie.

She liked what was happening but, at the same time, was fearful of what would happen next. She shifted her upper body forward in an attempt to put a little distance between them. It was to no avail; Rob's hand slid down to her right side and teased her side up and down with his fingers. It made her heart race even faster and her temperature seemed to rise, as well. *Oh no, what should I do if his hand ventures into the more guarded areas?* She had no quick answer. Think fast before it happens, she urged herself.

Even though she'd been married 10 years, she felt like a naïve 15-year-old virgin who couldn't decide what to do. She felt paralyzed. She knew she should get out of there, if she wasn't ready to deal with the escalating situation. But alas—a strong desire inside of her wanted to caress and kiss him.

Rob's hand rested more firmly on her waist. He pulled her closer to him. He moved Sandy's hair over to her right shoulder and then gave her a soft kiss on the nape … and then more.

Oh, my. Sandy sighed internally. Her body tingled all over. Her neck was one of the most sensuous parts of her body, and Rob's warm, tantalizing kisses were driving her crazy. Erotically crazy! She closed her eyes, which heightened her senses more.

She held her breath. She didn't want Rob to detect the wild beatings of her heart. Nothing seemed to help—she couldn't contain herself anymore. She uttered a drawn-out moan as Rob continued kissing her neck and shoulder. She could sense Rob getting more excited and aroused.

She didn't know what she should do. She would if she were with Steve. The movie in front of them kept on playing, but she was barely aware of it by now.

Rob laid her down gently on the sofa. She still had her eyes closed and was now in the midst of a moral struggle. Should I leave, or stay? Her mind was whirling. Her thoughts were racing. It clouded her judgment. As she contemplated her dilemma, she waited for Rob's next move. But Rob didn't move. She opened her eyes and saw him watching her.

When her star-struck eyes met his, she looked deeply into him, and felt him doing the same, probing, as she was, into the other's mind and soul. She sensed him pleading her to not reject his advances.

Oh, Rob, please have me now. She kept her thoughts to herself because she knew that many would suffer if she gave in to her lustful desires. "I'm sorry," she managed to say in a whimpering, whispery voice.

Rob stiffened and stopped, with a slight choking sound. He stood and waved his arms in the air. "I'm sorry, too. Don't know what got into me. I swear, I didn't invite you over with the intent to take advantage of you."

Sandy stood also. "I know you didn't, Rob. Sorry, for leading you on." She went over to give him a hug to let him know she wasn't upset with him. Rob reciprocated and kissed her on the forehead. Sandy's hardened nipples against his chest hungered for his mouth. She was well aware of Rob's hard arousal. She felt guilty and miserable for their situation. But her moral values were too strong. They were in the way.

She hugged him tightly, in hopes that it would do the trick. It didn't, of course, but it just had to do.

"I should be going home now," Sandy muttered.

Rob nodded. He walked her to the door and waved to her when she'd gotten into the elevator.

* * *

Once Rob was alone, he smacked his right hand on the back of the couch so hard that it stung him badly. He sat on the sofa and rested his head back. He closed his eyes and let out a big sigh of frustration. He brought both his hands up and clapped the sides of his forehead as he scolded himself.

What were you thinking? Dumb. Dumb. Dumb. Dumb. Dumb! He dropped his hands to his sides. *After telling yourself a million times that you're done with women, what did you do? Make a real ass of yourself. You're such an idiot.*

He brought his hands back up and rubbed his face, in hopes of getting rid of everything that was bothering him. It didn't. He stopped the movie, which, by now, was showing the last of the credits. Then he turned off the TV before going to the bathroom to take a cold North Dakota shower. *Burr!*

CHAPTER 16

When Sandy left Rob's place, she went to pick up Sheyenne and Taurea from school before heading home. The children were talking with excitement about their day, but Sandy was distracted with the day's events. She was oblivious to her children's yapping and to her driving. She got the scare of her life when they arrived home and realized she couldn't remember the details of her driving.

How in the world did I manage to drive home? She placed her left fingers over her lips. *Oh, my gosh, I honestly can't remember much of the drive. Lord, thank you for bringing us home safely.*

Sandy didn't talk to Carrie as much as she normally did. She felt guilty; she couldn't look Carrie in the eye. She couldn't confide in her little sister, who adored Steve as if he were the brother she never had. Sandy busied herself with dinner, while Carrie talked about school.

"I have a book report to write for my abnormal psychology class, and I have to study for my anatomy and physiology quiz. *I'm so stressed out.*"

After dinner, Carrie helped Sandy clear the table and wash the dishes. "Have you heard from Steve lately?" Carrie said.

The mere mention of her husband's name—somehow rattled her. She nearly dropped the rinsed plate in her hand. "Not in a month ... why?"

"Well, he's been gone almost six months and we haven't heard from him in a while. Aren't you counting the days until he comes home?"

"I am. I try not to dwell on it every minute of the day." She snapped her fingers. "Oh, I just remembered—I didn't bring the mail in. Kindly get it for me?"

When Carrie went out of the room, Sandy smacked her forehead.

All of my thoughts are so much on Rob, that I've hardly thought about Steve lately. I've forgotten this is his sixth month of deployment already. I'm so ashamed that my sister had to be the one to remind me about it.

"There's one from Steve," Carrie squealed as she brought the mail in. Sandy opened the envelope and read it. She noticed that the letter was dated two weeks ago.

Sept. 28, 1999

Dear Sandy,

I received the package you sent me. Thanks for all the goodies, especially the homemade chocolate chip cookies. They remained intact in the tins you sent them in. The other guys appreciated them, too, as much as I have.

How are you and the kids holding up? I'm sorry I'm not there to help you care for them. Hope Carrie is still enjoying her stay with you.

I thought that my unit would be coming home in April, but Uncle Sam just extended our stay until next September. I'm sorry. I'm sure it's not what you want to hear. You can just imagine how bummed we were when we found out about it.

Our role has become more of a humanitarian one since the war ended. These days, we see more local folks— mostly Albanians and some Serbians—than soldiers.

The locals really appreciate our presence here. We've been putting in a lot of hours treating them. We're so short-handed with doctors, nurses, and techs. This is one of the reasons that I haven't been able to write to you as often as I'd like.

> *Give Sheyenne and Taurea my love, hugs and kisses.*
> *Keep most of it for yourself. Say hi to Carrie for me. Also,*
> *give my regards to Mom and Dad. I miss you tons.*
>
> *All My Love,*
> *Steve*

Sandy handed the letter to Carrie, who was waiting ever so patiently. While Carrie read Steve's letter, Sandy went to take a shower. When she finished, she said goodnight to the girls and gave each a hug and a good night kiss before letting them go back to playing with their toys on the floor. "Daddy wants me to tell you both that he loves you."

"When is Daddy coming home," Sheyenne asked.

"Next September, sweetie … the Air Force wants him to stay there for additional six months."

"I miss Daddy very much," Sheyenne said.

"I miss Daddy, too," Taurea said.

"I know, sweeties. By the time we know it, he'll be back home. We'll just have to be patient, okay?" Sandy gathered the girls into her arms again and gave them more hugs and kisses. At that moment, Sandy missed Steve too. Her eyes moistened.

Sandy went to say goodnight to Carrie as well. She hoped Carrie hadn't noticed anything different about her today. Sandy didn't know exactly how she felt about Steve's letter. She was more preoccupied with the thought of Rob leaving than with the thought of Steve not coming home until next September. *What's wrong with me? What kind of a wife am I? I'm afraid I am straying away from my marriage vows.*

In bed, she tossed and turned. She had the hardest time falling asleep. The events that took place that afternoon kept replaying in her head. She was relieved nothing more had happened between her and Rob beyond the couch incident. But, at the same time, she also couldn't help but feel disappointed. Sleep finally came to her, but the alarm clock sounded off only an hour later—and she hit the snooze button. She was so tired and sleepy that she didn't get out of bed until after the third time the alarm went off.

CHAPTER 17

When Sandy arrived at work, she went straight to her designated work area in the chemistry department. She avoided Rob, but stole a few quick looks. At around 3:00 a.m., Rob approached her.

"Sandy."

"Yes?"

Rob got closer to her. "Are you okay?"

"Yeah." Sandy avoided his eyes as she continued doing her work.

"Look, Sandy, if you're mad at me because of what happened yesterday, I understand. I was wrong, and I'm sorry."

She raised her eyes to meet his. "But I'm not mad at you. I thought you'd be mad at me."

"For what?"

Sandy noticed the confusion in his face as he said his words. "You know … leaving you the way I did."

"I was mad at myself but not at you."

She stopped what she was doing to face him. She thanked him for his kind words. Her eyes started welling up. Soon her tears began to inch down her cheeks.

He gave her a concerned look. "Did I say something wrong?"

"No, no. Not wrong. Good."

"So, why're you crying then? I don't get it."

"You, apologizing for yesterday, touched me deeply. And because you'll be leaving soon. It saddens me a great deal."

"Thank you. Those are the sweetest words I've heard in a very long time."

Sandy wanted to give him a hug, but with Celia just around the corner, she held back. She accepted the box of Kleenex Rob handed her. "Thank you," she said. She pulled three sheets of tissue out and dabbed her eyes and cheeks. There was a long silence between them before Rob finally spoke.

"Hey, since next Friday is my last day at work, how about you and I go out for a drink at the Starlight Club next Saturday night?"

"Sure," she said without hesitation. She dabbed her eyes and cheeks again with more Kleenex, trying to compose herself.

"You sure you can make it?"

"I'll be off, so I can make it."

Rob appeared happy to hear this.

* * *

Saturday evening came. It took her a long time to get ready. She loosened her tight curls by using a large rod curling iron. Instead of putting her hair up in a bun, this time she let her hair hang down to her waist. The few strands that draped down on the right side of her face made her look even more alluring. She applied heavier make up this time.

Usually she dressed rather conservatively, but this time she wore some of her more provocative clothes. It had been quite a while since she had worn them. At first, she felt a little uncomfortable, but she liked what she saw in the mirror. To complete the presentation, she dabbed her earlobes with her favorite White Diamonds perfume.

"Mommy, you look *beautiful*." Sheyenne's eyes and face lit up in amazement at seeing her mother.

"Wow," Carrie said. She was also captivated.

Even Taurea expressed her approval when she woke up from all the raucous exchanged.

Sandy blushed from all the accolades. She hoped she hadn't overdone it. She thanked them gracefully and gave each one a hug and a kiss before she left.

❋ ❋ ❋

Rob, having been at the club for half an hour by now, was getting antsy. He hadn't had any mixed drinks in quite some time. Tonight, he decided to drink gin and tonics, instead of his usual Bud Light. He looked at his watch again. 8:35 p.m. He began to entertain the possibility that Sandy had stood him up.

"Hi! Dee!" Rob heard someone yell over all the noise. He looked around and saw Dee, looking ravishing. She was wearing the same outfit from the last time he had seen her—black tight-fitting jeans, a black stretchable blouse that showed off her figure well, and a pair of black boots. She wore the same silver necklace with tiny diamonds throughout. Rob realized then; he had forgotten all about her. As of late, he had been focusing all his thoughts and attention to Sandy.

"Oh … *hi Angela*," Dee shouted back. Rob saw Dee give Angela a hug. They chatted for a short while and then Dee looked around. She waved, smiled, and started going in his direction. Rob looked on both sides to see to whom she was waving at and to whom she was directing her smiles.

"Hi there Rob," Dee said.

Confused, Rob stood, not sure how to act. With reluctance, he said, "Hello."

Dee crinkled her forehead. "You look as if you've seen a ghost or something."

"You know me?"

"Of course, I know you. Hello, we work together? Geez … it's me, *Sandy*." The different pitch and volume of Sandy's voice over the loud noise altered the sound of her voice. "Well, who do you think I am?"

"Well … you don't look like the Sandy I know, but you sure

look like Dee who used to sing here. First of all, I've never seen Sandy dressed this way and, second of all, Sandy wears glasses." He pulled out a chair for her to sit on.

"Well, I'm one and the same. Of course, you haven't seen me wear clothes like this to work. Not appropriate. As for my glasses, I'm always in too much of a hurry to put my contacts on. So ... you've come here before and seen me sing?"

"Yeah, I came here the first three weekends after I arrived. So why did you sing just twice?"

"I was just filling in for Cindy. I used to sing with the band during jam sessions, and they liked my singing. So, when Cindy went on vacation, the band asked me if I could fill in for her."

Rob was astounded with what he was hearing. For six months, he'd been working with 'Dee', the woman he thought he'd lost before he even had a chance to meet her. "You look magnificent." He couldn't take his eyes off of her.

Reddening, she said, "Please, don't stare at me like that. You're making me feel uncomfortable."

"I'm sorry. It's just that I still can't wrap my head around this ... that you, Sandy, are also Dee, and you look absolutely gorgeous. But I've told you that many times already."

"Yes, and thank you very much. You look very handsome yourself."

Sandy's compliment flattered him. He ordered a Long Island Iced Tea for her when a waitress came to their table. It was difficult talking over the band's music and the background noise of people talking; they mostly looked at each other and smiled. He pulled his chair over next to Sandy's and put his right arm over her right shoulder. She didn't object, instead she leaned her body against him. He was surprised she did that. He enjoyed the warm feeling they were sharing as they sat next to each other, and could tell she felt the same. They listened to the band and watched the people dance.

"I need to use the men's room," Rob said. He was only gone three minutes but, when he came back, he didn't see Sandy. He looked around everywhere. He waited five minutes, thinking she might have gone to the ladies' room also, but Sandy didn't come back. He waited a little while longer, but still no Sandy. He thought she'd abandoned him. The thought angered him, and he started cursing to himself.

Miffed, he gulped his drink and then slammed the glass down on the table. As he was heading for the door, he heard an announcement.

"We have a guest singer tonight, folks. Some of you might recognize her. She hasn't been here in a while, but tonight she's here to sing for us again. Please welcome Dee back to the stage!"

Rob turned around and saw Sandy walking up to the microphone. Excitement rushed over him, and he couldn't help but smile and shake his head. He hurried back to take a seat in the chair he had vacated. He was now sorry he cursed her in his mind. People clapped and whistled. When she was ready, she started out with one of Reba McIntire's songs, *One Promise Too Late*.

When she finished, the crowd clapped and whistled again. They chanted, "More! More! More!" She smiled sheepishly at the crowd and at the band's leader. He signaled for her to go on and sing some more. She stepped up to him to have a short conversation before she took center stage again. This time, she sang one of Dolly Parton's songs, *I Will Always Love You*.

When she finished, she rejoined Rob. She found him a little choked up. "Are you okay?"

"Yeah. Your songs got to me a tiny bit."

"Really? Did you like them?"

He coughed to clear his throat. "Uh-huh. I enjoyed your singing the very first time I heard you. You have an outstanding voice. Were those songs meant for me?"

"Thank you for your compliment," she said. "And, yes, I sang them for you." Her lips curled up into a smile.

"I'm very touched."

Sandy gave his forearm a gentle squeeze. She looked at her watch. "Five past eleven, I guess it's time for me to go home. I'm sure you want to get some rest and do some packing."

Rob agreed. As they walked outside toward Sandy's car, they strolled side by side with one arm around each other's waist. The month of October in North Dakota was cold already. Even with a heavy jacket on, Rob could sense that Sandy was cold, so he pulled her closer to him. "Still cold?"

"Not so much anymore. Thank you."

"Good."

"The sky is so clear in deep midnight blue. It's absolutely beautiful and enchanting," Sandy gushed.

Rob looked up. "Indeed."

They stopped walking to observe the Little Dipper and the Big Dipper. Rob used his extensive knowledge of astronomy, pointing out and naming all the visible constellations in the sky to impress her.

"Wow, you know so much about astronomy," she said. "Aside from knowing some of the commonly known constellations, I know nothing more about it. You're talking way beyond my knowledge level. I feel stupid."

"Thanks. But please don't feel stupid." He pulled her in more toward him and kissed her forehead. "It's been one of my hobbies. I've a huge telescope that I had lugged up in high places, away from city lights. That sucker can magnify the stars and planets like you wouldn't believe."

"*Awesome.* Do you have it with you here in Minot?"

"No, it's in my storage place in Pennsylvania. Did you see the shooting star whizz by?"

"No, I didn't. I was preoccupied with what you were saying. Sorry." She smiled at him. He smiled back.

Rob trained his eyes on the night sky. "Look, there's another one … and another." He pointed each one with his left index finger. Sandy squealed each time. They resumed strolling across the parking lot. When they reached Sandy's car, they stopped to say goodbye.

"I'll give you a call once I get settled," he said. His face turned solemn. "Try not to cry."

"I'll try … have a safe trip … keep in touch."

He noticed her voice breaking. It tugged at his heart, especially when he noticed her eyes glistening and moistening. His own mouth felt dry and a big lump formed in his throat. He almost couldn't breathe. He wanted to plead to her, *"Please come with me."*

He wished he had the nerve to say exactly how he felt about her—the fact that he was truly, madly in love with her. For heaven's sake, he'd fallen in love with her twice. Hasn't he? Granted, he hadn't known, 'till now, that she and Dee were one and the same person. Still, why didn't he have the courage to tell her? It's for fear of rejection, as simple as that, he reasoned.

He realized he never told Sandy his true feelings for her ... only in subtle ways. Even now, he resolved his unspoken feelings and unspoken sentiments by hugging her one last time.

After a long and tight embrace, they finally bade farewell. They got into their own vehicles and drove off, each going their separate way.

CHAPTER 18

Sandy unleashed her pent-up emotions, which she had managed to restrain until she got into her car. She cried all the way home. After parking in her driveway, she stayed inside the car to cry some more.

She had been crying for five minutes since she parked her car in the driveway. Her eyes were red and puffy, and her chest was aching from heaving so much. Light taps on the window disrupted her private moment of agony. Startled, she lifted her head from the window where she had it rested. She saw Rob bent forward with his left arm on top of her car as he peered inside, facing her. Feeling frantic, her heart began to pound.

Why is he here? Fumbling, she swept her tears away with the back of her two index fingers before lowering her window. "Why are you here?"

Rob looked at the ground, closed his eyes, and took a deep breath, as if trying to gather his courage. He faced her again. He looked deeply into her eyes. "May I kiss you?"

Huh? "Why?"

"Because I love you. When I drove away from the Starlight parking lot after we said goodbye, I regretted that I didn't kiss you. *Dammit*, even if I can't have you, I will at least kiss you to let you know I love you. I'm standing here right now, feeling stupid and nervous, waiting for your reply."

Sandy's heart jumped for joy to hear those words uttered from Rob's lips. "Oh, Rob, *I love you, too.*"

"You do?"

"Yes, I do, and I'd love for you to kiss me, but not here. What would my neighbors—or my sister—say if they happen to see us kissing?"

"Well … would you like to come to my place, then?"

"Uhm … I'm not sure that's a good idea. I feel very vulnerable right now."

"Are you saying no?"

"*No* … I mean I want to go with you, but I'm afraid. I might do something I'll regret in the morning." She was vacillating big time. *I want to go. No, I shouldn't. But I really want to go. No, don't go.*

He straightened up his back from his hunched position, looked up to heaven and at the same time taking a deep breath, then letting it out in a huge sigh. He looked downward and honed his eyes on her. "Sandy."

"Yes?" She looked up at him.

"I'm not one who readily expresses his inner feelings … but, you must know that my heart is pretty broken up right now. The joy I felt just seconds ago … is now sinking fast—deep into the abyss."

Rob's words tore Sandy's heart apart. She felt his pain. Looking into his eyes, she said in a sympathetic voice, "I'm so sorry, Rob."

"I'm sorry, too … is there something I can say to make you change your mind?" His voice, now pleading.

"I don't know." She still felt unsure and wavering, not knowing which way to go. "I'm really struggling with this dilemma. I truly want to go with you right now—more than you know. It's just that I'm really torn. I hope you can understand my situation. It's not easy for me to make up my mind just like that. I have a husband and kids to think of."

"In that case, I have to say goodbye." Before walking away, he said, "Sorry I ever came," his voice mixed with anger, sarcasm, and sadness.

"Please don't go," she said, but Rob was still walking toward his car. His pace quickened. Sandy snatched her handbag and ran after him. She caught up to him. Crying, she said, "Okay, I'll go with you."

"Please, Sandy; don't make this any harder for me than what it already is right now."

"But I really want to go with you." She insisted.

"*Not* if you're going to *regret* it in the *morning*." He got into his car, slammed the door, and drove off, screeching his tires as he pulled away.

Sandy fell apart. She sat on the curb, crying her eyes out as the obtrusive street lamp cast its light down on her.

Rob's red corvette came to a stop at the stop sign at the end of the street. It did not move forward.

Sandy looked. *What is he doing?* She observed him peering in his rearview mirror, then smacking his forehead. He shouted something. A couple seconds later, she saw his car back up and make a U-turn, coming back. It pulled up curbside alongside of her. He got out and picked her up in his arms.

"I'm sorry I made you cry." His voice was now soft and comforting. "You sure you want to come over to my place?"

"Yes," she said in almost a whisper. In an instant, she went from a rational, sensible person with good judgement to someone completely the opposite.

At the apartment, Rob turned on the stereo and put on a CD of classical Beethoven compositions. He asked Sandy if the lighting in the room was okay, saying the one lit lamp was already on its lowest setting. She nodded, indicating it was fine.

"Would you like something to drink?"

Sandy performed one of her classic nose wrinkles and shook her head in declining.

"Do you mind if I take a shower first? Even though I tolerate cigarette smoke in the clubs, I can't stand their lingering smell."

"Yeah, me either. No, go ahead. I'll just sit and listen to your music, if you don't mind." Sandy liked that Rob was concerned about hygiene. It was important to her, too. She sat on the sofa and picked up a copy of *Scientific American* from the coffee table. She leafed through the magazine and started reading an article on "Embryonic Stem Cells for Medicine." It was mindless observation, really, her mind was somewhere else—with Rob— to be precise. So, she was not really able to digest anything from what she was reading.

She let her imagination run wild as Beethoven's *Moonlight Sonata* played in the background. She wondered what it would be like to be in the shower with him right now. *Hmmm....*

Sandy was caught off-guard at the sight of Rob when he emerged in front of her. She didn't expect him to be coming out with just a towel around his waist. She was embarrassed to look up at him, so she lowered her eyes to the floor. She could smell his Brut cologne and his fresh breath as he approached her.

Rob took her hand and raised her to her feet. Her heart skipped. Warm fuzzy feelings came over her. He brought her closer to him. Before he could kiss her, she said, "May I use your bathroom?"

Even though she heard Rob say, "sure," she noticed his reluctance in releasing her. When he let her go, she picked up her handbag and went off to the bathroom.

After she finished showering, she took her toothbrush and toothpaste from her handbag and brushed her teeth. She didn't think Rob would mind if she gargled with some of his mouthwash, so she did. After that, she applied a generous amount of body lotion on herself. She had already folded her clothes and had hung them on one side of the towel bar before she jumped into the shower. She was grateful Rob didn't wear his polyester bathrobe that was hanging on a hook on the door. She put it on. It was big and long for her, but she didn't mind. She smelled the faint scent of Rob's Brute cologne on it. It pleased her. She stepped out of the bathroom with her hair still wet, which made her hair look a lot curlier.

Rob was sitting on the sofa with his head leaned back. He had his eyes shut as he listened to the Elvis Presley CD.

Sandy couldn't help herself anymore. She came up from behind and put her arms around him. She kissed his forehead, and then rested her head on his left shoulder.

Rob took her hands and kissed them. He rose from the sofa, still holding her hands. "May I have this dance?" He came around and drew her toward him. Sandy nestled her head into his neck and shoulder and smiled at the romanticism going on between them. She was enjoying every second of it.

"Wise men say only fools rush in," the song played, *"But I can't help falling in love with you. Shall I stay? Would it be a sin? If I can't help falling in love with you."*

They swayed to the music and moved together as one. Rob lifted her chin and then lowered his lips to hers. He kissed her tenderly and then hungrily in complete abandon, to which Sandy responded just the same. Sandy had her arms around Rob's neck, stroking it and playing with his hair. She felt Rob's arms around her back, caressing the small of her back sensuously with his fingertips.

"I hope you don't mind me wearing your bathrobe," she said coyly when they stopped kissing.

Half grinning, he said, "I do mind." His tone was playful.

Her eyebrows furrowed. "What do you mean? You don't want me wearing it?"

With an impish smile, he said, "That's right … I prefer you wear it … like this." He pulled the robe off and over her shoulders in a teasing, slow motion while kissing her first on the mouth, then neck, and shoulders. Sandy felt her heart and his beating in a furious unison. His kisses electrified her all over.

She closed her eyes and her senses heightened. They danced their way to the bedroom as the music continued to play. Her bathrobe now fell to the floor. As did his towel. All at once, their bodies were touching, skin to skin. She was on fire. Oh, my! There was no holding back now. Their nakedness intensified her burning desire for him.

Once in the bedroom, she abandoned any inhibitions. She let the heat of passion engulf her, guide her, and rule over her. She explored him with her hands and tongue. She whispered words of "Oh! Rob, I love you, too" in response to Rob's "Sandy

I love you." Rob made his move to get on top of her. She didn't object. Instead, she parted her long, slim legs to await his next move. Rob made his gentle entrance into that small—but most coveted—entryway between her legs. She hadn't had sex in ten months, so she was fairly tight on the first few tries.

"Am I hurting you?" he asked with a gentle voice.

"No. I'm okay." Oh, how she loved him more for his considerate nature. As they made love, she responded to Rob's every move. At the height of her passion, she cried out in ecstasy. At the same time, she heard Rob moan and call her name. Afterward, she felt his muscles contract and then convulse on top of her. As the orgasmic sensations subsided within her, she collapsed in fatigued relaxation.

✻ ✻ ✻

Sandy bolted out of bed when she realized she had to get home. She had dozed off, along with Rob, after their passionate lovemaking. She checked the time on Rob's alarm clock. It read a quarter to two. She had to get home or else her sister would be getting anxious about her. *Granted, Carrie is probably fast asleep already. Still, I still need to go home, just in case she's waiting up on me.*

Rob stirred. "You okay?"

"Yes," Sandy said, while heading to the bathroom, "I promised my sister I'd be home by two o'clock. I just need to shower first."

"Wait. It just dawned on me. I have to give you a ride home."

"Oh, yeah. I forgot. I'm sorry."

"No, no. Don't be. But is it okay if I take a shower with you to save some time?"

"Uh … sure." Her heart palpitated again. She picked up the robe from the floor and put it on. Rob picked up the towel and wrapped it around his waist.

As soon as Rob had the water temperature regulated, he let

her step into the shower tub first. Once in the shower, Sandy could not ignore Rob's eyes on her naked body and the erection he was displaying as a response. As a result, it awakened her womanhood also. She went to him, and they made passionate love once more.

Sandy imagined no more what it would be like being in the shower with him. She was living it! It was everything she had imagined it to be … and more.

Still breathless, Rob whispered in her ear, "I love you."

"I love you, too," she replied in her sultry voice.

Rob kissed her once more. Before releasing her, he said, "Thanks for tonight. I shall treasure it always."

Sandy was touched by his sentiment. She acknowledged him, and then started crying at the realization that this would most likely be it for them. She was glad Rob hugged her, to comfort her now aching heart.

❋ ❋ ❋

Makenna had been typing away at her keyboard for seven and a half hours straight, working throughout the night while her husband and daughter were sleeping. She stopped only for occasional coffee and bathroom breaks. For the entire month of April and through the third week of May, she had dedicated a large share of her time to writing this novel. Reaching this point in the story, she felt comfortable in taking a break for a little while.

Even though her laptop had the time displayed, she still looked up at the clock on the wall. Oh, my goodness, it's almost five o'clock already. Her husband, Clint, would be waking up soon. She stretched her upper body and shrugged her shoulders.

Tomorrow at 11:00 a.m., she would be having lunch with her childhood best friend, Nina, the senior editor for Lover's Lane Publishing Company in Loveland, Colorado. She was excited about their lunch date. But, for now, she had to get breakfast ready for Clint and Chloe, their daughter.

CHAPTER 19

On May 30, 2007, the weather outside was sunny. There were a few scattered, white puffy clouds high up in the sky. The temperature was a comfortable 74 degrees. Inside Applebee's restaurant in Fort Collins, Colorado, Makenna and Nina were having lunch together. Makenna was having an oriental chicken wrap and some unsweetened iced tea, while Nina was having the five cheese chicken penne and some unsweetened iced tea, as well. It had been a year since they'd last seen each other. Their busy work schedules were always getting in the way whenever they tried to have a get-together. It seemed as if they were always busy meeting deadlines in their line of work.

While they ate, they enjoyed a lively conversation. They talked about their families, life in general, the weather, and finally about work.

"Remember when you called me on my cell phone three years ago and asked if I'd be interested in writing romance novels?" Makenna said.

Nina remembered it. She was just a month into her new job as chief editor of a newly formed publishing company, which she'd helped grow from ground up. There were hardly any clients at the time, and she was recruiting writers she knew. "Uh-huh … and you said that you weren't yet ready to give up doing children's books and … not yet ready to plunge into a different genre."

"Ah ... ," Makenna said. Her face brightened as she opened her eyes more and smiled wide. "But now, I am so ready." She relaxed her smile. "Anyway, I've been working on this novel for almost two months now. I'm wondering if you're still interested."

Nina swallowed her food and took a drink of tea before she replied. "Of course. Why the change of heart?"

"A revelation made to me five years ago got me thinking. It hurt me terribly for a very long time, but I've finally accepted the truth and have come to terms with it."

"Is it something you'd like to talk about?"

"No, not really. In due time, perhaps. But for now, let's just say I'm inspired."

"I understand. Just mail the manuscript to me, or email it as an attachment, or bring it with you the next time you come this way."

Makenna's face lit up in excitement with Nina's expressed interest in her novel. "Actually," she said, looking timid, "I brought it with me now. It's only partially written, but I'd like to know what you think first before I go any further. I've tried to edit it as much as I could but, of course, you're the expert. You'll let me know."

Nina put a forkful of pasta into her mouth. After she chewed and swallowed, she drank some iced tea. "That's better yet," she said. "If you still have errands to do in town, I'll take the manuscript home and read it today. Just come by the house before you go home."

"I'm not imposing, am I?"

"Ab. So. Lute. Ly. *Not*."

＊ ＊ ＊

It was 4:00 p.m. when Makenna arrived at Nina's house. She rang the doorbell, and it was Trevor, Nina's husband, who opened the door. They gave each other a hug and exchanged greetings. He led her to the formal living room and offered her a seat on the chocolate-colored leather sofa. "Let me get Nina for you."

After a minute, he returned from the sunroom. "Nina should be here soon. She said she's down to the last two pages. Don't know what you've written, but it sure made her cry."

"Really?" Makenna was amused.

"Yep." He smiled. "I'm leaving to go to the hardware store, but may I get you something to drink before I go?"

Trevor was a big man and slightly on the heavy side. Makenna likened him to a gentle giant because, in spite of his size, he was sensitive and always jovial to everyone.

"Just a glass of water, please. Thank you."

Makenna was drinking her water when Nina emerged from the sunroom. She put her glass down and looked at Nina, who was waving the manuscript toward her, but not saying anything. Nina was smiling, but her eyes were damp. Makenna looked at her with much anticipation. She was hoping Nina would say something, but she didn't. Instead, Nina sat on the sofa opposite her. Makenna couldn't take the suspense any longer. "So?..." she said. Her eyes were searching Nina's, "What do you think?"

"This is very good. I can't wait 'til you finish it to see how it ends. The part where Sandy and Rob drove off their separate ways and then Sandy letting go of her pent-up emotions really got to me. Remember when Trevor and I were just friends?"

"How can I forget? You drove me insane. You were like 'Trevor this' and 'Trevor that' from the time you woke up 'til the time you went to bed."

"I was not." Nina pouted like a child.

"Yeah, hah." Makenna wagged her head.

"We went to school, too, so I couldn't have been that way *all* the time."

"True, except that we attended the same classes and majored in the same field. Remember?"

Nina laughed at the realization. "Was I really that bad?"

"Uh, huh." The bantering going on between them was a loving and sisterly kind. At that moment, Makenna felt like the two of them were young adults once again.

"Sorry, and thanks for putting up with me. Anyway, I felt the same way Sandy felt in that scene. Trevor didn't know it at the time, but I was *so* in love with him. I wanted so bad to tell him that I loved him and was desperately hoping to hear him say the same thing to me that night before he left for Germany."

"I remember you telling me that vividly. That's what I used when I wrote that particular scene."

"Seriously?"

Makenna smiled and nodded. "Sorry, I stole that from you. But I created my own version of it."

"Yes, you did. You made it more exciting and heart-wrenching by making her a married woman. Wow, who would have thought that I'd play a role in your novel writing someday?"

"Thanks to you, I was able to write that part effectively and convincingly."

"Glad to be of help. Anyway, going back to your novel," Nina said as she composed herself and assumed her professional role. "I really like it and definitely will consider it. Do you have any idea when you'll finish it?"

"I'll try to finish it after my surgery. So, hopefully, in five to ten months, depending on how fast I can recover."

"Surgery?"

"Uh huh … double mastectomy on June eighteenth."

"*Oh, Makenna.* Why didn't you tell me your cancer's back?" Her face turned somber. She scooted over to Makenna and hugged her.

After they hugged, Makenna said, "It's no big deal. Besides, I didn't want it to affect your decision about my novel."

"But this is a big deal, Makenna. How are you holding up?"

"Physically? I feel fine. Emotionally? That's another story. I get depressed and cry every time I think about losing both my breasts. I don't know how Clint is going to react toward me without them." Makenna was tearing up now.

"If Clint truly loves you, he'll love you no matter what. This will test his true love for you."

"But I don't want to lose my breasts to find out. I'd much rather not know as long as I have my healthy breasts."

"I'm sorry, Makenna. That was very insensitive of me."

"Don't worry about it, Nina." Makenna forced a smile for Nina, who was obviously feeling terrible about her comment.

"I should be going home now. I don't want to drive through the mountains in the dark if I don't have to."

"If there's anything I can do for you, please let me know."

"I sure will. Thanks." They hugged again before saying goodbye.

As Nina watched Makenna walk toward her car, a scene of their first meeting, thirty years ago, played out in her mind.

They were both five years old at the time. She strolled into Makenna's driveway one day, shortly after she and her family moved into the neighborhood. She remembered Makenna wearing a purple dress with medium-sized, white polka dots and a pair of light purple flip-flops. She stopped and stood there watching while Makenna busily drew on the driveway with different colors of chalk.

"Hi. What's your name," Makenna had asked when she noticed her.

"Nina," she'd said. She remembered herself wearing her favorite dark green knit shorts with a light green tank top. She also remembered wearing her favorite pair of white shoes with neon green shoelaces.

Makenna squinted as she glanced at her. "Where do you live?"

She had her hands together behind her back, swiveling her body back and forth while she spoke. "I used to live in America, but now I live in Cheyenne."

Nina smiled in her remembrance. At five years old, she thought that Casper, Wyoming was America and that Cheyenne, Wyoming was somewhere else in a foreign land.

"What's your name?" she asked.

"Makenna," Makenna had said without looking. She continued to draw until she spoke again. "Would you like to draw with me? Here, you can have this green chalk, and I'll have the purple chalk." Thus, began their lifelong friendship.

Nina waved her hand now while Makenna pulled away from the driveway, still continuing her recollections.

She remembered attending school together since kindergarten all through college. They attended journalism school at the University of Wyoming. And they were dorm mates, too. She was thankful they got along so well.

She recalled a conversation during one of their previous visits when she had said, "Remember when we both had this *big* dream of traveling the world to cover world events for CNN? We were pretty sure of ourselves then, weren't we?"

Makenna had laughed. "Instead, we had to settle for the not-so-glamorous little, obscured outfits here in Wyoming and South Dakota. What an eye opener that was."

"Don't forget North Dakota."

"There was a reason I left that one out. Even though it's my birthplace, what a God-forsaken place that was. Everything stays frozen for months up there. The first snowfall never melts until *spring*."

Of course, that was in their first three years after they had finished college. Later on, she landed a job as an assistant editor at the Wyoming Tribune Eagle in Cheyenne until she got her present job as chief editor for Lover's Lane Publishing Company in Loveland. During that time, Makenna still worked part time for CBS television in Cheyenne. A year after marrying Clint Wilde, Makenna finally did get her dream job at CNN. That was ten years ago.

CHAPTER 20

S andy, are you okay?" Celia asked. "I think so." Sandy was puzzled. "Why?"

"You look sad. You always come to work with smiles, but not so much lately."

"I've just been feeling tired lately. I think this shift is finally getting to me," she lied.

There was no way she would confide in Celia. She knew Celia's husband left her for another woman after twenty-six years of marriage. For sure, Celia would never understand her predicament. "I apologize if I've been acting a little off," Sandy said.

"Oh, no. Don't apologize. I just want to make sure you're okay," Celia said in her thick, but soothing Filipino accent.

"I'm okay, Celia. Thanks for your concern." She was sincere in her gratitude. She hated that her face was most likely giving away way too much of how she was feeling inside. She'd tried to be her usual happy-go-lucky self in the days and weeks that followed her tryst with Rob. But the minute she was in her own department, melancholy still dwelled within her, gnawing at her and dragging her down.

She had been missing Rob. It had been a month and a half, and still no word from him. She felt miserable. Her monthly menstrual cycle that usually arrived like clockwork hadn't come. She was edgy. She had stopped taking her birth control pills after Steve left for Kosovo. She hated taking them then, so she figured why keep taking them if there was no reason to. Unfortunately, she had no protection against pregnancy when she and Rob spent—what she considered— "a magical night together".

Her heart hammered with anticipation and then stopped for a moment when the home pregnancy test kit showed a strong blue dot in the middle. She let out a deep gush of utter disappointment. It confirmed her fear and suspicion. The blood drained from her face. She was lost. She hadn't planned for this. She didn't know how to deal with it. *What should I do?* She didn't believe in abortion—not even an option. *Should I tell Steve? Should I leave Steve? Or should I tell Rob?* She decided to follow through on the latter.

The phone rang three times. No answer. Rob's cell phone always went to his voice mail on the fourth ring. She repeated the process every other day for a week with no luck. She also sent him numerous emails: "Please call me. I need to talk to you. I miss you so much." All went unanswered. She wondered if the love she gave him had been worth the risk of losing her family and dignity. Not to mention the degrading of her moral values to their lowest, especially now that Rob was incommunicado.

* * *

Today, she was able to connect with Rob—almost two months after he left North Dakota.

"I suggest that you refrain from calling or contacting me." He almost shouted, "*I don't love you.* And I don't have any desire to get involved with anyone else, especially not with you."

She was stunned. *Did he really mean what he said? Wasn't he the same man who told me how much he loved me before he left North Dakota? Wasn't he the same man who seduced me, for whom I had entrusted my heart—the only other person—after giving it first to my husband? Most importantly, wasn't he the same man with whom I eventually spent an intimate and passionate night—against everything I morally believed in—when he came after me, after we had said what I thought were our final goodbyes?*

Wham! Rob's words slapped her across the face with such force it shook her entire being. She felt numb. She was caught off-guard and completely dumbfounded. All she could manage to say was, "Thank you for your honesty," before she hung up.

It took a few minutes before his words really sank in. When they did, her heart and lungs seemed to collapse. She felt as if all the blood was draining from her entire body. She felt light-headed. Her breathing became shallow, and her vision turned black.

The next thing she knew, she was lying face down on the kitchen floor. She rolled over on her back and looked around. She slowly picked herself up and sat on one of the dining room chairs to regain her bearing. She was still in a daze, trying to figure out how she ended up on the kitchen floor. Her head pounded, which nauseated her. She scurried to the bathroom to throw up. When she lifted her head from the sink and looked at herself in the mirror, she noticed a cut and some dried blood on the right side of her forehead. She also noticed a large bruise around the right corner of her right eyelid.

I must have hit the corner of the kitchen table when I passed out, she thought. She remembered making the phone call at 11 a.m. The clock in the bathroom showed 2 p.m. *What? I was unconscious for three whole hours? Oh, my God!*

When her mind cleared, Rob's unkind words and his angry tone of voice came through to her again like a dagger, stabbing her heart, repeatedly, shredding it into a million pieces. With each stab, pain radiated to every nerve and fiber of her body.

She cried in private for days and was distraught for weeks, then months. Somehow, she managed to hide her distress from everyone else. It was hard enough that she was hurting; it was unbearable that she had no one to talk to about the pain she was going through. The feelings tormented her.

As a married woman, she wasn't at all proud of her extramarital affair. Definitely, no one in her social circles would sympathize with her. Instead, they'd ostracize and banish her, never to let her into their tight groups again. It would be just like what had happened to one of her friends, Sarah. In fact, Sandy was one of the people who stopped being friends with Sarah when Sarah found herself in a similar situation a few years back.

Sandy thought of her now, and oh, how she wished she could have been more understanding and sympathetic, instead of being judgmental, critical, and dismissive when Sarah confided in her.

"How could you cheat on Brad like that? Are you ready to sacrifice your marriage and family because of your lust?" Sandy hadn't, for the life of her, been able to understand why anybody would do such a thing.

"Did you think I went looking for a man, intending to fall in love so I can carry on an affair? It just … just … *happened.*" Sarah had sobbed and cried inconsolably as she talked to Sandy. "If I were married with someone else before I met Brad, it would not have stopped me from falling in love with him, either. Besides, I didn't come to you for a lecture. I came to you for moral support because I'm feeling miserable with all these confusing emotions I've been feeling."

Sandy now understood what Sarah must have felt and must have gone through. She still didn't know how and why she fell for Rob. She sure hadn't gone looking, either. It simply happened. She still loved Steve very much, but she also loved Rob. How could she have denied her love for Rob if she loved him just as much? Now she suffered and agonized on an emotional level, just as Sarah had.

* * *

Makenna felt drained from writing this chapter, for it had affected her in an intimate way. Even so, she found writing it both therapeutic and cathartic. She had felt betrayed after learning the truth. "Why wasn't I told about this sooner," she had asked.

"We didn't think it was necessary to tell you," her dad had

said. She wished she'd never known the truth. But now, she was grateful. Without her knowing the truth, she might have gone through with the divorce and lost Clint, the love of her life.

Clint was now making noise in the bathroom. She could hear him flush the toilet and turn the faucet on. She decided to stop writing for now, so she could get their breakfast ready.

CHAPTER 21

Sandy had been feeling nauseated a week before she performed the home pregnancy test, but now she started to throw up.

"What's the matter? Are you sick?" Carrie asked her on one of those episodes.

"I think I have a stomach flu."

"Oh, *great*. That means we're all gonna get sick too. I can't afford to get sick. I have semi-finals next week."

Sandy waved her off. "Don't worry you won't get sick."

Carrie grasped her arms together under her breasts. "How would you know?" She peeled her right arm out of the fold to hold out an open hand. "That's supposed to be very contagious, right?"

"I'll make sure you won't get sick," Sandy said with a wave back and forth of her hand.

Both arms came out, in an imploring gesture. "If you weren't able to keep yourself from getting sick, how would you keep me from getting sick?"

For the first time since Carrie came to live with her, Sandy expressed a bit of irritation toward her. "Look, if I said you're not going to get sick, you're not, okay?" As soon as she scolded her sister, she regretted it. Especially when Carrie fell instantly mum, pivoted around, and marched off to her room.

The following week, she was still vomiting and was feeling sicker. She did not have the energy to spend much time with her children after they came home from school. She called in sick the day she passed out, and it was fortuitous, too. She hadn't felt well for the rest of the day. She was scheduled to be off the next night for working the coming weekend, which gave her more time to recuperate.

"Where's Mommy," Sheyenne asked.

"She's sick," Carrie said, stroking Sheyenne's hair, "so she asked me to come get you and Taurea."

"Mommy, please don't die," Sheyenne said, with Taurea whimpering and nodding in agreement when they found their mother in bed after they arrived home from school. It was the first time Carrie was the one to get them from school. Naturally, they were worried.

"Mommy's okay, sweeties," Sandy assured them.

"May I come to bed, Mommy?" Sheyenne said.

"May I come, too, Mommy?" Taurea said.

Sandy agreed and welcomed them to her bed. Sheyenne went to her right side, and Taurea cuddled up to her left. They all hugged and snuggled in bed. Their presence and chattering somewhat relieved her thoughts from Rob's hurtful words.

CHAPTER 22

"What's with the bruises?" Joe said.

"What bruises?"

He huffed and pointed. "On your forehead and eyelid, that's what."

"Oh, those," she said with a dismissive wag of her hand. "I got up too fast, felt dizzy, and fainted." Sandy had been giving the same untruth to everybody who asked. She didn't tell Joe or anyone about the phone call she made to Rob, either. She thought her pregnancy probably made her more susceptible to fainting.

"You didn't hurt yourself anywhere else, too, did you?" Joe seemed concerned.

"I don't think so."

"How long were you out?"

"Three hours, I think."

"Woo … that's a long time. Did you go see a doctor to check you out?"

"No." Tears threatened. She looked upward, hoping to hold them back. Her nose flared a bit at the onset of a cry.

"Did I say something wrong?" Joe's eyebrows furrowed as he looked closely at her.

She blew out a deep sigh of resignation, and said, "Joe, I'm pregnant."

"*Congratulations*," he let out with a whoop and his hands clasping his face.

She rushed a finger to her lips in a 'shhh' signal. "You

don't understand. *This is not Steve's,*" Sandy said in a desperate controlled voice, making sure no one overheard her. She was now crying.

"*Oh.*" Joe's face showed his shock. "I'm … I'm … *speechless.*" His face became somber, showing concern and sympathy for her.

"Please don't say anything about this to anybody." Joe had been a good friend and a coworker to her. Now he was going to be her life-long confidante.

"I promise." He placed a reassuring hand on her shoulder. "I won't. But what are you going to do now?"

"I don't know." She sniffled. "I don't know."

"Why don't you go take a break if it makes you feel better."

"Thanks. I think I'm going outside to my car for a short while, if that's okay."

"Sure. Take your time. I'll cover for you."

"Thanks again." She went outside after she put on her winter coat. The crisp, frozen air of the winter night numbed her face as soon as she stepped out of the building. She shivered. The foot of snow that blanketed the ground and the shrubs made everything bright. She looked up at the sky. Billions of stars shone brightly against the clear dark-blue, almost black, heavens. It reminded her of the night she and Rob were walking outside the Starlight Club almost two months ago—such a stark contrast to how it was for her tonight.

Inside her car, she cried some more when she thought of Rob's hurtful words. But, her cry of pain and sorrow was mixed with some anger and fury. She was angry at Steve, at Rob, and at herself. *If Steve had loved me more, showed me some affection, and paid more attention to me, Rob's seduction would not have had any effect on me.*

She was also angry at Rob for seducing her in the first place, knowing she was a married woman. She was furious with him for making love to her, and then, after that, treating her the way he did. Ultimately, she was incensed at herself for being weak and stupid, and angry for giving into the wishes and desires of her heart rather than taking heed to the sensibilities of her head. Ooh, she hated herself. The angrier she got the less she cried. She finally calmed down and gathered herself together.

"Feeling better?" Joe asked when she returned.

"Yes. Thank you." Joe nodded, spun around on his heel, and walked away. She was grateful he didn't ask questions, because any more inquiries or even talk about this catastrophe would surely make her start crying again.

Before they left work that morning, Joe went to check up on her. "How're you feelin'?"

"Better, I think. Thank you."

"I think you should go see a doctor as soon as possible." He placed a hand on her shoulder. "Sandy … fainting, and falling unconscious for three hours, you have me concerned about you. Especially now, knowing you are pregnant."

"I will," she assured him. Joe started to leave when she called out to him. "And Joe, thanks again."

"Anytime, Sandy."

The next day, Sandy contemplated where to go for her prenatal check-up. *Should I go to the Base Hospital or go downtown? If I go downtown, my laboratory tests will be done where I work. I cannot lie about my pregnancy to my coworkers if they ask me. And, I don't want to have to deal with any of their questions. If I go to the Base Hospital, there could be a possibility that somebody I know will run into me and become too nosy. Steve might find out through them.*

In the end, she made the decision to go to the base hospital. She called to make an appointment at Minot Air Force Base's OB clinic and took her chances. While she spoke with a scheduler on the phone, Sandy took notes. On a piece of paper, she wrote: OB Appt.—Dec. 15, Monday @ 0900.

CHAPTER 23

The weekend was a busy one for Makenna. She helped Clint fix some fences around their property that had come loose or damaged. She was too tired to do any writing during the nights. Instead, she relaxed and spent some family time with Clint and their daughter, Chloe.

Today, after a good night's sleep, and after Clint left for work, she felt ready to continue writing. She wanted to write before Chloe woke up.

She poured herself some hot coffee, then added some creamer into it. She sat on the sofa with her back against the armrest, stretched her legs to the length of the sofa, placed her computer on her lap and turned it on. She took sips of her coffee while her laptop booted up. After logging in and a few clicks, she was in the chapter she had been working on. She read a few sentences to jog her memory, in hopes for ideas to start flowing in. At last, she started to type.

* * *

On the day of her first prenatal appointment, Sandy went in early to fill out pages of forms. A staff sergeant, who was an Air Force medical assistant, called her name in the waiting room. Sandy got up and followed her to a room.

In the room, Sandy's height and weight were measured. Her blood pressure was read. Then all the data was noted in her medical chart.

"Make sure to wear short sleeves on your next visits so it's easier to take your blood pressure readings," the staff sergeant said. "When was the first day of your last menstrual period?"

Sandy thought a moment and said, "I believe September seventeenth." The sergeant asked her more questions and then wrote more notes on Sandy's chart.

"Go ahead, undress and put the gown on with the opening to the front. The doctor should be here soon." The sergeant walked out of the room.

"Hello, Misses Richardson. I'm Doctor Moran." Dr. Moran wore captain bars on each side of her lapels. "I assume you are Doctor Richardson's wife? I noticed him as your spouse, according to your chart."

"Yes, I am. Nice to meet you, Doctor Moran." *Great*, Sandy thought, just what I need.

"When does he come back from Kosovo?"

"Next September. His tour of duty there got extended." Sandy had a feeling that Dr. Moran suspected the pregnancy was not with Steve. She was relieved when she didn't ask any more questions about him.

Dr. Moran proceeded with Sandy's physical and prenatal examination, which included the collection of samples for a Pap smear and swabs for wet prep, Group B Streptococcus test, and Chlamydia and Gonorrhea tests. She wrote a prescription for prenatal vitamins and a requisition for prenatal laboratory tests. She also wrote her a requisition to take to the Family Practice Clinic.

"Everything seems to be okay. Unless you're having problems, I'll see you in four weeks. Do you have any questions so far?"

"Not at the moment."

At that, Dr. Moran smiled at her as she handed her the orders she had written.

Sandy went to the laboratory to have her tests done. An airman first class—AIC, with two stripes on her uniform sleeves, called her name. As she followed her into the drawing room, she saw Joe in his office. He was seated behind a mahogany desk, writing. Sandy did not disturb him.

"May I speak with Joe before I leave," Sandy asked the young woman after her blood was drawn.

"Joe?" The young woman appeared confused.

"Yes. The man in the office we passed coming here."

"*Oh*. You mean Sergeant Webber?"

Sandy nodded.

"We know him as Technical Sergeant Webber, but we call him Sergeant Webber for short. Sure, you may."

Before Sandy left the lab, she stuck her head inside Joe's open office door and said, "Knock, knock," in rhythm with a couple raps on the door jamb.

"*Sandy*," Joe said as he looked up, beaming with a pleasantly surprised face. He hadn't seen her for a few days, due to conflicting schedules. He stood and motioned her to have a seat opposite his. "What brought you here?"

"I went to my prenatal appointment." Sandy was astonished. Joe looked sharp and distinguished in his crisply ironed light-blue Air Force uniform. "You certainly look different in your uniform. Almost like a different person."

"Just the uniform differentiates Sergeant Webber from the Joe you work with in scrubs at Trinity," he said with a chortle.

"No. It's not just the uniform. Even with the way you act and talk."

"Git outta here," he said, blushing into the color of a ripe tomato. "So … what did the doctor say?"

"Everything looks good. I'll see her in four weeks unless I have problems between now and then."

"That's good. Did you mention to the doctor about you passing out for three hours?" Sandy appreciated his, once again, showing concern, and took it as a show of his affection.

"I did. First, I have to go to the Family Practice Clinic. Then the Family Practice Physician will evaluate me to see if I need to see a neurologist."

"I'm glad you're taking my advice. Would you be going to see a doctor about it if I hadn't said anything?"

"Probably not. Thanks for looking after me."

"Well, somebody has to," he said with a satisfied smile.

"I guess I should be going now and leave you to your work. I still have to go to the pharmacy to pick up my prenatal vitamins and to make my appointment at the Family Practice Clinic."

"I'll see you Wednesday night."

"Okay."

After what seemed like a decade at the base hospital doing this and that, Sandy finally headed home. After she parked her car in the drive way, she went inside the house and hung her coat in the closet by the hallway to the living room. She was surprised to find her mother with Carrie in the living room.

"Mom, *what a surprise*." Sandy went to hug her mother. "Is everything okay? Is Dad Okay? Why didn't you tell me you were coming? Did you know Mom was coming, Carrie?" Sandy was truly perplexed.

"Everything is okay. Your dad is okay. But what Carrie's telling me is that you're not okay."

"*What?*" Sandy glared at Carrie. She felt the pupils in her eyes narrowing to a pinpoint and her cheeks started smoldering. "So, what exactly have you been telling Mom and Dad about me?"

"Please don't be angry at your sister. She's just concerned," her mother said. Carrie stood and left the room immediately without looking at her sister, who was still casting her a deadly glare.

When Carrie disappeared into her room, her mom spoke again in a motherly and non-confrontational voice. "Your sister said that she found a positive pregnancy kit in the trash can while she was emptying your bathroom trash two weeks ago. Then you got sick with the ... *flu* ... that lasted a while, and then you started acting weird about every little thing. It's so unlike you at all, Punkin'. Because she was concerned, she talked to me about it, and so I decided to come here."

Sandy's voice elevated in temper. "It would have been nice

if she talked to me first before going straight to you."

"Well, are you okay, Sandy?" Her mother looked at her with intensity.

Sandy was fuming. "I'm okay, and I'll take care of it if there's anything wrong." Sandy stormed out of the living room, went into her bedroom, and slammed the door behind her.

* * *

When Sandy had left the living room, Carrie emerged from her room, crying, and then went to hug her mother.

"I'm sorry Mom," she said.

Christina hugged her back. In a soft and motherly voice, she said, "For what sweetie?"

"I shouldn't have said anything to you. I should have just kept quiet about the whole thing."

"Shh…," her mother said, patting her back to soothe her.

"Now she hates me. She probably wants me to leave. Because of me, she yelled at you, Mom. I've never heard her talk to you that way before. Oh, Mom, I'm so sorry."

"No, my baby," her mother said, still embracing and consoling her. "You did the right thing. Your sister needs our help. She's just upset right now. And, don't think for one minute that she hates you. We'll just leave her be for now. She'll come to her senses soon, I'm sure."

"Thank you, Mom."

"You're welcome, my baby."

* * *

Inside the bedroom, Sandy was furious. She forced herself to go to sleep. She was awakened by knocks on her door. "Yes?"

"Do you have to go to work tonight?" her mother said.

"Yes." Sandy looked at the clock. 10:00 p.m. "Oh—*shit*," she said, surprising herself for saying it. Cussing was never a part of her vocabulary. She bolted out of bed and opened the door. "Thanks Mom."

"You're welcome. Carrie went to pick up Sheyenne and Taurea at school. They're both asleep now, so don't worry about them."

Sandy felt so irresponsible for forgetting about her kids and for not setting her alarm clock on. How could she then tell her mother that she was a responsible adult to deal with whatever problem came her way? Ooh, she felt small and helpless. She rushed to get ready for work, and went to check on her kids. Her mother and sister were still awake, watching the news in the family room. She went to put her arms around her mother and squeezed.

"Mom, I'm sorry about earlier."

"No problem, Punkin. Don't work too hard."

Sandy moved on to give Carrie a hug "I'm sorry Carrie, for getting angry at you. Thanks for your concern. We'll talk more tomorrow."

Carrie's eyes filled up. "I'm glad," she said, almost choking with emotion, "you're not mad at me anymore."

"I'm sorry again. I love you ... and you, too, Mom. I've gotta go. See you both in the morning."

CHAPTER 24

T he night felt magical as the stars twinkled brightly in the sky. Clint and Makenna sat outside in an open deck, out in the country, enjoying their solitude. They were drinking some unsweetened iced tea. The hoots of owls, howls of coyotes, and the sound of crickets and other creatures of the night provided the soundtrack to the scene.

"Are you going to bed now," Makenna asked when Clint stood after he finished his tea.

"Yeah, I think I should, since I have to get up early in the morning. I'm going to Cheyenne to represent a young couple in court. I'd like to make sure I have everything I need before going."

"I think I'm going to do some more writing tonight, so don't wait for me."

"Okay. Just don't stay up all night."

They gave each other a hug and a wet kiss before saying goodnight. Clint went to the bedroom, while Makenna went to where her laptop sat. Makenna started typing the next chapter of her novel.

* * *

Sandy was met by blasts of freezing winds as she stepped out of the house. She held the hood of her winter jacket tight to her face, fighting her way to her car parked in the driveway. She was appreciative of having a four-wheel-drive Honda CR-V EX to get around in that nasty weather. She drove much slower than usual; she could only see one car-length in front of her.

A usual fifteen-minute drive on a nice weather day took her forty-five minutes. The wind had subsided from when she left the base. As Sandy walked from the parking lot to the hospital, the snow made crunchy sounds with each step she took. Her breath gave off steam.

An ambulance, with its siren blaring and lights flashing, pulled up to the emergency room entrance door. Sandy heard the overhead announcement for a "Trauma Respond" as she entered the building.

As soon as she had clocked-in and put her lab coat on, she went to work right away. Lana briefed her with what was going on in the blood bank department before handing the department over to her.

"Pending list is clear, except for the trauma respond that just arrived. Except for one trauma patient from a car accident earlier, it has been a quiet evening. You shouldn't have to order anymore blood products from United Blood Services. There's enough in our inventory."

"Thank you, Lana." Sandy went ahead and processed four units of O Negative blood and delivered them to the emergency room for the new trauma patient. The night shift went from a relatively quiet evening to a very busy night. They were able to get their lunch breaks, though.

※ ※ ※

When Sandy arrived home in the morning, Taurea went running toward her as soon as she saw her enter the door.

"Mommy, Mommy, I missed you so much." She was crying as she gave Sandy a tight hug. She clung to Sandy's neck as if she was afraid of letting go. Sheyenne came out of the bathroom, ran up to Sandy and hugged her tightly also. She joined her sister in crying while Sandy tried to console them.

"I'm sorry you didn't get to see me last night. I promise, tonight, we'll order pizza and we'll have a pizza party with Grandma and Aunt Carrie, okay?"

"Okay," the two responded together.

"Go finish getting ready, so I'll drive you to school."

Sheyenne and Taurea obeyed with happy faces.

After Sandy drove the children to school, and after Carrie left for school, Sandy and her mother went to the living room. Sandy opened the picture window's curtains. She stayed standing by the right side of the window, looking out. She placed both hands in her uniform pockets. "Sure is a beautiful day," she said. She saw the sky was clear. There were no clouds in sight as the sun radiated from the east. The freshly fallen snow on the front yard looked pristine. It glistened in the sun's rays.

Christina joined her, but stood more in the middle of the window. She had her arms crossed over her chest. "It sure is," she said. She looked in Sandy's way. "How're you feeling, Punkin? You must be tired and ready to go to bed."

Sandy turned her head and body half way toward her mother. "I'm okay, Mom. I feel fine right now. I think I have my second wind." She was looking forward to talking to her mother about her dilemma. She'd thought about it during the night while at work. She realized she truly needed her family's support.

She took her eyes off her mother and looked outside again. "Mom, I know you'll be very disappointed with me when I tell you I'm two months pregnant with another man's baby."

"Well ... I sort of suspected as much before coming here." Her mother directed her eyes outside.

"I haven't told this to Steve, yet," Sandy said, still looking out.

"Good. In that case, I suggest you should get an abortion."

Her mother's words shocked her. She abruptly snapped her head to face Christina. "*Mother*. How could you even suggest such a thing?" Sandy's voice raised in volume and intensity. "Of all people, you're the last person I thought would suggest to me to get an abortion." She went to flop on one end of the long sofa after removing her shoes.

Her mother went to sit on the loveseat catty-corner to her, resting her right arm on the armrest. She crossed her left leg over her right leg in a lady-like pose, with her left shoe's tip pointing downward. "Normally, I would not suggest such a thing. But under this circumstance, abortion is inevitable unless you're ready for a divorce from Steve. You and Steve are perfect for each other. You have the perfect marriage and a beautiful family. Are you ready to risk all of these?"

"Mother, I want you to know that my marriage is far from perfect. If it were, I wouldn't be in this situation."

Her mother's eyes shot wide open. "What … what are you saying?"

Sandy's face fell. She gave a little whimper and said in a moan, "That I have been unhappy for a very long time." She looked up at her mom and then her head went back down. "I need a man who loves me and who can actually show me his love. I want to truly feel what love is, Mother." Sandy by now was sobbing. She felt like her heart was spilling out of her mouth until her chest was a vacuous chamber of misery.

"I'm sorry, Punkin." Her mother rose, went over to her, and pulled her into her embrace. "I didn't know you've been unhappy for a long time now. Why didn't you tell me sooner?"

"Because I didn't think it's something I should be telling you about. You, Dad, and Carrie think so highly of Steve that I didn't want his reputation marred in your eyes."

"Has he been abusive to you in any way?"

"See, that's the hardest thing," she said, easing out of her mother's arms, sniffling and wiping away the tears, "because he's never been physically or verbally abusive, but … I feel emotionally abused. He ignores me, is impatient with me, and acts grouchy around me most of the time. He's such a perfectionist that when things don't turn out just the way he expects them to be, he gets angry and then takes it out on me by ignoring me and by not speaking to me … Mom," she squeezed her eyes shut, with more tears oozing out, "Mom, sometimes for days!"

Sandy forced herself to regain a measure of composure. She went into the kitchen to pull a sheet of paper towel off the roll. As Sandy sat again, she dabbed her eyes and said, "Don't think that he's a terrible person, Mom, because he's not. He gives me all the material things I need. He's never cheated on me, that I know. But he's emotionally detached and physically aloof. What I'm longing mostly for from him is his love and affection, but he's incapable of showing or giving it. So, when Rob showed and gave me the things that were lacking in my marriage, I fell for him and this is where I am now."

"This Rob, where is he now? Does he know that you're pregnant with his child?"

Sandy buried her face in her hands. She took a deep breath and exhaled, loud, long and heavy. "That's another thing, Mom. I tried to contact him to tell him about it, but he shut me out." Mother and daughter locked eyes in a moment of horrific understanding. "I thought for sure he loved me, but …" Sandy started weeping again at the thought, then anger took hold of her. She spat out, "But he told me a week ago on the phone that he doesn't love me. He didn't even give me a chance to tell him I'm pregnant with his baby. I certainly don't want him to know about it now, knowing that he doesn't love me. I hate men! *They're all the same.* They're all so nice until they get you in bed, and then they treat you like nothing after that!"

"Oh, honey," her mother opened her arms wide, "not all men are bad. Look at your dad. He's a wonderful man."

Sandy snorted, then gave a little dip of the head in acknowledgement. "Dad is the exception."

After an awkward, prolonged silence, Sandy's mother said, in a quiet, consoling voice, "What do you want to do now, sweetie? If you want to preserve your marriage, my suggestion is for you to get an abortion."

"I don't think I can go through with it, Mom, even if I want to stay married. I think I'll just tell Steve and take my chances."

"Whatever you decide, we'll be here for you." There was another long silence between them before Christina spoke. "I think that, for now, you should go to sleep and get some rest. We'll talk some more when you're well rested."

Sandy pulled her face up out of her hands, where they had been buried again. "Sounds like a good idea. I do kinda feel tired now. Thanks, Mom, for being here for me right now. I'm sorry again for yelling at you last night." They hugged before Sandy traipsed off to the bedroom.

❋ ❋ ❋

As Sandy had promised Sheyenne and Taurea, she called in an order for a couple pizzas before picking them up from school. The children acted like they were back to their normal routine when their mother was the one who picked them up at school. The doorbell rang a few minutes after they arrived home.

"*Pizza is here*," Sheyenne and Taurea shouted as they ran to open the door, with Sandy right behind them. The delivery man came in, and placed the still piping-hot pizzas on the table. Just then, Carrie arrived home from school. The children were antsy about getting started.

"Keep your pants on," Sandy said. Instantly, the two became silent. With perplexed looks on their faces, they looked down to check their pants. They grabbed their pants and held onto them. It took a few seconds for Sandy, Carrie, and their mom, Christina, to figure out what was happening with the two. After that, the three adults let out their boisterous laughter, a prelude to a good and happy evening for all of them.

Since Sandy was off that night, she was able to mingle with the rest until they all retired to their own rooms. For once in a very long time, she felt loved and happy—the kind of love and happiness without guilt and reservation whatsoever. She let out a sigh of complete contentment. Sleep came to her effortlessly.

The next thing she knew, it was already six-thirty in the morning. She felt relaxed and well rested. She went about her daily routine with Sheyenne and Taurea. She visited with her mother until she had to go to sleep, before going to work.

CHAPTER 25

During their drive from their home in Elk Mountain to Cheyenne, Chloe said, "Mommy, where are we going?"

"We're going to Cheyenne to see Grandma and Grandpa. You're going to stay with them while I go to my doctor's appointment, okay? Also, Mommy's going to order her wig today."

"What's a wig, Mommy?"

"Well, it's somebody's hair that I buy in a store, which I'll be wearing when I lose my own hair."

"Why are you going to lose your hair, Mommy?"

"Remember when Daddy and I talked about you staying with Grandma and Grandpa when I go to the hospital?"

Chloe nodded.

"Well, after my surgery, my doctor will give me treatments called chemotherapy, which will make me lose my hair." At her age, she thought, she could only give her the short version about the whole process.

Excited, Chloe said, "Oh, oh, then you wear your wig, Mommy?"

"Very good, Honey. You're so smart."

Chloe's smile and body language let Makenna know she was feeling happy and proud with herself.

When they returned home, she and Chloe took a long nap. At night, after Chloe and Clint went to sleep, Makenna was again in front of her laptop to continue her writing. I have to hurry up with my writing if I want to accomplish as much as I can before my surgery, she told herself.

* * *

Three days had passed since Christina arrived in Minot. It was time for her to go back to Minnesota.

"Mom, thanks again for coming here. I love you. Please tell Dad I love him too," Sandy said as she hugged her mother.

"Gramma, when do you come see us again?" Sheyenne said.

"Christmas, I hope."

"Gramma," Taurea piped in as she tugged at her grandma's jacket. She was not going to be left out in saying goodbye. Grandma picked her up.

"Yes, sweetie."

"Please bring Grampa when you come back."

"Of course, honey. Both of us will come to see all of you at Christmas time. In the meantime, you both behave yourselves, okay?" She put Taurea down, hugged Sheyenne, then gave her attention to her own baby.

"Carrie ..."

"Mom ..."

"Good luck to you with your finals next week," Christina said as they held each other close.

"Thanks, Mom. I sure need it; especially now that my classes are getting harder. I love you ... and Dad, too."

"Flight Two Eighteen to Minneapolis is ready for boarding," was announced overhead.

"That's my flight number. I have to go, my darlings. I love you all. I had a real good time." Christina gave each one a hug and a kiss one more time before entering the gate. All of them stayed at the airport until the plane left the ground. They stayed, watching until the plane disappeared into the horizon. Before heading home, they stopped at Dairy Queen for some treats.

CHAPTER 26

Makenna got up from her chair. She stretched her body upward and from side to side. Ooh, that feels so good, she thought, and then gave out a big sigh when she completed her stretches.

She was having difficulty coming up with more ideas to write for her novel.

Think - think - think.

Hot cappuccino at 2 a.m. sounds like a good idea right now, she figured. She hoped the cappuccino would invigorate her overworked, sleepy brain cells.

When she finished making her concoction, she took a few sips. Mm … yummy. She savored the taste and warmth of her cappuccino as it traveled over her palate and down her throat. After a few more sips and a little more brainstorming, she thought she was ready to type again.

✳ ✳ ✳

"How did your visit with the doctor go today," Joe asked Sandy when they worked together that night. He'd been interested in Sandy's well-being ever since he found out she was pregnant, and she had fainted for three hours. He had so much compassion for her that he took it upon himself to look after her in her husband's absence.

Each time Joe looked at Sandy now, he didn't see a self-confident, independent, attractive, mature woman. Instead, he saw a vulnerable, fragile, naïve woman who needed someone to protect her. He felt compelled to somehow shield her from anything that would harm her.

"Doctor Reynolds, the Neurologist who saw me today, said that, based on what I told him, he doesn't think there was anything more to it than I just flat out fainted. However, he went ahead and made an appointment for me to have an EEG tomorrow. I'm happy that the base hospital granted my request to see a Neurologist downtown and for these tests to be done in town. It's also better than the original plan of sending me all the way to Fitzsimmons Army Medical Center in Denver, Colorado."

"No kidding," Joe said, nodding. "So, what exactly is he looking for in the EEG?"

The phone rang, and he had to answer it. He looked in the computer and then said, "Yes, it's finished. Try refreshing your screen, and see if that does the trick." After a few seconds he said, "You're welcome," and hung up.

"Sorry about that," he said to Sandy.

"Eh, no problem. Anyway, to answer your question about the EEG, Doctor Reynolds wants to make sure I didn't have a seizure, and to rule out epilepsy."

"Epilepsy?" Joe stiffened.

"Yeah. I said the same thing when he said that. I know I don't have epilepsy and that I didn't have a seizure." Sandy rolled her eyes and bobbed her head. "But, whatever ..." She waved off the notion, "Doctor Reynolds also said that if the EEG comes out abnormal, it means I have epilepsy. So, each time there's a sudden surge of disorganized electrical impulses in my brain, then I'll have a seizure."

Joe flipped a palm up. "Then what?"

"Then ... he's going to order CT Scan and MRI to see what's causing my epilepsy. He mentioned possible brain tumors or other brain diseases and infections. Maybe I have a brain tumor." Her shoulders rose and fell. "Who knows?"

Joe placed both hands on her shoulders and looked her in

the eye. "I don't think you have any of those," he said in a consoling tone, then released her from his hold.

"I put a STAT specimen for type and cross in blood bank," Carmen said.

"Thanks Carmen," Sandy said, then turned to Joe. "Guess I have to go take care of that now."

CHAPTER 27

J oe?" Sandy said when she was delivering some specimens to his department the next time they worked.

"Yes?" Joe said from where he was standing, hunched over, cleaning the sample and reagent probes of the chemistry analyzer.

Sandy moved closer to him. "May I have a word with you when you're not busy?"

"Sure … just need to finish up here, and then I'll come over."

"Okay … thanks."

When Joe finished loading his QC materials, he went over to Sandy's department. He sat on a rolling chair near where Sandy was seated while she was reviewing results in the computer before finalizing them. "So … what'd'ya wanna talk to me about?"

Sandy faced Joe after she finalized the last result. She looked around before she started talking in a hushed voice. "I know you told me before that you don't want to hear about Rob and me if it goes beyond the songs."

"Yes, I remember telling you that." He was bobbing his head up and down. "So?" He searched Sandy's eyes. "Oh, geez. He's your baby's father?"

Sandy bowed her head in shame and then nodded.

"So, why do you want to tell me this?"

"Joe, I have no one to talk to about my problem other than my mom. I feel so alone." Her voice was breaking and eyes beading. "Besides, I thought you'd like to know."

"I'm so sorry, Sandy. I'm such a jerk. Of, course. Thanks for letting me know. I'd been wanting to ask, but I knew it wasn't my place, so I didn't bother."

"Thanks, Joe. I know I can count on you." She wiped her tears with some Kleenex tissue.

"Does Rob know?"

Sandy shook her head.

"And, why not?" His brows narrowed.

"Remember when I fainted and ended up with bruises?"

"Uhuh. Geez, he didn't beat you up, did he?"

"No, no. Not physically, but he might as well have." Sandy related to him about the phone call and the conversation.

"Shame on him. He should be shot." His words were intentionally stern and angry. "I liked the guy, you know? Now, I detest him for what he's done to you."

"Thank you, Joe. Your words of support mean so much. I don't feel so alone anymore."

"You're welcome. Hey, come talk to me anytime, okay?"

"Okay. Thanks … please keep my situation just between you and me?"

"Of course." He made a zip sign on his lips before he left.

CHAPTER 28

C hristmas 1999 came in a big way. Sandy's parents, Larry and Christina, arrived two days before Christmas.

"Wow, your Christmas tree is *beautiful*," Sandy's mother marveled at the seven-foot tall live tree placed in a corner of the living room. Her father also expressed his admiration.

"Oh, Mom and Dad, you should have seen us when we went to get it," Sandy said.

"Why?" her father said.

"Well, first off, we had walked through almost the entire plant nursery before we chose that one. Sheyenne would pick out a tree and then all of us would gather around it. Then, we'd mull over it as we critiqued it. One of us would point out a missing branch at the bottom, not full enough at the top, not straight enough, or there's a big gap on the other side." Sandy could see by her mother and father's eyes and facial expressions that both of them were amused.

"Of course, every Christmas tree candidate was evaluated by the same strict criteria as the first one. Knowing the process involved, Sheyenne was so happy and proud of herself for finding our *perfect* Christmas tree this year."

"That sounds exciting, honey. I bet that would have been a sight to see ... I love how you decorated it," her mother said.

"Thanks, Mom. Sheyenne and Taurea made those cutout white paper angels, birds, and stars at school. All of us made those strings of popcorn," Sandy said, pointing them out as she talked.

The strings of popcorn draped up and down, round and round the tree like laces, crisscrossing with the strings of multicolored Christmas lights. The ornaments Sandy and Steve had collected over the years also decorated it. Underneath the tree were the wrapped presents.

On Christmas Eve, Sheyenne and Taurea placed a plate with cookies and a glass of milk by the fireplace. Leaning against the glass of milk were two letters to Santa from them. In past years, Steve would fire up the fireplace during cold winter nights, and Sandy would sit in the rocking chair in front of the fireplace and just watch the fire until she fell into a deep trance. Alas, this winter was not the norm. Steve was not home for Christmas.

No matter, Sandy thought, *I will keep up with yet another family tradition.* She fired up the fireplace and stationed herself in the rocking chair as she always had. The logs crackled as they burned. Their flames danced from log to log, displaying their captivating hues of blue, red, orange and yellow flames. The flames enthralled and mesmerized her. The scent of pines emanating from the logs brought back wonderful memories of her childhood, camping with her family in the deepest woods of Minnesota.

Having a campfire was the reason Sandy had enjoyed going camping. She and her family would gather around the fire to roast marshmallows, tell stories, and get warmed up from the chill of the night. As the night progressed and the family's conversations became far in between, they'd still sit around the pit to watch the fire dance and change colors. Camping without a campfire, according to her, just wasn't the same.

Sheyenne's voice awakened Sandy from her trance. "Is Santa going to burn when he comes down the chimney, Mama?"

"No sweetie, because I'm going to put out the fire by pouring some water on it before I go to bed," Sandy assured her and Taurea, who was sitting next to Sheyenne by the fireplace.

The children were having a hard time staying awake till midnight. So Sandy put them to bed at 11:00 pm. After that, Sandy, Carrie, and Mr. and Mrs. Christensen put some small boxed presents in each of the children's Christmas stockings. The fasteners weren't strong enough to hold the weight. Therefore, Sandy put the stockings on the floor, in front of the fireplace.

As soon as the clock ticked midnight, everyone got up to give one another a hug and a kiss, while saying 'Merry Christmas'. It was the first time in a long time the foursome was together, celebrating the arrival of Christmas.

"Mom and Dad, this is like old times. It reminds me of my younger days still living at home," Sandy said. The couple agreed.

"And, you, Carrie, were always the center of attraction," Sandy said.

"Why's that?"

"'Because you were always entertaining us with your singing and dancing. You were so *cute*."

Carrie giggled. "Yeah, that's right. I'd forgotten all about that. Seems so long ago."

When their conversations stopped, Sandy stayed reflective of the past. The memories warmed her, and lingered with her until she fell asleep.

✻ ✻ ✻

Makenna had started writing this chapter early yesterday morning. She took a break when Chloe woke up at 9 a.m., and resumed it when Chloe went to nap at 2 p.m. When she felt tired and sleepy, she took a nap herself for almost an hour. When she woke up, she fixed dinner before Clint arrived home. They had their usual family get together in the family room after dinner, watching the news, playing with Chloe, or just talking about the day's events.

"How's your novel coming along?"

"Slowly, but surely. I've got to finish at least two-thirds of it before my surgery."

"Talking about your surgery, I'm taking two weeks off from work."

"Oh Clint, that's so sweet of you. But is it necessary for you to take two weeks? Mom and Dad will be able to stay with me some time. I'd hate for you to get so far behind and be buried with work when you get back."

"Darlin', you are more important to me than my work," Clint said as he winked at her. Makenna's heart fluttered each time Clint flirted with her like that. Even after seven years of marriage and a near divorce situation between them, Clint still had that kind of dizzying effect on her. She was forever thankful to her father, who had talked her into seeing the *bigger picture* of their lives, marriage, and family dynamics before making her final decision about getting a divorce.

At 11 p.m. earlier, Makenna had resumed her writing until she finished it. It was now 3 a.m. Her vision was distorted, making her see doubles. But now that this chapter was finished, she could go to sleep... soundly, she hoped.

CHAPTER 29

Makenna's concentration from her writing was distracted when her cell phone played ABBA's *Mamma Mia* ring tone.

"Hi Mom," she said, and then listened intently. "Oh, my goodness, I completely forgot about it. Thanks for reminding me, Mom." She looked at the clock on the living room wall. 8 a.m. "Do you think you and Dad would like to have lunch with Chloe and me if we come to Cheyenne around noon?"

Makenna paused again to listen. She waited while her mother checked with her father about having lunch. "Good. We'll come by your house to pick you guys up. We might as well ride in one vehicle to save a parking space at Applebee's. You know how bad it can get there during lunch hour. So hard to find parking most times." Her mother agreed and started talking again about their trip.

"So, you'll fly to Anchorage and then board the Carnival Cruise ship in Anchorage?" Her mother acknowledged her question and then expressed some reservations about her going. "Mom, I'll be fine. My surgery is not 'til the eighteenth, so you'll be back by then." She paused again. "Yes, Mom. I'll be sure to eat well and take my daily vitamins. I don't want you to go there, worrying 'bout me here. Otherwise, you're not going to enjoy yourself and will have just wasted your money. I still remember you talking about how much fun you both had on your first honeymoon to Australia. So, I want you and Dad to go to your second honeymoon and have another fun time. You both deserve this long-awaited cruise to Alaska."

Makenna looked at the clock again, and got up to go to the kitchen. She heated some water in her mug. "Okay, Mom. I'm just gonna finish this chapter I'm working on before Chloe wakes up." She stirred a scoopful of Mocha flavored powder in her mug. "See you soon. Love you, too, Mom. Give Dad my love. Bye." She took more sips of her mocha before taking her usual spot on the sofa.

✳ ✳ ✳

"*Merry Christmas*." It was Steve, calling from Kosovo.

"Merry Christmas to you, too, honey." Sandy was still sleepy when she answered the phone. "How are you?"

"Oh, I'm okay. Heard you got dumped on with three feet of snow yesterday."

"Yeah, and nobody's moving much in the neighborhood, except for the ones with snowmobiles. I'm glad I'm on vacation for the entire week. I don't have to go out in this weather. I'm thankful I heard the weather reports, warning of the blizzard. I went shopping ahead of time. The house is well stocked; we should have plenty of necessities as we wait out the storm and for things to return to normal."

"Good to know. What time is it there now?"

Sandy peeked over her pillow to check the time in her radio/alarm clock. "Six a.m.."

"Two in the afternoon here. We already had our Christmas lunch with all the trimmings. What about you? Are you going to have a turkey?"

"Of course, hon, except Mom will be the one cooking the turkey. I prepared the stuffing for her last night. Be making the side dishes today. Carrie said she's gonna make a dessert and a salad. Dad said he and the kids will be going outside to make a snowman. He's also going to build a mound of snow where Sheyenne and Taurea can sled down."

"Thanks again for the goodies and for my Christmas presents you all sent me. Sorry I didn't get you much for Christmas, but I'll make it up to you when I come home in September. I miss you all so much, but mostly you. Maybe you and I will finally go to our honeymoon that we never had? Hawaii sounds good, or do you prefer Australia or New Zealand?"

Sandy was getting choked up at Steve's expression of love for her. *If he only knew what I've done, he definitely would not be telling me those things. Oh, hon, I wish I could tell you. I keep telling myself to tell you about my situation before you come home. But I don't have the nerve, and this just isn't the right time. But when is it the right time to tell someone that you deceived him or her?*

"Sandy? Are you still there?"

Sandy swallowed hard to clear her throat before she spoke, but her voice cracked anyway, "Y-yes, honey."

"Is everything okay?"

"I'm just missing you so much, too." She was crying now. She really was missing him, but at the same time was overcome with a tremendous feeling of guilt. She had committed the gravest sin in her marriage.

"I'm sorry, Sandy. Just hang in there a little bit longer. Only nine more months. By the time you know it, I'll be home. I'm going to love you like no other. I'm going to hold you in my arms forever and never let go."

Oh, Steve, now you are expressing true love to me? She shook all over with grief. *The horrible irony of it—the more you say these things, the more ashamed and miserable I feel. I am so undeserving of any of this. God, I wish I could just drop dead.*

"Before I go, I'd like to speak to the kids."

Sandy pulled her fragmented self together enough to say, "Sure, honey." She went to wake up the kids. "They're coming."

"Oh good. I love you and just hang in there a little longer, okay?"

"Okay hon … I love you, too," she said as she cried some more.

Sheyenne and Taurea got on the phone and peppered their dad with all kinds of questions. They were full of excitement as they told him all the things they had done at school. They couldn't stop telling him how much they missed him and how much they loved him. They also kept asking when he'd come home. After what seemed like an endless interrogation and reporting by the children, Sandy handed the phone to Carrie.

Afterwards, Steve talked to Larry and Christina. The couple had welcomed him into the family and loved him as the true son they'd never had. They respected him for what he'd done for himself, considering the circumstances in his life. Orphaned at twelve and never knew his father. As for Steve, he considered them more as parents than as parents-in-law.

CHAPTER 30

Major Ben Harris, Steve's best friend in North Dakota, was having dinner with his wife, Beth. "I have to say, sweetie, this stuff is so good. What is it? He took another big bite and chewed it with gusto.

Beth swallowed her food before she spoke. "Thanks, Babe. It's called chicken delight."

"I don't think you made this before."

"No, I haven't. I got the recipe from my newly-found friend, Sandy."

"Oh, yeah?"

"Uhuh. I met her at the OB clinic yesterday. We were talking about cooking, and she shared me this recipe. I shared her my smothered burrito recipe."

"That's good, Babe. I'm glad you're making new friends." He took another bite.

"Yeah, me, too, especially she seems very nice. I feel bad for her, though."

"Why's that? he said before he drank some of his water.

"Because her husband is sent to Kosovo." She made a sad face.

"What's her name again?"

"Sandy Richardson."

Ben's ears perked up. "Sandy Richardson?"

"Uhuh."

"And her husband is in Kosovo?"

"Yep."

"Did she say if her husband's a doctor?"

Beth finished drinking her sweetened iced tea before she said, "As a matter of fact, she did say that. Do you know her?"

Ben picked up on the annoyance in her voice. "Yes sweetheart ... she's married to my buddy, Steve, who's now in Kosovo. What was she doing in the OB clinic?"

"For prenatal check-up. She said she's five months pregnant."

Even though Ben and Steve were best friends, Beth and Sandy had never met. Ben married Beth in Ohio after Steve was shipped out to Kosovo. Ben never got the opportunity to introduce his wife to Sandy.

"Hm ... interesting," Ben said. He did a quick mathematical calculation in his head and came to the conclusion there was no way the baby could be Steve's. He instructed Beth not to mention to Sandy about their conversation and not to reveal to Sandy that she's married to Steve's best friend. He explained to Beth about his suspicion. Given that information, Beth agreed.

For a few days, Ben mulled over as to whether or not to call Steve.

CHAPTER 31

Kosovo: March 21, 2000

H i, Ben. What's up? Good to hear from you." Steve was surprised to get a phone call from his friend. The last time he'd heard from Ben was at Christmas time when he received a card from him. They had talked on the phone four times since he arrived in Kosovo, but it was he who made the call each time. So, for Ben to be making the call was somewhat out of the ordinary.

"I'm good. What about you? How're things over there?"

"As good as can be expected in a war-torn country."

"Hey, have you heard from Sandy lately?"

"Yeah, a week ago. Why?"

"How'd it go?"

"Good … what're you getting at, Ben?"

"You didn't happen to come home to Minot from Kosovo since you left, without me knowing it, did you?"

"Now Ben, you really are putting me in a pissy mood. What's going on? Somethin' I should know about?"

"Sandy didn't mention anything unusual to you, did she?"

"None. *Dammit* Ben … just tell me what it is you want to say. Is Sandy running around on me?" Steve grated his teeth, clenching his jaw in response to his rising anger at the thought.

"You sittin' down?"

"Who cares whether I'm sitting down or standing up," growled Steve, but still in a low, controlled voice.

"Look, I don't know whether she is or not. All I know is that Beth, my wife, had met Sandy in the OB clinic, and the two of them have been talking when they see each other there. And, from what Beth tells me, Sandy is five months pregnant. That's why … I'm curious to know if you happened to come home to Minot without me knowing it."

A long silence ensued. Steve was not a very vocal person when angry, but by now his blood was burning in his veins. He felt his eyes turning glassy, filled with fury. His vision turned the color of his blood that was gathering, collecting, and streaming through the capillary veins in his eyes. His heart was beating an erratic rhythm and his breathing was irregular. The veins in his temples pulsated, bulging in and out. His jaw was a tightened vise, and his right hand formed into a prize fighter's fist.

How could Sandy allow me to speak lovingly to her all those months we spoke on the phone, and all the while she had been unfaithful to me? The thought sickened him. Bile came up from his gut to lend its bitter taste into his mouth. Oh, how he detested her. He regretted expressing his love for her in the most amorous way and for revealing his innermost secret fantasies for her when they spoke on Valentine's Day. He wished he could take them all back. His love for her had vanished that very instant.

"Steve, are you still there?"

Steve said nothing.

"I'm sorry, man. I feel bad to have to be the one to let you know about it. At least you won't be shocked when you come home in a few months."

Steve still didn't respond.

"Call me when you're ready to talk." The line stayed open on Ben's end.

Steve pounded his fist on his desk. He spoke, at last, after what seemed like a century. "Damn her!" His voice blasted like a ton of TNT, reverberating throughout the facility. People nearby were jolted out of their seats at his explosion. All eyes were directed toward him, but he scarcely noticed. Fury and disgust took over his whole being; he didn't have a care in the world who was hearing him.

"I want her out of the house right now! I don't want to see her there when I come home!"

People nearby started murmuring, acting shocked. Steve was peripherally aware, but didn't give a damn.

They knew him as, always, the soft-spoken and easy going kind of guy, so his shouting in such a rage had to be unsettling and baffling to them. *Mind your own business—get back to your work, people.*

Oddly enough, they seemed to hear his thoughts, because they did just that, albeit tentatively and looking confused.

"How about your kids?" Ben's query jolted him back.

"Don't know, but I sure's *hell* don't want my kids around her. I don't want them seeing what their mother is doing. I'm gonna get ahold of Colonel Morrow to see if I can leave sooner to deal with her."

After their conversation, Steve's initial reaction was to confront Sandy. Still raging, he dialed his house in North Dakota. No answer. Next, he dialed Sandy's cell phone. It went to her voicemail. He slammed the phone down and spewed out expletives. He stood, shoved and jammed his chair against his desk, making a clunking noise, before he left to go outside. He went to his room in the makeshift barracks and snatched his metal bat. Outside, he approached the nearest big tree. He beat at the poor tree until his strength was drained and his anger subsided enough to think clearer.

CHAPTER 32

C lint was outside on the patio, drinking a beer, his second. Leaning against the patio railing, he watched Makenna through the sliding screen door talking on the phone. He heard her wishing her mom and dad a happy bon voyage for their trip tomorrow.

From his vantage point, he could see Makenna's profile as she leaned back on the kitchen counter with her left elbow resting on the counter. Clint looked up at the night sky and gazed at the billions of stars above, twinkling with brilliance. Returning his gaze to Makenna, his eyes traced the contours of her body, lingering on her beautiful face and on her well-endowed breasts. Warm sensations emanated from his groin, affecting the rest of him, as he allowed himself to lust and fantasize about her. It had been a while since he'd laid eyes on his wife's flat-bellied, curvaceous figure.

Drawing in a deep breath, he closed his eyes and tried to imagine Makenna without her breasts after her surgery in nine more days. He hadn't given it much thought before tonight. He opened his eyes and he only could see her with them on. And tonight, she looked pretty darn hot in her fitted jeans and dark green tee shirt tucked inside her jeans. His beer consumption was—no doubt—helping stir up his longing for her as well. As soon as Makenna stepped out to the patio to join him after she finished talking on the phone, he said, "Darlin', come over here and give this cowboy some hot lovin' tonight."

Makenna, with her flirtatious smile, went to him, took the bottle away from him and put it on the patio table. In a provocative look and tone, she said, "Wha'd'ya say, cowboy?"

"I said, come over here and gimme some hot lovin' tonight." He drew her toward him.

"Ah, ah, ah. Only if ya promise to respect me in the mornin' after makin' love to me," she teased.

"Cross ma' heart 'n' pray to die, baby doll," he said, and gave her an irresistible wink and a smile. He was feeling impassioned toward her tonight; especially with Chloe spending the night at a friend's house. He loved her dearly, but he also welcomed some moments like this without her presence. It allowed him and Makenna to be lovers again. With the way Makenna was reacting toward him, he knew she felt the same way about everything he was thinking and feeling.

"In that case, I hope you have a lotta lovin' to give back, 'cause baby, I'm so ready for ya." Makenna teased him by giving him quick little kisses to the lips, neck, and chest as she unbuttoned his shirt in slow motion.

"Darlin', can you make it a little faster? You're killin' me with anticipation."

"Nope. I want it to go slow and take my time until you can't wait any longer."

"Heck, can't wait any longer, darlin', so I'm gonna do it my way." He took Makenna into his arms and kissed her ravenously. His hands were busy undressing her, while Makenna's hands were busy unzipping him. When their clothes had fallen on the floor, Clint carried Makenna to the hot tub. Using his right big toe, he pushed a button and the cover retracted to one side. He pushed another button and the water jets came alive. He pushed yet another button and the music came on with a Tracy Byrd tune: *The Keeper of the Stars*.

He placed her in the hot tub and proceeded to kiss her. Makenna moaned, arching her back when Clint kissed her voluptuous mounds sensuously.

Being ten miles away from their nearest neighbor, they had

the luxury of indulging each other in the hot tub outside the house without offending anyone. When they finished with their foreplay, they proceeded to perform the main act in the art of making love. Gasping for air to catch their breaths at the height of their love-making, they stayed glued to each other for a long moment until that most electrifying and all-engulfing sensation exploded beyond the threshold, leaving them completely drained, but totally fulfilled.

CHAPTER 33

Kosovo: March 28, 2000.

D octor Richardson, Colonel Morrow's on the phone for you!"
"Coming! Thanks, Sergeant Williams!" Steve shouted
back. He was outside of one of the trailers that served as the
hospital squadron's field office, talking to Dr. Rogers when he
was called in. Even though Steve had the rank of major in the Air
Force he was still called *doctor.*

"Hello, Colonel Morrow." Colonel Morrow was his hospital
commander in Minot and was also a doctor, but everybody called
him colonel. He didn't practice medicine much anymore, since
he was serving more as an administrator than as a physician.

After beating the helpless tree into almost a pulp a week
ago, Steve had gone to his quarters to gather his thoughts. He
hadn't felt like talking to Sandy anymore, so he hadn't tried to
call her again. Instead, he'd sent Col. Morrow an e-mail the next
day.

"Hello, Steve. I was away on vacation for a week, so I just
now read your e-mail. I'm sorry to hear about what's going on
with your personal life. Are you okay?"

"No, sir. *I'm mad as hell.*" Steve and the colonel always
had a good non-working friendly relationship, so Steve felt
comfortable saying the truth, with harsh words if need be.

"As to be expected. I truly empathize with you, Steve. And
I know you want to go home immediately, but I think it's not in
your best interest, nor your family's. Your emotions are running

high right now, which is understandably so."

"But Sir, I jus—"

"Tell you what, Steve, give it two weeks, and if you still want to go home then I'll see what I can do. This will give time for the tides to settle down. Whadaya think?"

"Ah, well ... sure. I mean, yes ... yes Sir," Steve said, trying to control his temper. He was incensed at the colonel for what he considered as blatant, callous insensitivity toward his predicament.

* * *

Sandy was at her prenatal appointment at the Minot Air Force Base Fifth Medical Group Hospital. It was time for her first ultrasound. She wasn't able to make her appointment a month ago, so her ultrasound had gone beyond the usual 16 to 20-week range.

The technician called her into the ultrasound room. "Did you remember to drink lots of water before you came?"

"Sure did. Feels like my bladder's about to burst."

"Let's get to it right away then."

Sandy changed into a hospital gown and settled on the ultrasound bed. She watched as the technician turned the machine on, programmed some specific settings, and entered the necessary information.

"This is going to feel cold when I put some on your belly," the technician said.

Sandy gave a squeal when the gel touched her skin. "You were not kidding. I should know it, too. But I'd forgotten." They both laughed.

"Sorry about that. But I warned ya," the technician said, grinning.

"Yes, you did, and I appreciated it." She continued to look on as the technician put a disposable plastic cover on the ultrasound machine's transducer probe. She and the technician watched the monitor as the technician glided the probe around on her belly.

Sandy was excited when the technician showed her the baby's head, stomach, legs, and heart. She was elated to see the baby's heart beating.

"I'll give you copies of the static pictures I've taken of your baby, so you have something to show to your family. Right now, I'm taking measurements of your baby's head, feet, body, and vital organs for the doctor to analyze when she comes in to talk to you."

"Can you tell whether it's a boy or a girl?"

"Doctor Moran will be able to tell you. I'm not allowed to give ultrasound results. She should be in soon to go over it with you."

After a short time, Dr. Moran showed up. She gave Sandy a warm smile.

"Hello, Misses Richardson."

"Hi, Doctor Moran."

Dr. Moran reviewed the ultrasound pictures, graphs, and other data. "According to the measurements taken today, your baby's twenty-five weeks old, which puts your due date between July tenth and July fifteenth. Dr. Moran took the transducer probe that was lying on top of Sandy's belly. She resumed gliding it over Sandy's belly while she watched the monitor.

"Can you to tell the sex of the baby from the ultrasound?" In the past, Sandy never wanted to know the sex of her babies. For some reason, she was curious about it this time. She told herself she didn't care whether her baby was a boy or a girl, just as long as the baby was healthy. Deep down inside, though, she was hoping for a boy since she had two girls already. "Since there's no protrusion present in this area, most likely your baby's a girl."

Sandy felt a pang of disappointment.

"Do you have other questions?"

"Don't think so."

Dr. Moran removed the disposable plastic covering of the transducer probe and then wiped off the gel from Sandy's abdomen before washing her hands.

"May I use the restroom? I don't think I can hold my bladder anymore."

"Yes, of course. You may get dressed after that, and you're free to go. I'll see you in two weeks." After Dr. Moran left, Sandy hurried to the restroom.

CHAPTER 34

A cross the Atlantic Ocean, on the other side of the globe from Sandy, Steve had never been the same since receiving the devastating news. He became withdrawn, moody, and impatient, especially to those who were below his rank. He'd snap at them when they made mistakes or when they did not work fast enough. His tolerance to such behaviors became nil. His easy-going kind of demeanor was replaced with harshness, full of sarcasm and cynicism.

He'd gone a little mad also, by having Ben spy on Sandy and then having Ben call him almost every day with updates.

"Any incriminating pictures you'll take of her with her boyfriend will give me solid grounds for a divorce. And, if I have proof of her infidelity, the judge will find her an unfit mother, which will guarantee me to have custody of our kids," Steve told Ben when Ben asked him why it was necessary to spy on Sandy.

"What about paternity testing? Isn't that proof enough?"

"Only after the baby's born is a paternity testing done. I can't wait 'til then."

"So, you got this all figured out now, huh?"

"What do you want me to do, Ben? Just sit around and do nothin'? Have that bitch run me down the way she did'n' then, in the end, get alimony and custody of our kids? No Sirree! So, yeah, you're damn right, I have it all figured out to look after my interests!"

"Oh, Lordy, what have I gotten myself into?" Ben sighed.

"Steve, I'm not too keen about doing it. But I'll do it, since I was the one who notified you about it in the first place."

In the days and weeks that followed, Ben spied on Sandy and took pictures from the distance. He did his spying after work and during his days off. Eventually, he'd had enough

"Look, Steve, for two weeks now, I haven't seen anything unusual to tell you about Sandy, and I haven't seen her with a man. So far, all I've seen was her going to work, to the commissary, and picking up the kids from school and then taking them to the park. The only person I've seen other than Sandy and your kids is a young woman."

"That's Carrie, her sister."

"I really don't want to do this anymore. I feel like a creep and a stalker. This has been weighing on me heavily, and it's affecting my marriage, too. Do you know what'll happen if your neighbors or Sandy get suspicious and report me? It will cost me my job. My career. My marriage."

Steve knew by Ben's tone he'd been wanting to express his concerns and uneasiness about the situation he'd been put in for some time now. After a long silence, pondering, he came to his senses. He sure didn't want Ben get into any trouble, which could ruin his career and marriage.

He sighed into the phone. "You're right, Ben. This is all insane. Sorry I got you involved. I appreciate you bringing some sense back into my head. I'll go ahead with another request to come home soon."

"When you come back, what exactly are you gonna do?"

"Don't know. All I know is that I should be there to deal with her."

"When you say *deal* with her," Ben sounded adamant, "what exactly do you mean?"

"I don't know, Ben. *Deal with her.* You know? Like get her out of the house—away from the kids. Find a good divorce lawyer." Steve was livid, and knew he sounded like it. "*That sort of thing.*"

"You're not going to hurt her, Steve, are you? I mean, like, attack and beat her?"

Steve stopped to consider. After a few seconds, he said, "No, Ben, I would never do that. I just have to confront her, straight up and no BS."

Ben sounded relieved as he sighed, and said, "Good—glad to know physical harm is not one of your objectives."

Steve sent another email to Col. Morrow. He knew this request would have a negative impact on his career and on his military record, but he decided his marital problem was something he could not ignore.

3 May *2000*

Dear Colonel Morrow,

It's been two weeks since our last conversation. I have given it considerable thought, and I still feel that I need to come home now to attend to my personal affairs. I hope you will give my request your full attention and consideration. I'm sure you understand that, if it weren't for this situation, I would intend to remain here for as long as I'm needed. Thank you in advance for taking the time to consider my urgent request for an early release from my current post here in Kosovo.

Sincerely,
Major Steven L. Richardson

❊ ❊ ❊

Makenna thought this scene was a good stopping point for her writing for the night. Her eyelids were feeling burdensome to where she could hardly keep them opened. She finished drinking her lukewarm cappuccino, and headed toward the bedroom.

CHAPTER 35

S teve didn't hear from the colonel right away. Finally, ten days after sending the email, Col. Morrow called him.

"Steve, sorry for taking so long to get back to you. I was busy having consultations with Colonel Hastings and Colonel Warren, your base commander there in Kosovo. Eventually, after consultations in person or through e-mails and phone calls, the three of us concurred that we will allow you to go home. But," he paused, then said, "with some conditions."

"What conditions, sir?" Steve was apprehensive.

"First, I need to know if you have any guns at your base housing."

"Yes, sir, I have several." Steve became suspicious and even more apprehensive.

"Will you agree to come directly to my office when you arrive in Minot?"

"Yes, sir." Steve now felt like he was definitely not going to like the next question.

"Will you agree to have your guns stored at the armory for an undisclosed amount of time?"

"What are you saying, sir? You're going to confiscate my guns and ammo?"

"No, Steve. Just for temporary safekeeping. This is what Colonel Hastings, Colonel Warren and I have decided to do—for your own safety and your family's—while you and your wife resolve your marital issues. Do you have any qualms about this?"

"No, sir." Steve shook his head. *What else can I say?*

"Okay, if you agree to these conditions, I'll fax Colonel Warren a copy of these conditions, which you have to date and sign to give back to him. He'll also give you a copy of the letter of approval."

"Thank you, sir, for approving my request." Upon considering the conditions put forth on him, with the colonel's explanation, he decided they didn't seem too unreasonable.

* * *

In Minot, Sandy went about her daily routines. She and Carrie got along remarkably well. She was thankful to her every day for being there, helping her with the children. Carrie seemed to be just as happy to be of help. Sandy thought Carrie was just like their mother—so giving and charitable in every way.

A month before, Sandy had stopped getting morning sickness and had regained her appetite. She craved anything with vinegar and anything that was sour. Her coworkers had noticed her eating a lot more, especially when she started putting on some weight. When kidded about it, she shrugged it off and blamed it on her big appetite lately.

"Hey Sandy," Anne, one of the night shift phlebotomists, asked one morning, "we're goin' to breakfast after work. Wudja like to join us at the cafeteria?"

Sandy had clicked well with Anne ever since Anne started three months ago. She was a talker, and Sandy found her very entertaining. She also loved Anne's southern drawl, especially when Anne tried to emphasize things in her accents. Most of all, she liked Anne for being a conscientious, hard-working, and enthusiastic phlebotomist. Sandy could tell Anne truly loved her work. "Who's we?" Sandy wanted to know.

"The gals'n' me."

"Sure. Just let me know when you're about to leave." With her increased appetite, Sandy piled her plate up with scrambled eggs, pancakes, sausages, bacon strips, and lots of hashed browns when they arrived at the cafeteria.

"Have enough food there, Missy?" Anne said, smiling at Sandy. "No wonder you've put on some weight." Anne was a no-nonsense person when it came to voicing her thoughts and opinions.

"*Hush.* I'm hungry, okay?" Sandy countered. She didn't mind that kind of talk as long as it came from Anne. It must have been with the way Anne said things in a teasing way, yet in a loving and affectionate voice why Sandy didn't get bothered by her comments. The other women's faces also showed amazement—as if they were all in silent agreement with Anne about the amount of food she had on her plate.

After they got a good chuckle out of Anne's comments, they proceeded to eat. They gossiped and laughed as they ate. They needed that kind of camaraderie after a busy and stressful night like they had last night. They felt good leaving work on a happy note.

The first four months of her pregnancy, Sandy's loose-fitting scrubs were able to hide the bulge growing inside her belly. But on her sixth month, they couldn't hide her pregnancy anymore. It was obvious to everyone at work, she could sense it. So, when a coworker asked if she was pregnant, she admitted it. The news spread in the lab like an Australian outback brushfire. One by one, her co-workers went to congratulate her.

Thank God, none of them seem to suspect that my pregnancy isn't with Steve. After all, none of them, except Joe, know he'd been deployed to Kosovo for so long.

CHAPTER 36

Makenna closed her cell phone when she finished talking with her surgeon's nurse. The nurse had called to remind her of her pre-op appointment with Dr. Cassidy tomorrow, Friday. The nurse also reminded her of her surgery on Monday, June 18, 2007.

Sandy's mom and dad had arrived, back from their Alaskan cruise, late Tuesday evening. When she, Clint, and Chloe went to visit them on Wednesday, Chloe stayed behind because she said she missed her gramma and grampa very much.

On the way home Wednesday, Makenna had said, "It works out pretty well that Mom and Dad are keeping Chloe for a few days."

"Why's that?"

"I'll be able to have more time to work on my novel before my surgery."

"Ah."

Makenna could tell from Clint's voice and demeanor that he was disappointed with her answer. "And, make love to you, since we might not be able to do it for a while after my surgery," she said with a smile.

Clint's demeanor perked up. "That's my gal," he said with a wink. And, so, they made love until they were fully satisfied.

Today, soon after Clint left for work and after she had finished talking to the nurse, Makenna showered and dressed. She went to the kitchen and opened the cupboard where her supply of beverages was kept. Makenna looked at the different types of beverages she had available. *I think I'm going to have some hot green tea today.* She got her mug filled with water and placed it the microwave oven to heat. After the water was heated to a boil, she dropped a bag of green tea into it, then stirred in a spoonful of honey.

She went to sit on her favorite side of the sofa in the living room. As long as Clint and Chloe were sleeping or not home, she preferred working in the living room than in her home office. She propped her computer up on her lap after she stretched her legs out on the sofa. She took a sip of her hot tea. *Hmmm ... perfect.* Now, she was all set to resume her wild imaginings to be put into written words.

* * *

Feeling anxious, Steve looked at his airline ticket for the umpteenth time. And, for the umpteenth time, he read the date on it: May 15, 2000. The trip from Kosovo to Germany and then to Minnesota was extensive and tiresome. It gave him ample time to think and reflect on a lot of things in his life: *What went wrong in my marriage? I thought mine was the best—the kind that everyone envies.*

He tried to think of the last time he looked at Sandy's face and the last time he gazed into her once elusive, verdant eyes, in ways he used to gaze into them, endlessly, in the beginning of their relationship. He had forgotten how magnificent she was. He couldn't remember the last time he'd made love to her or the last time he held her in a sensual way that made her feel wanted and special. It seemed so long ago.

He did, however, remember the one time they'd had a major argument. It was vivid, just the way it happened over a year ago.

Their children were having a sleepover at their friends' house. He and Sandy were seated adjacent to each other in the living room—he, in the big sofa, and she in the love seat, when Sandy spewed her accusations in one long tirade.

"You don't even *make love* to me anymore. And, I bet you could care less about it, either. You never have time for me and the kids. All you do is work, read, and surf the internet!"

He'd been taken aback and stunned momentarily by her outburst. Even so, he was ready to retort. "Oh, so now, it's my fault for not making love to you? It's a two-way street, if you ask me. And don't pull that crap about me not caring enough, because I sure haven't seen you make any effort, yourself. You're either sleeping or working when I'm home. Besides, what do you want me to do? Come and rape you in the middle of your sleep or come after you and make love to you at work?"

"Don't patronize me like that!" Sandy had started to cry.

"No, seriously, tell me, because I don't see any other way. Do you?"

"It's not like I work every night."

"And I'm supposed to read your mind?"

"Yes—that's exactly what I wish for, for you to be a sensitive enough husband and lover to be able to read me, feel what my body is telling you, and ... and get *some kind of response from you*?"

"Oh, puhleese...!" As he spoke, he rolled his eyes in disdain.

"Forget it," Sandy shouted as she sobbed more in frustration.

"Oh, no. You just don't open a can of worms like that and then tell me to forget about it. And as far as me not spending time with the kids, who do you think is taking care of them when you're sleeping or working, huh?"

"Okay! *So you are.* And that's fine and dandy, but what about me? I need you just as much as they do."

"There you are again." He felt like he was having to scold a selfish child. "Has it ever occurred to you that if you get off the night shift and move to the day shift, you and I can actually connect? Have you ever thought of that, huh?"

"And you think that I like being on the night shift? As much as I complain about being on the night shift, you still think that? I'd be on the day shift in a heartbeat if it were that easy. Believe me!"

"Well," he remembered saying, with a snort, "until that happens, I don't want to hear any more of this crap about us not having time together."

She glowered at him. "Fine!"

"About that crap of me reading and surfing, you know exactly the reasons why. You've never heard me complain when you ignored me and the kids, completely, each time you crammed to finish your competencies online."

"No, because I'm not constantly online like you are."

"I'm a doctor; I need to be more informed than you. So, naturally, I read more and research more, you ... you bitch!"

Without warning, Sandy had grabbed a small potted plant from an end table and threw it at him.It hit the wall, just missing his face, with a loud shattering crash. He'd jumped to his feet from where he sat. Soil from the shattered planter covered him all over.

"What the hell! You're lucky it didn't hit my face," he'd said with a crimson face and his hands clenched into fists.

"That's for calling me a bitch. That was uncalled for. And don't you ever, ever call me bitch again!"

"And you, throwing things at me, is called for?"

"Well, you made me!"

"Don't give me that shit! This is getting out of hand. I better go downstairs to watch TV before one of us gets killed. Because right now, all I wanna do is to strangle you to death."

"Yeah, go for it," Sandy had mumbled, but loud enough for him to hear.

"What, go for it and strangle you?"

"You think I'm crazy? I meant go for it and watch TV. That's what you do anyway. If you're not reading or online surfing, you're watching sports. That's why we never get to do any family activities together."

"So now, it's also a crime for me to watch sports? Is that it?"

"I didn't say that. *And you know it.*" Sandy heaved a sigh, burying her head in her hands, sobbing.

"I guess from now on, I have to ask permission before I can watch TV."

She'd lifted her tear-soaked face. "You're so sarcastic. I hate you!"

"Who says I'm being sarcastic? I'm just making a point."

"The kids and I will leave as soon as they get home in the morning. So, you can do whatever you want."

"You can leave anytime, but not with the kids. You got that? Just remember one thing: once you walk out that door," he pointed at it, "you're never coming back."

"I know you don't love me anymore and don't even care if I leave."

"Think what you want, but don't be putting words into my mouth."

Steve's full bladder brought him back to the present. *Thank goodness*, he thought, because he didn't want that part of his life consuming his thoughts forever. He got up to go to the restroom.

When he returned and got situated, his reminiscing shifted to the time when he first met Sandy, sixteen years ago.

There she was with her three friends, bowling at the opposite lane where he and his buddies were bowling. Standing five feet, seven inches tall in her slim, well-toned body, Sandy looked stunning. He remembered liking Sandy's layered, medium-brown hair, with its natural tight waves. Her mixed race gave her a smooth, natural light tan skin.

His eyes caressed her as he watched her every move, each time she took two steps forward, gliding her left foot on the floor before delivering the ball. She impressed him with her strong and accurate delivery.

He knew that Sandy's beauty, with or without makeup on, could easily grace any of the beauty magazines' covers. But it was her shyness and her elusiveness that challenged him to go after her. Even though the other girls were flirting with him, Sandy was the one he had his eyes on. Sandy was the recipient of his full attention that night. Each time he looked her way, she'd smile and then jerk her eyes away. He'd wanted so much to lock his eyes onto those eyes of hers.

Unusual, he remembered thinking, because green eyes are normally seen in people with light or white skins and not on people with darker skins. Her shy smile, her deep dimples, and everything about her attracted him more to her.

Steve's reminiscing of that episode of his life calmed his nerves. They softened his hardened heart. He longed for the days when their love was fresh and sweet to come back to him. He wished for those feelings of always wanting to hold and wanting to touch her—just like the feelings he felt for her in the beginning of their relationship, when he couldn't keep his hands off her.

His deep thoughts were interrupted when he repositioned his body to alleviate the discomfort from the cramps of his seat. They occurred often when he dozed off, when he got up to go to the restroom, or when he ate his meals.

He asked himself several questions. Will I be able to control my anger when I see her? Will I be able to give her so much as a hug, or will I completely ignore her? What will her reaction be when she sees me? A flash of rage flooded throughout his being when he thought of Sandy being unfaithful to him. The thought of her in the arms of another man riled up his killer instincts.

He assured himself that whatever he didn't do for her didn't justify her infidelity, whatsoever! He despised her with bitterness and hatred. He fantasized destroying her beautiful face until no one could ever love her again, or kicking her to the ground until she begged him to stop.

Yes, stop. What are you thinking? He chastised himself when he brought himself back to his senses. A devilish chill snaked its way down his spine. He tried to shake it off. His head throbbed— too many negative thoughts. He was not a very religious person, but, somehow that moment, he felt compelled to pray.

That's not how I want to handle this. Lord, please give me the strength to fight these evil thoughts. And please don't allow these thoughts to materialize at all. I beg for your forgiveness, Lord. Amen.

He stood, retrieved his carry-on bag from the overhead storage compartment and took a bottle of Tylenol out from his small medical bag. He dislodged two capsules from the bottle, called the attention of one of the attendants on duty, and asked for some water. As soon as the attendant brought him a cup of water, he popped the pills into his mouth and downed them with it. He continued drinking the water until it was gone.

He settled himself back in his chair and closed his eyes again. This time, images of a woman in his past appeared to him.

"These are beautiful paintings," the woman had commented the first time he brought her to the house that he and Sandy were renting at a secluded area in Omaha.

"My wife painted them while taking an Art class for one of her electives in college," he had said.

Oh, Cathy, why now? Steve grumbled to himself. This was one chapter in his life he wasn't proud of about himself. He tried to erase this chapter from his memory. He hated it that it had come back to haunt him now.

The affair had occurred during his last year at Creighton University—four years after he and Sandy were married. Cathy was his research partner for their project in Oncology their final year of medical school. They'd spent extensive time together. In the end, they'd succumbed to the temptations of lust and passion. Most of Steve and Cathy's activities happened at Cathy's. Being a single woman, she had no one to worry about observing them.

On the occasions that Sandy went home to Minnesota, Steve had brought Cathy to the house he and Sandy shared. The affair ended a few months after Cathy moved northeast to Boston to do her residency and after he told Cathy he wasn't going to divorce Sandy for her.

How can I criticize my wife for being unfaithful when I, myself, is just as guilty? Ah ..., that was then and this is now. She didn't know about mine, but I know about hers. Plus, I didn't have a child as evidence, and she's going to have one to complicate our lives. I know Sandy never suspected my affair. I haven't seen signs that indicated to me in any way that she thought I might have been unfaithful to her.

He tried to justify himself in his mind. He could go on justifying himself, but that wouldn't make him any better than his wife. He was thankful his unpleasant thoughts were interrupted by the captain's overhead announcement. He perked up and opened his eyes while he listened to the announcement.

"This is your captain speaking. We're now flying over Chicago at an altitude of thirty thousand feet. The current local time is two-fifteen in the afternoon, and our estimated time of arrival at Minneapolis-Saint Paul is three o'clock in the afternoon. We'll start our descent to twenty-two thousand feet in fifteen minutes in preparation for our approach at Minneapolis-Saint Paul International Airport. Current conditions are clear and sunny at forty-five degrees Fahrenheit."

He was glad, but felt apprehensive at the same time, to be home soon at last.

CHAPTER 37

Makenna was so engrossed with her writing that she hadn't noticed the time. "Oh, my goodness," she declared. She'd been on her computer since 3 am. The clock on the wall showed 7 a.m. She took a deep breath and let out a big sigh. With reluctance, she lifted her hands off the keyboard. She reread the chapter she'd just written and decided to stop writing for a while.

For over three weeks since meeting with Nina, Makenna had pounded out her novel. She had to stop for the time being, for the next day, June 15, 2007, she and Clint would be going to Cheyenne to meet with Dr. Cassidy, the surgeon, to get her lab tests done.

She had to take care of the bills, clean the house, and do the laundry because she wanted everything to be in order before her surgery. Her surgery date worked out well, since it was during school vacation. Chloe would be staying with her grandparents while she was in the hospital. Clint, for his part, was going to be off for two weeks.

* * *

The drive from their place at the base of Elk Mountain to the on-ramp for Interstate 80 was spectacular. Makenna felt pensive as she took in all the breathtaking scenery of the mountains' peaks, sprawling valleys, and the trees that covered them either entirely or in quilt-like patches. She never got tired of gazing at the view.

Even after they were on the highway, where all she could see were miles and miles of nothing, she still enjoyed looking out there—imagining the plains in a time long ago, with Native Americans on their horses, herds of stampeding buffalo, and cowboys, herding their cattle. The scenery inspired the writer in her to imagine all sorts of things, bringing to life the empty, open prairie that surrounded her.

Every weekend during the spring, summer, and early fall months, she and Clint rode their horses across the prairies and into the mountains. Those outings would have to be put on hold for a while until she recovered completely from her surgery. Her thoughts were now with the handsome cowboy beside her. She squinted as the morning sun hit her eyes.

"Are you okay?" Clint said when he noticed her ponderous mood.

"Yeah," she said, and paused, briefly, before she spoke again. "Will you be okay without me?"

"I'll fall apart and die without'cha," he said, and then winked at her, letting a smile ease across his face.

"You're patronizing me," she said in a childish pout.

"Darlin', I'm dead serious. I meant what I said. But I don't want you worryin' 'bout me. Just concentrate on getting well so you can come home to me ... pronto." He extended his tanned, long, muscular arm to touch her blushing into soft pink cheeks. Makenna met his touch by pressing her face toward his hand. When their eyes met, they both smiled, and Clint winked at her again.

Makenna winked back, her oceanic eyes twinkling with love and happiness. She closed them and reminisced of the time she interviewed Clint during Cheyenne Frontier Days in July of 1996 for the local TV station —the day they fell in love and became inseparable.

At present, Makenna moaned with her eyes still closed.

"Are you awake?" Clint gave her a soft nudge with his elbow.

Makenna opened her eyes, her lips curling into a smile. "You said something?"

"Yeah. What were you moanin' and smilin' about?"

"What do you mean I was moaning and smiling?"

"Exactly that."

Makenna was kind of embarrassed. "What else did I do?"

"Nothin'. Just heard you, so I looked, and there you were, moanin' with your eyes closed."

"Oh, just remembering the time we first met. Do you remember our first date?"

"Of course, sweetheart. You were batting your big, blue eyes and thick, long lashes at me the entire time you were interviewing me. I thought, damn, she's gorgeous. I'd be damned if I'd let the day go by without arranging a date with her."

"Oh, *stop it*," Makenna said in a playful gesture while grinning at the same time. Deep down, she was cherishing Clint's every word. It warmed her heart.

"I wanted so badly to impress you that night by winning that gray elephant for you. I wasn't gonna give up until I won. I was gettin' real frustrated. Sure was happy I won when I did."

"I didn't realize you were getting frustrated."

"Worked out good, too. Or else you might have left me out in the cold and wouldn't have had the chance to kiss you that night." He poked her in play. "Plus, we might not be here together talkin' about it now."

"Maybe, maybe not," Makenna said, remembering what a heavenly kiss that was.

After Clint won the plush elephant, they had walked to Makenna's car and dropped off the stuffed animal. Clint suggested going to Sloans Lake, two blocks away from Frontier Park. She agreed. As they walked around the sandy beaches, she could hear George Strait's music bringing the house down as he entertained the crowd after a day filled with rodeo events and hot sun. The stars were out, decorating the night sky. When George sang one of his mellow songs, *I Cross My Heart*, Clint had taken her hand and asked if he could have a dance.

"Right here?"

"Why not?"

And so, she enjoyed a slow dance with him without a care who might have been watching them. When the music stopped, she looked up and met Clint's entranced eyes. She saw him guide his lips onto hers, which she readily accepted and, in return, she offered hers to him. She was caught up in the allure of the night, the stars, the music, and the sensuous smell of his cologne. She tasted him as her tongue teased, played, and intertwined with his in a lingering passionate kiss. *Oh, that was such a blissful night.*

CHAPTER 38

G ood Morning Doctor Cassidy," Makenna said in response to the doctor's greeting. They shook hands. Her nervousness was put at ease as soon as she saw Dr. Cassidy's contagious smile and uplifting persona. Since it was Dr. Cassidy who performed a lumpectomy on her left breast three years ago, she felt more comfortable, too.

* * *

About a month ago, Makenna had felt lumps in her left breast—the same familiar lumps she'd felt before. She knew, with her history of breast cancer, she should have been more diligent at checking and examining her breasts for lumps, more than the every-now-and-then-just-whenever-she-remembered. For the first two years after her first surgery, she'd done what she was advised to do, taking her monthly self-breast examinations to heart. After that, sadly, she had to admit, she'd become complacent.

"Oh! *God. No*. Not again!" Makenna was panic-stricken when she'd felt the lumps. She held her breath for such a long while she almost fainted. A tremendous feeling of anxiety and defeat descended upon her. When she resumed breathing, she inhaled deep and exhaled slow a few times. She allowed her body to slump completely on the bed where she was already reclining.

Who knows how long those lumps have been there? She'd

wondered. Gosh, it had to be at least eight months ago when I last checked. She tried, but couldn't remember for sure. When she had regained her color and composure, she made an appointment with her primary doctor that same day.

Dr. Eileen Fletcher had shared her concern. She wrote Makenna a STAT order for a mammogram test. The mammogram showed three masses, the size of snow peas. A biopsy performed two days later confirmed the masses to be malignant. Dr. Fletcher had referred her to Dr. Cassidy right away.

"I like Doctor Cassidy," Makenna had said to Clint. "Not only is she highly competent as a surgeon, she also has a warm, nurturing, and compassionate bedside manner—a rarity in doctors these days, especially now that doctors are always so busy."

"I like her, too, sweetheart. She's definitely perfect for her calling. That's why I feel as comfortable as you are about her doing your surgery again."

"Yes, I wish there were more like her."

* * *

"There are three options we're going to discuss today," Dr. Cassidy had said. "First option, you'll have another lumpectomy and hope the cancer will not come back. Second option, you'll have a radical left breast mastectomy so that you have the least worry about it coming back in that breast. In this procedure your breast will be completely removed, along with the lymph nodes, for good measure."

"No …," Makenna remembered crying softly, feeling deflated. She hadn't considered her breast to be completely removed. She'd anticipated having the same procedure as she had before. Tears were rolling down her face. She'd looked at Clint, who was seated to her left. Clint hugged her while she buried her face in his chest.

"Shh...," Clint said. Clint's hug and simple expression of empathy had helped soothe and console her anguish.

"I'm so sorry, Makenna," Dr. Cassidy had consoled her. There was a long, agonizing pause afterward.

Even in her condition at that time, Makenna was able to sense Dr. Cassidy's hesitation to continue. When she glanced at her, she had noticed the genuine compassion on the doctor's face. "I'm sorry, Doctor Cassidy," Makenna had said. She straightened herself after she regained her composure. She plucked some tissue from the table and wiped the tears off her face.

"No problem, Makenna. Would you like me to leave you two alone for a while?"

"No, that's okay. If I have to get rid of my cancer, then I must hear the rest of it," she'd said in between sniffles. She tried to be brave and strong after that.

"The third option," Dr. Cassidy continued, "you'll get a radical double mastectomy as a preventive measure. It's to ensure that the cancer is not going to also grow in your right breast later on. It's a drastic measure to take, I know, but with your history—cancer coming back—I recommend the double mastectomy."

As much as Makenna had tried to be stoic, she couldn't help from tearing up again as she contemplated the possibility of a double mastectomy. Clint took her left hand into his hands and held them on his lap.

"You don't have to decide right now, of course. I'd like for you to go home, consider the options, mull over each one, and then call me back later with your decision." Dr. Cassidy had provided this counsel three weeks ago.

✽ ✽ ✽

For a week, Makenna and Clint discussed the different options.

"Honey, which one do you think I should go for?"

"It's entirely up to you, darlin', but if you really want my opinion on the matter, I have to agree with doctor Cassidy."

Makenna thought for a long while before she spoke. "We're talking about me losing *both my breasts, honey*."

"I realize that, sweetheart."

"If I choose the double mastectomy, will you still love me?"

"Oh, come on now," he gave her an incredulous, yet endearing look, "I didn't fall in love with you for your *breasts*. Sure, they were definitely a plus, but they were not the reason I fell in love with ya."

Makenna had struggled to make her decision. She mulled over and over the different options before she called Dr. Cassidy to tell her of her decision: a double mastectomy.

＊ ＊ ＊

Today, Makenna asked more questions, which the doctor answered to Makenna's satisfaction. She and Clint left the clinic to go over to the hospital and do all her pre-op tests. It was already twelve thirty in the afternoon when she and Clint were finished. They then headed out to Makenna's parents' house.

CHAPTER 39

As soon as Makenna opened the door, she was greeted by the aroma of her mom's cooking, which Clint's appreciative sniffing of the air let her know he was equally pleased by. By the time they had made their way into the living room, it was delightfully obvious the aromatic nose teaser was permeating the entire house.

"Hmm … barbecue pork ribs," Makenna said as she inhaled through her nose. "I'm starved."

She was thankful her mother was cooking ribs. As a child, she had always requested them on her birthday. It was her favorite.

"Mommy! Daddy!" Chloe said. She came running from the kitchen. Makenna heard her mother squealing, but also chuckling. "My goodness, child, you nearly knocked over the stool you were sitting on." She chortled again. "Ya think she's glad to see you two?"

Chloe extended both arms so Makenna could pick her up. They hugged and kissed as if they hadn't seen each other for weeks. Next, Chloe extended her arms to Clint, and Clint took her from Makenna. They kissed and hugged the same way.

"Hello, Mother," Makenna said in her high-pitched enthusiastic voice when she joined her in the kitchen. She hugged her mother and planted a warm kiss on her cheek.

Cassandra reciprocated and then cupped Makenna's face. "How's my beautiful baby?"

"I'm good," Makenna said. Her mother removed her hands from her face. "I like your new hair color, Mother."

"Thank you, honey. I'm happy with it myself. My hairdresser called it medium ash color. I think I'm going to stay with this color for a while."

Makenna had observed over the years that her mother had her hair colored anywhere from dark to light brown shades with blond or reddish highlights. "You should, Mom. I think you look best in that shade. The color makes you look younger."

Makenna knew how to flatter her mother. But she wasn't just flattering her, she truly thought her mother looked much younger than her actual sixty-seven-years. She also thought her mother was attractive and even more so when she was younger. She could prove it to anyone by showing their family portrait that hung on the living room wall. Or, perhaps, dig up one of the many photo albums that were stored away somewhere.

She commended both her parents for staying fit. She wished when she and Clint got to her parents' age, they'd do the same for health's sake. Riding horses out in the country was not much of an exercise for the whole body.

"Anyway, honey, is everything squared away with Doctor Cassidy and at the hospital for your surgery?"

"Yep, all done."

Clint and Chloe joined them in the kitchen. Clint was still carrying Chloe in his arms. "That sure smells good," he said. He put Chloe down before he went to give Cassandra a hug.

"We're having ribs tonight."

"I thought so," Clint said, beaming.

"I want to feast today," said Makenna, "for Sunday evening there will be no eating for me. I must go into surgery with an empty stomach."

Richard, Makenna's dad, emerged from the family room where he said he had been watching TV. Both he and Cassandra were retired. He extended his hand to Clint and they shook hands and patted each other on the shoulder. Makenna gave her dad a kiss and a hug. Her dad's hair was mostly white, which he kept fairly short. He also kept his face clean-shaven—'to the delight of my wife,' he often quipped. Even with a starter's beer belly, Dad is still handsome, Makenna thought.

Cassandra offered everyone something to drink, then she said, "Let's go make ourselves comfortable in the living room for now. The food has some cooking time left to go yet. It's not good to hurry up the cooking process. Great barbecue pork ribs take time to cook to perfection."

Makenna marveled at her parent's newly built house—only a month old. "Mom and Dad, I love your house," she said as she looked at the expansive living room with its high ceilings, which extended through the entire house.

"Thank you, honey," the couple said. They all stayed standing instead of sitting.

Makenna looked at the ceiling again. "I love the high ceiling and the open concept. It makes the entire house look airy and more spacious. I also like the idea of leaving the huge wood beams in the living room, dining room, and in the kitchen areas exposed. For sure, they add special effects to the overall aesthetic beauty of the house."

Next, she stared at the chandelier overhead, observing that it was made of antlers—moose antlers to be precise. "Of course," she said, "Dad has to decorate the house with his own touch and style." She saw her dad grin when she glanced at him.

She left her parents standing where they were as she went to inspect each artwork and paintings of moose, elks, and bears close up and personal. There was quite a collection of them displayed or hung neatly throughout the living room and dining room. Ah … my avid outdoorsman father, Makenna thought as she admired the artwork pieces.

When she finished, she noticed Clint standing in front of a family portrait, which was hanging directly above the living room fireplace. He had his arms crossed over on his chest and his legs spread a foot apart. She went to join him and wrapped her left arm around his waist.

"What's up?"

"Oh, nothin'. Just admirin' your family portrait."

"But you've seen that before already, Clint."

"Don't matter. I still like looking at it. You look darn cute there even though you're missing your two front teeth." Clint unraveled his arms, wrapped his right arm around her, and kissed her smiling lips.

"How old were you there?"

"I believe I was six. My older sisters always teased me how goofy I looked without my front teeth."

Her father was wearing his Air Force formal dress uniform. The right chest area of his uniform was decorated with several medals, which he mostly earned during his service in Vietnam as a medical doctor.

"What do the two silver maple leaves on his shoulders mean?" said Clint.

"They denote his rank as Lieutenant Colonel."

"Ah ... I know nothin' 'bout military ranks. I'm just a simple cowboy."

"Well, how would you know, honey. You haven't been around military people. And when you met my dad, he was already out of the military and in his private practice. And by the way, you're much more than a simple cowboy. You're also an excellent lawyer, if I may say so." She gave him a light squeeze on his left side.

"Why, thank you, Ma'am," he said, and then winked at her. "Your dad looks dashing and distinguished in that picture, while your mom looks radiant and captivating."

"Why, thank you, Sir," Makenna said, mimicking him. She felt happy and proud of both of her parents.

Cassandra excused herself to go to the kitchen to check on the barbecue and continue with her cooking. A few minutes later, she announced, *Food is served. Time to eat, everybody.*

Makenna and the rest moved to the dining room and took their seats around the enormous dining table.

Aside from the barbecue ribs, Makenna also had some garden salad, baked potatoes, steamed corn, and steamed asparagus. She feasted until her belly was satisfied and well-stretched. By the looks of the others, she thought they were just as stuffed as she was. When she finished eating, she carried her iced tea out to the patio, as the others did, in order to enjoy the nice weather and to let her meal settle.

It was a great day for all of them.

CHAPTER 40

June 18, 2007. Clint and Makenna woke up early to get ready to go to the hospital for Makenna's 8:00 a.m. surgery.

After kissing Chloe on the cheek, and after a short chat with Makenna's parents, followed by embraces and smooches, Clint and Makenna departed. During the drive to the hospital, they listened to KOLT FM. The radio announcer mentioned it was going to be in the low 80's during the day and in the low 50's overnight. It was going to be mostly sunny with no chance of precipitation. Following the weather report, *Western Skies*, a Chris LeDoux song, came on. Clint sang along and knew all the words.

Clint had expressed to her how much he agreed with and could relate to what Chris LeDoux was saying in his song. He often said he could not imagine a better place to live than in Wyoming. Chris LeDoux had been his childhood cowboy/singer idol. Every time Chris performed in a concert during Frontier Days, after Chris LeDoux retired from the rodeo, Clint had gone to see him, including his very last concert in 2004. He could also relate with Chris because they were both cowboys and rodeo men. Heck, they even attended the same community college up in Casper, only at different times.

Makenna knew his story, but she was different when it came to musical background. She had never been a country music fan until a few years after marrying Clint. Growing up, she and her friends hated it that most groups performing during Frontier Days were country bands.

Sure, she covered and reported the events during Frontier Days when she became a field reporter, but that was where her association with anything "country" stopped. Instead, she and her friends attended the few rock and roll performances. Her taste in music had made a big departure since then. Now, she listened mostly to country music.

"Honey, I'm so glad you convinced me to go to Chris LeDoux's concert in two thousand four. It would have been a shame if I hadn't gone, knowing now that he died the very next year. I'd be kicking myself now. So, thanks again for talking me into it."

"You're welcome, darlin'. Things happen for a purpose, don't they?"

"Uh-huh." The music and Clint's singing-along entertained Makenna's thoughts. In no time, they arrived at the hospital parking garage, winding their way up, looking for a parking space.

Once inside the hospital, Makenna checked in at the admissions office. A nurse's aide came to get her and Clint from the waiting area and took them to a private room on the third floor. Makenna was asked to change into a hospital gown. Different nurses and aides came and went. They asked her name and birthday before attaching monitors to track her vital signs, attaching a bag of IV fluid, and giving her forms to read and sign.

All standard procedure, she was told. They, the hospital and the doctors, just wanted to make sure they have the correct person. Makenna was comforted knowing Clint was a lawyer, and was paying close attention to all the procedures and forms.

Dr. Cassidy went in to talk to them, explaining that the procedure would take approximately four to five hours. She asked Makenna again if she had any last-minute questions or concerns. She had none.

Later, an anesthesiologist showed up. He asked many questions and then walked out of the room.

"Well, my love," Clint said, "are you ready?"

"I'm scared, honey. What if something goes wrong, and I

bleed to death, or have a deadly reaction to the anesthesia?"

"You shouldn't be thinkin' 'bout that now. You'll be just fine, sweetheart. Just know that I'll be thinkin' 'bout ya and prayin' for ya. I'll be here when ya wake up. Just like what the doctor said, all you'll remember is gettin' wheeled in and when you come to, you'd think you're still gettin' wheeled in. 'Sides, you've gone through worse than this and you've survived. You have nine lives, baby." Clint gave Makenna a kiss and then brushed the back of his hand lightly along her cheek. He smiled and winked at her.

For Makenna, it was enough to make her feel at ease and better. She smiled, winked back, and nodded. Winking was never her thing until she married him. During the course of their marriage, she'd learned how to wink. So now, she winked back each time he winked at her. She knew Clint got a kick out of her winking back.

The anesthesiologist returned, and administered the anesthesia to Makenna before she was taken to the operating room. Before she was wheeled out, Clint gave her another kiss, expressed again his love for her, and assured her that he'd be seeing her soon. He was still talking to her, assuring her, when she was being wheeled away, but the anesthesia had already taken effect because Makenna had faded into unconsciousness and hadn't responded to him.

❋ ❋ ❋

When Clint was alone in the room, he acknowledged the fact that he was just as scared as Makenna was. He just didn't want Makenna to know how afraid he was. He didn't want her to feel even more frightened. Instead, he'd expressed optimism just to ease her worries.

A nurse came in to ask if he wanted something to eat or drink. He said no. She said he could stay there or he could leave and come back later. He decided to head over to Makenna's parents' house. Dr. Cassidy had assured him earlier that she'd get in touch with him on his cell phone if he was not in the room after the surgery.

When Clint arrived at the house, his parents-in-law were anxiously awaiting to hear about Makenna's surgery. He relayed to them everything that he knew so far.

"Poor child," Makenna's mother said while wiping away some tears that almost trickled down her cheek, "For someone her age, she has gone through so much, more than anybody in the family."

"She's a fighter and a survivor, though, Cassie," Makenna's father said. "She survived a major surgery as an infant. She came through from the deadly gunshot wound she received in Gaza. She overcame her issue with endometriosis. And, yet again, overcame her first breast cancer." He walked to his wife and gave her a consoling hug.

That was something Clint noticed about the couple. *They truly love each other. Their love, compassion, and generosity had rubbed off onto their children, because Makenna and her sisters are just as loving, compassionate, and generous as they are.*

"Would you like something to eat or drink," Cassandra asked Clint.

"Thanks, but I think Chloe and I'll just get something to eat at the mall. I'd like to take her out today, to spend some time together. Is she awake now?"

"She's awake. I gave her a bath and have her dressed already. Oh, Clint," she said as an afterthought, and then continued, "you should have seen her earlier. She was so cute when she ran around the house, saying, 'Yee hah!' Just out of the blue, she said to me, 'Gramma, I want to grow up just like cowgirl Barbie.' She made me laugh so hard when she said that. She also told me how she'd like to have a cowgirl outfit just like cowgirl Barbie."

"That's my girl, like father like daughter. Yep, maybe it's time for me to teach her some ropin' skills," Clint said, feeling pleased.

"Oh, Clint. You're not even ..."

"Why not? She'll love it!"

"She's only five. She might get hurt." Cassandra said.

"Nah … my dad got me started when I was three. So, no, I don't think she's too young to start. Besides, she's only goin' to be ropin' a mechanical calf." Clint enjoyed bantering with his mother-in-law—as usual, nothing confrontational, simply taking opposing opinions.

"Only if Chloe shows an interest," Richard said.

"True," Clint agreed. "Well, I suppose I should go get my little cowgirl so she and I can go to the mall. I'd like to be back at the hospital before Makenna gets back to her room." The couple agreed with him. So they let him be.

"*Daddy—Daddy*," Chloe said in excitement. She laid down the cowgirl Barbie she was brushing. She jumped out of her bed as soon as Clint opened the door and stuck his head in. "Where's Mommy?"

"She's still in the hospital, and she'll be there for a few days."

"Oh." Chloe's face fell.

"How'd you like it if we go to the mall today?"

She glimmered. "And, and buy me cowgirl clothes like Barbie's?" She showed Clint her doll.

"Sure, if you like."

"Oh, Daddy, thank you. I love you." How could Clint say no when he heard her daughter talk to him like that? Sucker or not, he spoiled her for sure.

"Did you brush your teeth yet?"

"Oh, I still need to do that."

"Hurry. Cowgirls move fast, so you have to move fast, too."

"Okay, Daddy." She appeared happy to comply.

"Where'd she get a cowgirl Barbie, anyway?" Clint wanted to know when he rejoined the couple in the living room.

"Well," Cassandra said, "seeing that Chloe loves Barbie dolls, and that the only Barbie she doesn't have is a cowgirl, I wanted to get her one. I couldn't find any at the stores in town. But I found one on eBay a week ago. I had to get it for her. I gave it to her this morning when she was feeling a little sad that you left without her knowing it. You don't mind, do you, Clint?"

"Heck no, Mom. I don't see any harm in it. Just don't overdo it. She might get too spoiled."

"As if you don't spoil her already."

"Oh, I know. We're all guilty of that, aren't we?"

"That, we are," Richard said.

"Thank you, both, for having her stay with you for a while. I hope she isn't too much trouble for you?"

"No trouble at all, Clint. She's been so wonderful to us. Been a joy to have her around," Cassandra said.

Richard nodded and said, "She sure makes us feel young again."

"It's been ages since our baby left, so this is all so new to us again," Cassandra said.

"I'm ready now, Daddy," Chloe exclaimed. She and Clint said goodbye and off they went to the mall. Once at the mall, Clint asked her what she wanted to eat. She chose to have some orange juice and some freshly baked pretzels, buttered and lightly salted.

When they finished, Clint took her to Corral West store to shop for some cowgirl clothes. After going through rack after rack of kid's shirts and jeans, with the help of a forbearing sales lady, Chloe picked out the ones she liked. She chose a white long-sleeved shirt with purple material appliquéd in the center of the chest and on the front and back shoulders. Short fringe bordered the appliqué design.

To complete the look, Clint bought her a pair of black boots, which paired well with any color. Clint was delighted when he saw his daughter all decked out in her getup. *Yep, my daughter's a cowgirl.*

"Daddy, may I keep my cowgirl clothes on, please Daddy?" Chloe gave him her sad, pleading face.

"If you want to. Sure." *I can be such a pushover sometimes.*

Clint was about to say it was time to go home after he paid for his purchases when Chloe said, "Daddy, let's go play at the arcade." Pulling Clint's hand, she led him in that direction.

"Alright, but we can't stay very long." At the arcade, Clint let her pick a few games she wanted to play. They played until Clint said it was time to go. Chloe didn't complain much. But she tried to bargain for more time. Clint didn't give in this time. She exchanged her earned tickets for trinkets before heading home to her grandparents' house.

"I'll just drop you off at your grandma and grandpa's because I still need to go back to the hospital to see your mommy, okay?"

"Can I come to the hospital to see Mommy?"

"Not today, sweetheart, but maybe tomorrow. Grandma and Grandpa will bring you tomorrow, okay?"

"Okay. Is Mommy all right, Daddy?"

"Yes, sweetheart. She's having a surgery right now, and I'd like to be in her room when she's finished."

"What's a surgery, Daddy?" Clint explained to her the best he could without alarming her with any graphic details.

"Why is Mommy having a surgery, Daddy?"

"Well, sweetheart, your mommy has cancer and the doctor wants to remove the cancer before it gets worse."

"What's cancer, Daddy?" Poor Chloe, she was still too young to know what was going on. She had been kept in the dark about the specifics. Now, though, her incessant questioning was forcing Clint to explain more, making Chloe learn things that no five-year-old is usually ready to comprehend. Chloe finally stopped asking questions and quieted ... for a short time, before bursting into a fit of tears and crying.

"I don't want Mommy to die, Daddy. Please tell the doctor not to let Mommy die. Please, Daddy. And please ask God not to let Mommy die. Please, Daddy."

Clint was all choked up, seeing his daughter cry and hearing her say those things. "Oh, sweetheart..." he swallowed before he spoke again. "Mommy is, is ... going to be alright." He reached out his arm and stroked the back of his hand over Chloe's cheek.

When they arrived back at the house, Clint carried Chloe

inside, instead of the usual way of letting her walk to the house. Chloe gripped her arms around his neck. When he tried to put her down, she didn't want to let go. "Show Grandma and Grandpa your new outfit, sweetheart," he said, but she still didn't release him. She clung to him as if to say, I'm never gonna let you go.

"Chloe, remember? You want me to go talk to the doctor?" It was only then she eased her hold and let go of him. His parents-in-law were perplexed by his comment. Clint mouthed to them, *later*.

Outside, he heard the expressed delights of the couple about Chloe's new outfit. He was happy to hear her chirping away about what a great time she had with her daddy today.

Makenna was not yet out from surgery when he arrived back to her room. Fifteen minutes passed and still no sign of Makenna. Clint was getting antsy, so he wandered into the hallway, but didn't see anyone. No one was at the nurses' station either. He went back into the room and waited some more.

While he waited, he started thinking the worse, and it made him feel nervous and afraid. It brought back some horrible memories of when Makenna nearly died in the year 2001. Makenna was reporting for CNN from Gaza during one of the many clashes between the Palestinians and the Israelis.

He remembered how glad he was to see her, even if it was only through the tube. However, seeing her in a helmet and body armor in the midst of chaos, made him feel uncomfortable and fearful for her. A few minutes into Makenna's reporting, the most horrific scene played out in front of him—Makenna got shot in a crossfire, collapsing to the ground—on live TV.

At present, he bowed his head, burying his face into his hands while his arms and elbows rested on his knees. He proceeded to pray in silence as he did when Makenna got shot in Gaza.

Dear, God, please don't take her away from me so soon. Please bless her, and let her live. Amen.

As if his prayers were answered, soon after, Dr. Cassidy came into the room to update him. "The surgery went well. Unfortunately, the initial frozen section that was taken from her left axillary sentinel nodes, which was tested during the surgery, was found to be positive for cancer. We then performed a full-node dissection. The right side is negative, but we still removed the sentinel nodes and they'll be sent to the pathologist for further study and confirmation."

"How's Makenna doing?" Clint was still worrying about her.

"Makenna is now in the recovery room. Her blood pressure is a bit elevated, but nothing to worry about. As soon as it normalizes, she'll be moved back here. A nurse will come in to keep you up to date while she's still in the recovery room."

"Thanks again, Doctor Cassidy."

"You're welcome, Clint. I'll come by in the morning to check up on her. If you have any questions or concerns, just let her nurse know and she will get ahold of me, okay?"

As Dr. Cassidy assured him, Makenna's nurse had been updating him. An hour later, Makenna was at last wheeled back into the room. He walked toward her. He saw that her eyes were still closed.

"Is ... is," he looked at the nurse, feeling like a man standing trial facing a jury about to deliver the verdict, "is she alright?"

"Yes," the nurse said. "Her blood pressure has finally come down. She's still pretty groggy from the anesthesia, that's all." Clint felt relieved to hear that.

He got closer to Makenna, took her hand, and started talking to her. Makenna slightly opened her heavy eyelids and smiled at Clint. She gave Clint's hand a weak squeeze. Clint could feel how little strength she had.

"I'm so tired and sleepy. May I just please sleep for now?" she begged and pleaded like a little child.

"I'm sorry Misses Wilde, but the doctor wants to make sure you get something to drink. She also wants you to stay awake to make sure the effect of the anesthesia wears off completely before we let you go back to sleep. It's also important that you give us some urine to make sure your kidneys are working properly."

"But, I'm so sleepy," she said in a mere whisper. Clint saw how everyone was fussing about her, while all Makenna wanted was to be left alone, so she could go to sleep.

"Makenna, Baby, I know you feel very tired and sleepy, but you must try to wake up," Clint pleaded. For the next hour, Clint tried cajoling her into waking up. Makenna kept trying to open her eyes, but Clint could see and feel the incredible feeling of sleepiness keeping ahold of her. Makenna eventually managed to get up to go to the bathroom and was able to provide urine to the nurse. After the nurse measured Makenna's urine, she dumped it into the toilet bowl to flush. The nurse was satisfied.

When Makenna went back to bed, Clint used a cold compress on her face, making sure to run it under cold water every time it warmed up. That seemed to do the trick, as Makenna was starting to keep her eyes open for longer periods now. Or, it could be the effect of the anesthesia wearing off, Clint thought. Whichever it was, Clint and the nurse were happy that Makenna was finally waking up.

CHAPTER 41

M ommy, Mommy," Chloe squealed as she entered the room. She let go of Grandma's hand and ran to her mother's bed.

"Shh ... , not so loud, sweetheart," Clint said in a hushed tone. As promised, Chloe was brought over to visit her mother today. Chloe was yearning to jump onto the bed with Makenna. "Easy on Mommy, not to hurt her chest," Clint said. He lifted Chloe up to kiss her mother. Makenna made room for Chloe on the bed.

"I missed you *so* much, Mommy," Chloe said as she snuggled with Makenna.

"I missed you so much, too, sweetie. *Look at you,*" Makenna said as she admired Chloe's cowgirl outfit. Chloe was, for sure, a blessing. It wasn't very long ago that Makenna didn't want anything to do with her, whatsoever. To think of it now made her cringe and felt guilty.

"Are you okay, Mommy?" Chloe's eyes were filled with tenderness.

"I'm okay, precious," Makenna jiggled Chloe's chin, "and how's my girl?"

"I'm okay, Mommy."

Mr. and Mrs. Stevens moved in to kiss their daughter and hold her hand.

"Hi, Mom. Hi, Dad."

"How are you feeling, honey?"

"In pain and exhausted from lack of sleep. If only I could get a solid four hours of sleep, I'd feel so much better. I'm so ready to get out of here."

"This is only your second day here, dear," her mother said.

"Oh, I know. It's just that I hate hospitals. They make me feel even sicker. I want to sleep in my own bed." Makenna was barely aware of her playing with Chloe's long brown hair by lifting her ponytail up and then slowly letting the strands drop down, repeating the process.

"When are they going to start you on chemo," asked her dad.

"In three weeks. I'm not looking forward to that one, either. But I suppose it has to be done."

"We know you can handle anything, honey. This, too, shall pass." Cassandra placed an assuring hand on Makenna's.

"You're a fighter, Makenna," Richard said. "You can get through this."

"Thanks Mom and Dad. Your words mean so much to me, especially now."

When it was getting close to Makenna's dinner time, Clint and the others went to the cafeteria to buy meals to bring back to the room. They ate together in the room before Chloe and her grandparents went home.

Makenna was being closely monitored and had been from the start. So closely, that she didn't get any rest. Family and friends went to visit her. She knew they all meant wel. But she wondered, how in the world will I ever get well if Ican't get any rest?

Makenna appreciated Clint spending the nights with her at the hospital. His presence calmed her anxieties. To see him give up the comfort of their cozy bed at home or at her parents', by sleeping at the hospital on the hard and narrow sofa bed next to the window, said something to her about Clint's love and dedication to her. It made her love him even more.

"Clint, I feel bad for you sleeping on that cramped bed," she said when he woke up.

"Baby, don't worry 'bout me." He got up and went to give her a kiss before he sat beside her. "Ya know? Bein' here with ya gives me a sense of reassurance that you'll be okay."

Makenna touched Clint's arm. "Aww ... your words moved me."

He took her hand into his. "How're ya feelin'?"

"Very sore."

"Just hang in there, Baby. You'll be out of here and be back home soon. For now, you should try to go back to sleep."

CHAPTER 42

B y the way, while you were still asleep, your nurse said that you may take a shower today. Would you like to join me when I take mine?"

Makenna looked away, obviously considering the idea, but then shook her head, lifted it, and said, "No … I … I'm just not ready yet for you to see me this way …" she looked down at her chest that was now missing its mounds. She heaved a sigh of sadness, but forced a smile, "Thanks anyway, hon, but I'll wait to go after you."

"Understand, darlin', but nah … you should go first, then."

A nurse's aide offered to assist her, but she refused. Makenna walked to the bathroom, her legs a little wobbly. She rotated the lever to where it was providing a comfortable stream of warm water before stepping into the shower. Still feeling unsteady, she held onto the wall-mounted bar and then positioned her body so her head was right under the shower. She enjoyed her scalp being massaged by the soothing water jets.

While in that position, she surveyed her chest. It was flat, all patched up with wide, thick gauze pads, and sealed and covered with broad waterproof tapes. Two drain tubes were inserted and two small bags were secured on each side. Gone were her beautiful, perky, voluptuous breasts that Clint had often admired and enjoyed. She would never feel Clint's sensuous touch on her magnificent breasts ever again. Nor would she feel the exciting suckling sensation from his mouth. She cried quietly.

She closed her eyes and tilted her face upward. The water washed away her tears. She shampooed her hair and agonized at the pain. She bit her lower lip and grimaced each time her surgical wounds were stretched or disturbed. She moved gingerly, but her wounds still throbbed. She brought her arms down to ease the pain. She continued taking her shower at the pace of an injured tortoise on Quaaludes. She whimpered and cried like a hurt puppy. A knock on the door distracted her.

"Are you okay, darlin?"

"Y-yeah, uh … h-honey."

"I'm coming in. You've been in there for thirty minutes and you don't sound well at all." Clint opened the door.

"Please, Clint, don't come in. I'm almost done," she begged. She was sobbing openly now.

"Well, sweetheart, you're cryin', and I'm worried."

"I swear, I'm gonna be done in a minute," she said, sniffling. Just then a wave of nausea came over her, making her dizzy. "Honey, I think I'm going to pass out."

Clint shoved the shower curtain to one side and caught her just in time. She fell limp into his arms, but she was still semi-conscious. "I'm sorry, Babe. Didn't want you to see me like this."

"Shh … " Clint sat on the toilet's lid and held Makenna on his lap. He reached for a towel to dry her off, being careful with her wounds. Makenna could feel his eyes lingering on her now leveled chest. "I think you're still gorgeous," he said. He put the clean gown on her and then carried her to her bed.

As a consolation for her ordeal, she now felt clean and refreshed. Sponge baths simply hadn't been enough. She felt exhausted. While Clint was brushing her hair, it relaxed her and she soon fell asleep.

❊ ❊ ❊

Cassandra arrived to relieve Clint. She whispered, "I'm glad she's sleeping."

"Taking a shower this morning exhausted her," Clint also whispered. They continued to speak in quiet voices.

"Bet that wasn't a whole lot of fun for her."

"No, it wasn't. She almost passed out." Clint related the event further.

"No wonder she's exhausted. Oh, my baby," Cassandra said as she gave her sleeping daughter a sympathetic look.

"When the nurse came to take her blood pressure reading, she slept through it. She moved a little, but never opened her eyes once. Didn't want to wake her up for lunch. I think she needs sleep more than food right now."

"I think you're right. As much as she complains about not getting enough sleep, I'm sure she'd rather sleep than eat. Sleep will do her good. Now, I think you should go to the house and get some sleep, too."

"Thanks, Mom." He left and went to his parents-in-law's house to get some much-needed rest. He didn't go to sleep right away. Not until after he visited with Richard and spent some time with Chloe. He finally went to sleep at 3 p.m. He was a little disoriented as to what time and day it was when he woke up at 9 p.m.

Cassandra was back from the hospital. "Chloe is already sleeping," she said, "and Richard is now at the hospital. I made some chicken and dumplings. I'm going to heat some up if you'd like to eat before going to the hospital."

"Sure," Clint said, beaming at the thought of eating some chicken and dumplings. "I haven't had any for a long time, and they're one of my favorite foods. Plus, you make the best chicken and dumplings ever—bar none. How can I say no?" Cassandra felt flattered with his compliment.

Clint ate his food with the gusto of a starved wildcat. Hospital food had never come close to his mother-in-law's home cooking and had never satisfied him. He was appreciative of how well Makenna had learned from her mother's cooking.

CHAPTER 43

At the hospital, Makenna and her dad were discussing her novel. It appeared that sleep had revitalized and energized her. Richard noticed the glow on her face and the life in her voice while they were talking.

"I'm curious as to what point in your novel you've gotten to."

"Well, I'm at the point where Steve has arrived at the Minneapolis Saint Paul International Airport."

"Very good. Very good." He and Makenna often discussed her book. He was intrigued by it and thought it was cute of Makenna for asking for his input. After all, he was never the romantic kind of guy and never in his wildest dreams imagined he'd be reading stuff like that. His interests were in medicine, sports, hunting, and fishing. Nevertheless, he and Makenna were bonding well because of it. Not that they weren't close before; they were much more so now.

"I can't wait to get done with it," Makenna was saying when Clint entered her room.

"What can't you wait to get done with?" He gave Makenna a peck on the lips.

"My novel."

"Oh." Clint turned to his father-in-law. "Dad, I didn't realize you knew she's writing a romance novel."

"Yeah, she had mentioned it to me a while back when she asked me how I met her mother."

"That's another reason why I can't wait to get out of here, is so I can finish it. Nina has been antsy about getting the rest of my manuscript. I've been sending her each chapter as I've finished it. As it gets further along, the more she gets impatient for the next chapter to be done. I'm hoping to write quite a bit before I start my chemo."

Her dad stroked his chin. "Nina Servino?"

"Yes, except she's Nina Jentzen now."

"So why are you sending your manuscript to her?"

"I'm sorry, Dad. I should have told you. Nina left her job at the Wyoming Tribune Eagle a while back. She's since been the chief editor at the Lover's Lane Publishing Company in Loveland. She's had that position since the beginning of the company. It's her company that's going to publish my book."

"Oh, so you have a publisher already. That's *wonderful*, Makenna."

"Thanks, Dad."

"For now, though, Makenna, I think you should take care of your health first before your novel?"

"But Dad, writing my novel will keep my mind occupied rather than allowing myself to wallow in self-pity. It'll help me get better sooner, I believe."

"Okay, if you think it'll help. I'm sure you'll know your limitations when the time comes." He went to give her a kiss on the forehead. "Well, I think I'm going to head home for now. I'll see you both tomorrow."

"Thanks, Dad," replied both Makenna and Clint.

CHAPTER 44

Today was Makenna's third day at the hospital—the day she had been looking forward to since day one. She was scheduled to be discharged this morning. She and Clint were waiting for a doctor to come around to give her the green light. She didn't know who was going to show up today. Every day was a different doctor.

A young nurse came in to take her vital signs. "Hi, my name is Diane. How're you doin' this morning?"

"Good," Makenna said, contrary to what she was feeling. Her blanket was wrapped around her nice and snug. She had a slight chill after a sponge bath this morning. After her ordeal yesterday, she'd decided on a sponge bath.

"I haven't seen you here before. Are you new?"

"No ma'am." "We, nurses, work seven-twelves on and seven-twelves off. Today is my first day back."

"Wow! So, you're well rested then?" Makenna pulled out her left arm from the blanket.

Diane clamped a pulse oximeter probe on Makenna's left index finger. "Not entirely. I was off for two days then I had to go to my part time job at Poudre Valley Hospital in Fort Collins for three days. I was off again for two days before coming back here. Many of the nurses I know do the same thing. They work at different clinics or hospitals, of course. I'm still paying off my student loan, so having that extra income helps a lot."

"Good for you," Makenna said.

"Very admirable thing you do," Clint said.

"Thanks," Diane said while pressing a button to activate the vital signs monitor. She wrapped the blood pressure cuff around Makenna's left arm and pressed more buttons on the monitor. Makenna felt the cuff inflate. Her arm was being squeezed to the point of it feeling tingly.

She noticed how focused Clint's eyes were on the monitor as he and Diane watched the numbers displayed. She heard Clint asking the nurse what the different numbers meant. Makenna concluded that, even though Clint was a highly educated lawyer, he was unable to interpret and decipher the numbers and graphs. She herself didn't know, either.

"I've decided," Clint said, grinning, "that the monitor was purposefully designed to be incoherent to non-medical people like me, just to provide additional leverage to you, medical staff." Makenna took notice of the way Clint spoke in a more professional tone rather than with his usual backwoods country style of talking.

The nurse chuckled. "Perhaps, you're right, Sir."

"The monitor appears totally different from what I remembered it looking three years ago."

"Yes," Diane said. "Technology sure changes rapidly." Makenna and Clint agreed with her.

"Hmmm," Diane expressed, as she wrote the numbers on Makenna's chart. Makenna couldn't see the monitor because it was situated beside her, past her head. Unless she tilted her head sideways and up, she couldn't see it. She felt the blood pressure cuff deflate around her arm and could feel her warm blood rush through her tingling arm once again.

"Do you have any history of high blood pressure?" Diane said.

"Not that I know of."

Diane turned the pages going backward, checking for previous readings.

"What reading did you get?"

"One thirty-seven over one-oh-one. According to your

chart, you had some high readings just after your surgery but none after that. Until now, of course. If you don't mind, I'd like to take another reading just to make sure. Before I do that, though, I'm going to take your temperature." She put a disposable plastic sheath on the thermometer probe and placed it in Makenna's mouth, underneath one side of her tongue. The nurse made a face and made the "hmmm" sound once again. "Are you feeling okay?" the nurse said with a concerned look.

"Well, to tell you the truth, I do have the chills. I thought it was because I'd just gotten my sponge bath this morning. And, now, I also have a headache. Why?"

"That explains it. You have a temperature of one hundred. I'm surprised you're not feeling lethargic."

"I think it's because I'm so excited about going home today. Does this mean that I won't be going home today?"

"I don't know. It all depends what the doctor decides." She took another blood pressure reading. She mumbled about the reading being even higher at 140 over 103. She looked at the monitor again, then turned to face Makenna. "Your heart rate has gone from sixty-five to seventy-seven. Are you, by any chance, feeling nervous right now?"

"Maybe, because of the possibility that I might not go home today." Makenna hoped that was all there was to it. She felt relieved to see doctor.

"Hi, I'm doctor Apollonia." Smiling, she said, "How's everybody today?"

"I'm ready to go home," Makenna said.

"She's running a fever," Clint said.

"Oh?" She took the chart from the nurse and read the notes. She went by the sink and dispensed some alcohol-based hand sanitizer on her palm, which she rubbed on until it dried. She touched Makenna's forehead, hand, and feet.

"You do feel warm." She applied more sanitizer on her hands. After the sanitizer dried, she put on a pair of gloves. She checked Makenna's legs, arms, and torso, muttering about looking for any sign of rash or petechiae. She put on her stethoscope and said, "Let me check on your lungs."

"Take a deep breath … exhale … once more … breathe normally … very good. Have the dressings been changed today?"

"Not yet," Diane said. She took out the items she needed from the cabinet above the sink. After she put a pair of gloves on, she cut out the waterproof tapes covering Makenna's wounds with a pair of sterile scissors. Makenna grimaced in pain as Diane peeled the tapes and gauze off her chest. Under the tape and gauze on each breast was a piece of sterile, medicated strip that covered the surgical wounds.

Dr. Apollonia removed one of the strips. She observed and assessed the condition of the stitches and wound. She did the same on the other side. "The wounds are a little red and inflamed." She checked the areas where the four tubes were inserted. The clear waterproof tape that held them in place allowed for easy observation and assessment of the condition of the portals. She instructed Diane to continue with changing the dressings.

"With you running a fever, blood pressure elevated, and your wounds still inflamed, I'd like to keep you for one more day of observation. I'm sure this is not what you want to hear today, but it's really in your best interest." When she finished talking, she added several notes to Makenna's chart.

Makenna sighed in disappointment. "Are you sure I can't go home today and just check back in if I'm feeling any worse?" she said in a cajoling and pleading way.

The doctor gave her a look. "*I'm sure*. It's important to keep you under observation. We want to see where this fever is going. What we don't want to see happening is for you to develop septicemia. Besides, it's easier for you, overall, should you have to come back in. You don't have to go through another admission and discharge process."

She wrote some more on the chart before talking again. "I'm going to have the lab draw two sets of blood cultures fifteen minutes apart. I'm going to prescribe some Tylenol for your fever and headache. As long as the Tylenol works, then you don't need anything stronger. If, for some reason, your temperature goes up to one-oh-one, or even if it comes back down, and you develop additional symptoms, the lab is going to draw another two sets of blood cultures, fifteen minutes apart. After the blood cultures are drawn, the nurse will give you some Erythromycin, a type of broad-spectrum antibiotic. She'll also give you some Vicodin."

"What symptoms should we be looking for?" Clint said.

"High fever, skin rash, low blood pressure, shivering, increased heart rate, sweating, chills, delirium, abdominal pain, and vomiting. These symptoms don't necessarily all present themselves."

"And what are the blood cultures for?"

"I want to rule out sepsis. And if she has sepsis, the sensitivity test will let me know what specific type of antibiotic to treat her with. Let's hope it won't come to that."

CHAPTER 45

M akenna's plan of doing more writing before her chemo was scrapped altogether. Due to the blood infection she acquired after her surgery, she spent seven additional days at the hospital. She also spent five days at her parents' house to recuperate. It was her parents' idea. She was thankful, for she was still weak after leaving the hospital. Instead of having three weeks to do some writing, now she had none. She decided to just take it easy and enjoy feeling good for a few days before she would start her sixteen weeks of chemotherapy.

Makenna's Oncologist, Dr. Luna, informed her that the pathology results of the axillary dissection were negative. "Based on these results," Dr. Luna had told her during her visit with him, before going home to Elk Mountain, "you don't need the five-week radiation therapy anymore after your chemo."

Makenna shed tears of happiness upon hearing the good news. She felt doubly blessed. Even so, she was not looking forward to losing her hair from the chemo, but she had no choice.

For now, Makenna was pleased to be home at last. She was able to sleep in her own bed. Oh, how she couldn't wait to put her tired body on the comfort of their bed and to cuddle with Clint. It's been a while, she thought.

After she arrived home, her days were occupied with changing the dressings of her wounds once a day. The wounds were healing well, but she still cried each time she looked at the two white patches where her large breasts used to be. She felt less of a woman without them.

"Darlin' I didn't marry you because of your breasts," she kept reminding herself of Clint's words—which he repeated often, "I married you because I love you and still do. Sure, your breasts were a plus, but hey, you still make this cowboy wild and crazy over you, even without them." He would tease, smiling and winking at her. He'd then gather her into his arms and give her hugs and kisses. His shows of love and affection comforted her enormously.

* * *

This was Makenna's third week of chemotherapy. *Chemo is supposed to treat my cancer. Instead, it's killing me.* At least that was what it felt like it to her when the side effects took their toll on her. As much as she wanted to stay upbeat, she didn't have the energy. She had no appetite for food whatsoever, either. The first three days, after each session, she spent much of the time in the bathroom sink, throwing up. As soon as she thought she felt better on the sixth or seventh day, it was time again for her next chemotherapy. It would start the whole cycle of feeling ill all over again. She was sick of feeling sick!

Her hair started to fall off in masses. She cried at the sight of herself every time she looked in the mirror. Everyday more hair was lost. Her hair came off when she slept, when she showered, and when she brushed it. It got to the point where she couldn't bear to see herself in the mirror anymore.

As far as she was concerned, losing her gorgeous dark brown hair, after losing her breasts, was the last straw. It stripped away anything left of her womanhood. She shaved off the few remaining strands of hair on her head that stuck out like the few trees still standing on a burned forest. The wig she wore didn't feel natural on her head. Her positive attitude and spunkiness only went so far. The toxic side effects of the chemotherapy had sucked the life out of her … almost.

CHAPTER 46

Makenna was lying on the living room sofa, feeling depressed. Even though the TV in front of her was on, she only stared blankly at it. She was feeling cold, too, so she had herself all bundled up in a thick fleece blanket. This had been the norm for her for six weeks now.

Her blank stare was rattled when her cell phone rang. She pulled her right arm out of the blanket and picked it up from the coffee table. She checked who was calling before she answered. "Hello, Nina," she said. Her voice seemed weak and lifeless.

"How are you doing, Makenna?" Nina said. Nina's voice was upbeat and full of life.

"Still not well, Nina. I'm now into my sixth-week of treatment. All I've done so far was go to my chemo and endure a four-hour long drug infusion once a week. For three days after that, I suffer from debilitating episodes of dizziness, headache, and nausea ... to the point where I end up throwing up the bile contents of my gut. I say that because I'm not able to keep anything in. I have no appetite at all. The only thing I can tolerate right now is Ensure protein drink." She coughed several times after that. Her coughs were weak, but they shook her frail and thin body each time.

"I'm so sorry to hear this, Makenna. I wish I were close by, so I could at least come help you in any way I can."

"Thanks, Nina. You, calling and checking up on me is already a big help."

"What about sleep? Are you able to sleep okay?"

"I sleep a lot, but only in short spurts. Most of the time, I close my eyes only to rest them."

"Please hang in there, Makenna. Stay strong and get well soon. Praying for your speedy recovery."

"Thanks so much, for your words of encouragement. They mean so much."

"You're welcome."

Makenna's conversation with Nina uplifted her spirits. Even though Nina hadn't visited her in person since her surgery, Nina had called her a couple times before this call.

Makenna's parents visited her often when they went to drop off Chloe on Fridays. They'd see her again on Tuesdays when she and Clint dropped Chloe off at their place before going to her chemo treatments. Makenna's sisters had also visited her a couple of times. They wanted to visit her more, they assured her, but Makenna understood. They both lived in other states, had jobs and families to take care of. Therefore, their visits were somewhat short and limited.

Clint's love, support, and understanding helped her cope with her depression and insecurity. He babied her and had been bending over backward taking care of her whenever he was home. Makenna was again happy she had listened to her dad's advice five years ago about forgiving him and saving their marriage.

She remembered her father's strong admonition, "Even if you can't forgive Clint, don't put the burden on the child. Instead, accept the child as your own. The child is not at fault here, Makenna." Makenna was going to divorce Clint when she found out about his affair.

"It was a one-night-stand," Clint had assured her. "I was drunk and wasn't in my best behavior when she seduced me. You're the one I love. Not her. It's you I want to spend the rest of my life with. I beg for your forgiveness, Babe."

The affair happened a month before she was shot in Gaza. When Chloe's biological mother gave birth to Chloe, she didn't want anything to do with Chloe. She gave full custody to Clint after a genetic testing proved Clint as the father.

"But, Dad," she remembered saying, "you don't know what it's like to be cheated on. And, the baby would always remind me of what he'd done to me."

Cassandra looked in the direction of her husband and saw the hurt on his face. "Makenna, I have to tell you something."

"Cassie, *please don't say it*." Makenna saw her dad turning pale. *What is he so fearful of her saying?*

"Yes, Richard, she *needs to know the truth*. I don't want to hide the truth from her any longer." She started crying. "What truth?" Makenna looked at both her parents in bewilderment.

"This is not the right time, Cassie."

"There is *never* going to be a *right time*, Hon." Cassie stood and planted her feet firmly on the floor as she spoke with emphatic resolve. "She needs to know the truth, especially now."

"Would you two please tell me what truth you're talking about?"

Cassandra went on to tell Makenna the truth of how she came into being.

"Mom, how could you have cheated on Dad like that?"

Her mother was crying and couldn't talk at that moment. So, her dad did the talking.

"Makenna, I've forgiven your mother a long time ago, so I'd appreciate if you would do the same. After all, you, my wonderful daughter, whom I've accepted and raised as my own, and then loved with all my heart, would not be here today if it weren't for your mother's mistake. I'm overjoyed, too, that she didn't opt to have you aborted in order to not face my wrath when I came home from Vietnam."

Makenna was now crying, too. "Why wasn't I told about this sooner? I wish I'd known it sooner."

"We didn't think that it was necessary for you to know." Her dad blew out air, his chest heaving and falling. "We were trying to protect you. As you can imagine, it's not something your mother would want to be talking about."

"Do Shay and Tori know?"

Dad raised a forefinger and nodded. "Yes."

Makenna's feelings were conflicted. On one hand, she felt angry and betrayed. On the other hand, she felt humbled and appreciative. She gave her dad a tight, long hug. "I'm so sorry, Dad, for what I said earlier about you not understanding my situation. Thank you so much for taking me in and raising me as your own. I love you so much."

"It's okay, honey. I love you, too. The words of advice I'd given you earlier were the exact same words of advice that your grandfather admonished me with, many years ago."

"It's a very sound word of advice," she'd said before giving her dad a hug again.

Makenna remembered giving her mother a warm, long hug also. "Mom, I'm sorry for criticizing you. Thanks a million times over for not having me aborted." Her mother had hugged her back with the same intensity, and her dad had joined them in a group hug.

* * *

Makenna was feeling great today. *Yay, I've survived my sixteen weeks of chemo,* she congratulated herself. She felt more amazing when Dr. Luna, her oncologist, gave her a clean bill of health during her one-month check-up after her chemo treatments. "You don't have to see me for three months. You may make your appointment now or may call later to make one."

"This calls for a celebration," Clint announced after relating all the good news to Makenna's parents. "Where does everybody want to go to eat? It's *my treat.*"

"Let Makenna pick, since she's the one we're celebrating for," Cassandra said.

Makenna thought for a few seconds, then said, "Since we haven't eaten at the Olive Garden yet, I'd say we go there if that's okay with everybody. I heard the food is wonderful."

"Olive Garden, it is," a jubilant Clint said. "Let's go."

They arrived mid-afternoon, before dinner rush hour, so they didn't have to wait long. Makenna's appetite was back. She relished every bite, and drank her raspberry tea with guilty pleasure. Her family all expressed how pleased they were to see her eating again. They also kidded her about needing to get more meat on her bony frame.

The next day, Makenna looked out the living room window. The morning view was so inviting, she had to step outside to the balcony. *Oh, what a glorious day it is.* She went to lean on the railing for support, closed her eyes, and breathed in the cool morning air. She tilted her face toward the morning sun, enjoying the warmth of it touching her face. She opened her eyes and saw the wonder of her surroundings. She was in awe. It was as if the first time she'd ever seen them. It was now the month of October. She noticed the prairies that stretched for miles and miles in front of her had now turned yellow. She also observed that the leaves of the aspen trees up on the mountainsides had turned into blazing and dazzling red, yellow, and orange colors. The chirping of birds coming from trees nearby was music to her ears. Even the sound of semi-trucks whizzing by on the interstate pleased her ears.

It's great to be feeling well again. All of my senses are now fully restored. I can even smell the inviting aroma of my coffee, brewing inside. Her nose led her to the kitchen. Makenna poured herself some freshly brewed coffee from the pot and stirred in some vanilla-flavored coffee creamer. She brought the mug close to her face and inhaled its rich aroma before sipping it in total delight.

I'm so excited to get back into my writing, she thought. She went to get her laptop from her study room and turned it on. She checked her emails and spent hours reading them, chuckling at funny jokes forwarded to her. She forwarded some she thought were most entertaining. After replying to her emails, at last, she was ready to resume her writing.

She opened her document folder and opened the last

chapter. She read the last five pages to refresh her memory. As soon as the ideas started flowing, she pounded them onto her keyboard.

CHAPTER 47

As soon as the plane landed and parked at Minneapolis-St. Paul International Airport, Steve disembarked along with the other passengers. He followed the crowd to the baggage area to retrieve his duffle bag and then went to the Avis office to rent a car. After he signed the lease and paid the bill, the agent called somebody over his cell phone to deliver the car.

Steve was somewhat nervous as he was approaching his in-law's house. He tried to rehearse his lines. He noticed the shock on his in-law's faces when they saw him at their doorstep, unannounced. Surely, they don't know what to make of this, he thought.

"What a nice surprise to see you, Steve," Larry said as he let him inside the house. This was the exact opposite of the reception he had gotten from Larry sixteen years ago.

"You may take your duffle bag up in the guest room, Steve," Christina said.

Steve obliged. When he came down, he went to give them each a hug. "So good to see you both and great to be back in the states," he proclaimed as he took a seat on the sofa.

"Would you like something to eat or drink?" Christina said.

"I'm a little hungry, but I can wait 'til dinner time. I'd like some ice tea, though, if you have any."

Christina went to fetch him some. When she came back, she placed it on the coffee table in front of him.

"Thanks, Mom."

"You're welcome, Steve, um … Sandy didn't tell us you're coming home."

"It's because she doesn't know. It's a surprise."

"*Oh*," the couple gushed, one after the other. Then they asked him lots of questions about his deployment. In a calm voice he related to them his experiences in Kosovo. In return, the couple listened intently.

* * *

Steve felt like he was experiencing a case of Deja vu. His mind drifted back sixteen years ago, when he had come to the same house to visit Sandy for the first time. He was shocked when he saw his boss at the door.

"Mister Christensen," he remembered saying, startled.

"Hello Steve." Larry looked strict and serious.

He became instantly uncomfortable and had to fumble for words to say, "I … I'm here to, um … to visit Sandy."

"Come in. We were expecting you."

"Please have a seat," Christina said with a smile. She was standing and waiting in the living room. She had an attractive, kind, and friendly face.

Steve noticed right away that Sandy got most of her looks from her mother, especially those unusual emerald eyes. *She definitely looks more Anglo-Saxon than a native Bolivian.* When Sandy told him her mother was from Bolivia, he had a vision that she'd look like one of those Hispanics he got accustomed to seeing around in Colorado. He noticed how well poised and graceful she walked and moved. He'd characterized her as the epitome of sophistication.

Steve thanked her and took a seat on the loveseat. He didn't lean back, instead, he leaned forward, resting his elbows on his knees with his hands clasped together. He tried to appear composed and at ease, but inside, he was a bundle of fried nerves. His heart was pounding and his gut was in a tight knot, especially when he didn't see Sandy anywhere.

He was face to face with her parents, who were seated on a sofa opposite him. He had no idea what was going on, or what to expect. He remembered thinking that Mr. Christensen must have read his mind, because not long after they were all seated, Larry started talking. His tone was stern and controlled.

"Steve, you're probably wondering what's this is all about, and why Sandy is not here right now."

Steve glanced over at Christina, whose eyes, at least, expressed sympathy to him.

"Is she okay?" Steve's eyebrows furrowed, and he'd felt his face turning ashen.

"Yes, she's okay," Larry said.

Steve noticed Larry's stern voice soften and his demeanor friendlier upon hearing him express his concern for Sandy.

"We want you to know, Steve," Larry held out his hands, in an imploring manner, "that we can't allow Sandy to date just yet. She's only fifteen."

Steve had felt like he'd been clobbered over the head with a baseball bat. His back stiffened as his posture shot erect in his seat. *"Fifteen? She told me she's eighteen."* Steve had to struggle to maintain his composure. This was shocking news, indeed.

"I hope, now," Larry said, "you understand why we're adamant about Sandy not going out on dates yet. If you're still interested in her in the future, you may come back when she's at least eighteen years old."

Larry, at least, allowed him and Sandy to have some private moments alone to say goodbye before he left.

He kept in touch with Sandy through letters and phone calls after that. Sure enough, the minute Sandy turned eighteen, he was at her doorstep with a birthday gift box and a bouquet of flowers. The attraction between them had never waned and was still there. He'd known all along they were meant for each other, and his heart assured him Sandy felt the same way. So, they married three months later. He could tell Sandy was in heaven as he was.

✳ ✳ ✳

Christina's voice brought him back to the present. "You two keep talking, while I go to fix dinner."

"Dad, I'm going to use the john. I'll be right back," Steve said.

"Okay, Steve. When you're done, just come join me in my study. I want to show you my new hobby."

"Okay, Dad," Steve said before he went to use the bathroom upstairs in the guest room.

Larry and Christina took the opportunity to have a quick hushed conversation in the kitchen. "I think I'm going to ask him straight away why he came back to the states earlier than scheduled."

Christina lifted her chin in thought, then placed a hand on the countertop. "Do you think he knows about Sandy's pregnancy? Or, do you think he got kicked out of the Air Force?"

"Don't know. Guess I'll try to find out."

"Now, you go easy on him. You don't want to put him on the defensive," Christina said.

"I better go to my office before he comes down."

✳ ✳ ✳

"Wow!" Your home office looks awesome, Dad," Steve exclaimed as he entered Larry's office. He was truly impressed. "The matching dark cherry desk and bookcases sure look great. They were not here the last time we visited you."

"Thanks, Steve. That's my sixty-fifth birthday gift from Christina."

"*Nice*. Belated happy birthday." Steve looked at family pictures hanging on the walls. The pictures made him miss Sandy and his children. When he noticed the painting of the bison, he said, "Isn't that the original painting you bought at an art gallery when you came to visit us in Minot two summers ago?"

"Yes, it is."

"I remember you going crazy, taking pictures of the bison when we took you to the South unit of the Theodore Roosevelt National Park."

"I was captivated by those magnificent creatures the moment I saw them. Since we don't have them here, the next best thing is to buy a painting of one. We sure had a great time that day."

"We absolutely did. Say, is this your new hobby you were talking about?"

"Yes, indeed."

"Why four identical sets?" Steve took a chair nearby and sat next to his father-in-law by the desk, examining the coin sets.

"One for Carrie, one for Sheyenne, and one for Taurea."

"And the fourth?"

"Steve, this is something you and I have to talk about. Why are you back in the states earlier than expected?"

This is it—the moment of truth. Steve closed his eyes and took a breath shallower than he wanted. He moved his chair by the window to face Mr. Christensen. He'd rehearsed, over and over in his head, the lines he was going to say and how to say them. But the circumstance now was so different from how he'd presented it to himself. The words he had rehearsed, now escaped him.

He knew. Even though they had always treated him like a son, they'd still be siding with Sandy. As is often stated, blood is thicker than water. In this situation, he was sure of this. He was encouraged, though, that Larry was the one who initiated this conversation. So, he took the opportunity to speak his mind.

"Dad, I'm sure you're already well aware that Sandy is pregnant with another man's child." He said it in a controlled and calculated tone, trying not to lose his temper. He noticed Larry squirm in his seat. "Dad, whatever's between Sandy and me, I want you to know that I hold no grudge against you, Mom, or Carrie. You've treated me like a son, and I thank you for that. So, what I'm asking of you and Mom is not to hold any grudge against me either. Now that I've decided to divorce Sandy for what she did to me."

He took another breath, this time longer and deeper. He thought he was doing okay, so far. "I thought it through during my trip back to the U.S. I've decided that divorce is the only option for us. I know that I can't, and will never, be able to forgive her for her infidelity. Her child will be a constant reminder of her cheating on me. Another deep breath followed. He waited forLarry to respond.

Larry was clearly in the most uncomfortable situation. After all, this was his daughter's infidelity that was at the crux of the conversation. Before he spoke, his chest rose and fell with an audible sigh. It was his turn.

"Steve, I'm not going to defend Sandy's infidelity. I agree with you. She wronged you in the worst way. However, I'd like for you not to hate the child. The child is not at fault here. Whatever sin Sandy and the other man committed should not be burdened on the child." He stopped and cocked his head slightly. "By the way, do you know who the other man is?"

Steve wiggled, side to side. "No, I don't. I thought you might."

"All we know is that he worked with Sandy in the lab for half a year, but left the area six months ago. He doesn't know about his unborn baby as far as we know. From what I gathered from Christina's conversations with Sandy, the man told Sandy he doesn't love her. Also told her to never, ever call him again. That was the first and the last communication they had since the man left Minot."

"Is that so?" Steve's eyebrows crinkled. "Did Sandy say anything to you about what she's going to do?"

"She said," he winced, "she's going to wait to see what you want to do when you get back."

"Well, if she thinks I'll be okay with everything, she's dead wrong. I'm going to find a divorce lawyer as soon as I get home.

I'll allow her to stay at our base housing, in a separate room, until she's strong enough to be on her own. Most likely that'll be twelve weeks or so after she delivers."

"Tell me, Steve, is your marriage important to you?"

"*Of course, it is.* But is it important to Sandy? She should be the one you'd be asking that. I'm not the one who was sleeping around. *She was.*"

Steve, get a grip. You're getting pretty riled up from this kind of questioning. He controlled his breathing, relaxed his tensed shoulders, and felt his temper settling down. At least now, Larry knew exactly how Steve felt about things with Sandy.

Larry was visibly more relaxed. An indication that he understood Steve's anger. Steve surmised he was imagining what he would feel in the same situation. *Even though he disagrees with my decision to divorce Sandy, in fairness, he has to appreciate my allowing Sandy to stay until after the baby will be three months old.*

A long silence between them was interrupted by a knock at the door.

"Dinner is served," Christina said.

"Okay, Honey."

"Don't wait too long. We don't want the food to get cold."

Larry got up from his chair. He walked toward Steve and patted him on the shoulder. "Let's go eat dinner."

Steve was thankful that his father-in-law was a fair-minded man.

The dinner was one of the best meals Steve had in a while. The mood was relaxed and happy. They talked, laughed, and discussed things amicably.

"Mom and Dad, I hope you can put up with me for a couple more days. I'd like to buy a truck tomorrow before going home to Minot. If I find one tomorrow, I'll leave the next day."

"Of course, Steve," Christina said, "You should know by now you're always welcome in this house. If it takes longer than two days for you to find the right vehicle you're looking for, then, by all means, stay here as long as it takes."

After dinner, they retreated to the family room to watch TV. Steve expressed his thanks to both, then excused himself. "I think I'll call it a night. Jet lag is catching up to me," he said, and then made a big yawn.

* * *

Steve woke up early in the morning to get ready to look for a truck. Even though he liked his Toyota SR5 truck in Minot, he was excited with the prospect of having one of those full-sized Dodge Ram models he'd seen advertised on TV on his way back to the U.S. It will be good during winter and during hunting trips, he figured. He even picked out a color - red. Just like the one he saw advertised. He thought red would give the truck a bold, yet sleek and sporty look.

Sometimes he suspected, though, the truck's main purpose was going to be a diversion from the uneasy situation he was going to be dealing with when he got home. True, in the beginning, he'd wanted to throw Sandy out of their base housing the minute he got home. Cut her off from him and the children. But he'd calmed down considerably since then. His more sensible and sensitive side changed his mind and position about the whole thing. That was how he came up with an arrangement he felt was more humane to Sandy and the baby.

Before he left the house, Steve borrowed Larry's computer. He Google searched for several Dodge dealerships in the Minneapolis/St. Paul area. He wrote down the addresses and phone numbers of the ones that had the truck he was looking for. Being a detail-oriented person, he wrote down the different specifications each truck had to offer. He compared them from one another before he settled on the one that satisfied all of his criteria. He visited each dealership and inspected each truck on his list.

He was also a tough negotiator when it came to buying big-ticket items. He haggled with the car salesman for a long while about the price. There was much offer and counter offer going on. In the end, he got the price he asked for. He was more than satisfied. After the documents were filled out and signed and a temporary plate put on his truck, Steve returned the rental car. He took a cab back to the dealership and drove his new truck home to his in-law's house. When he arrived, Larry and Christina went to check out his truck. They expressed their delight and approval, while walking around the truck. They even liked its *red* color. Steve was pleased.

* * *

In Minot, Sandy received a call from her parents while Steve went looking for a truck. She became emotional and cried for quite some time after the call. When she settled down from her tumultuous crying, she started moving her personal belongings to the guest room where Carrie was staying. She told herself that at least now Steve already knew. She won't have to be explaining her situation to him anymore. Also, now, she knew exactly what Steve wanted to do. As much as she wanted to stay married to him, she could not fault him with his decision. She probably would do the same thing in that situation. She was relieved to know Steve was still going to allow her to stay at the base housing until after the baby was born.

"What's going on? Why do you have all your stuff in my room," Carrie asked when she arrived from school. Sandy related to her what their parents said to her, which made her cry again. Carrie went to give her a consoling hug. "I'm *so* sorry, Sandy. Do you want me to move out now?"

"Not yet. You may stay here until after Steve arrives. You and I just have to share the room for one night after he arrives. I'm sure you'd like to see him. And I'm sure he wants to see you, too. From what Mom and Dad told me, Steve doesn't hold any grudges against any of you for what I've done to him. The issue is strictly between him and me."

Carrie whimpered, "Aww … are you going to be okay?"

"I hope so. I have to. It's my fault, you know?" Carrie hugged her again.

CHAPTER 48

S teve woke up at six in the morning to get ready for his long drive home to Minot. After he took a shower, he ate the breakfast Christina prepared for him. Last night at supper time, Larry and Chistina informed him that they had called Sandy and told her everything they had discussed and that he'd be leaving Minnesota the next morning. Steve was fine with that. Now, he thought, I won't have to explain to Sandy about the living arrangements. The less conversation we have, the better.

"Have a safe trip, Steve. Please call us when you get there, so we know you've arrived there safely."

"Okay, Mom. Thanks for everything," he said as he gave her a parting embrace. He also gave Larry a hug. He used to give him just a handshake but, in the last five years, he started hugging him like a son would his father.

"I'll call Sandy to let her know you're on your way."

"Thanks, Dad." He climbed into his truck and started the engine. He backed out of the driveway as the couple looked on, and waved at them one last time before driving away.

The weather was mostly sunny. Roads were good and clear on the interstate. The woodlands on either side of the highway looked lush. Fir trees appeared robustly green, and the shrubs were budding and greening. Steve was enjoying his ride. He was in a good mood. He sang along with the songs on the radio.

I might as well take advantage of this good mood I'm in now, for there will be none later on. Every now and then he stopped at rest stops, and once at Wendy's to buy a sandwich and some soda. He ate his sandwich as soon as he got back on the road, but took a swig of his soda every so often.

❋ ❋ ❋

At 8:30 a.m. Sandy received a phone call from her mother. "Hi Mom."

"How are you, Dear?"

"I'm okay, Mom. Just got back from dropping off the kids at school and am getting ready for bed."

"Sorry, Punkin. I'll be quick. I called to let you know Steve had left the house at 7:30 this morning."

"Thanks, for the update, Mom. By the way, I already moved out of our room and into the guest room." Her voice felt unsteady.

"Will you be okay, Sandy?"

Sandy took a swallow to ease the lump in her throat before she said, "I hope so, Mom. And, don't you be worrying about me. I'll be fine."

"Call us anytime. We're here for you."

After talking with her mother, Sandy went to sleep until 1:00 p.m. When she woke up, she hurried to clean the house and wash the dishes before taking a shower. After she got dressed, she applied light make-up and a spritz of her perfume. She checked herself in the mirror and thought she looked good enough.Then her whole demeanor collapsed. *Why do I even bother? I'm sure he could care less at this point how I look. I have to prepare myself for the worst.* She took out a container of frozen lasagna from the freezer and put it in the oven. It should be almost cooked by the time Steve arrived.

She fidgeted and felt uptight—unsure on how to approach Steve when he got there. She knew she wanted to hug him so much, but wasn't sure if he'd appreciate it. It was time for school to be dismissed in the afternoon. So, she went to pick the kids up. By the time they arrived, Carrie was home. Sheyenne and

Taurea went by the large picture window in the living room. They waited with much anticipation for their daddy's arrival.

"Daddy's here! Daddy's here!" the girls screamed as they ran outside to meet him in the driveway. Carrie ran after them, followed by Sandy, albeit with some hesitation. When Steve emerged from his spanking brand new muscular, blood red truck, he was sporting five days' worth of stubbles from not shaving since he left Kosovo.

Oh, he looks so handsome, Sandy thought. She wanted so much to run to him to kiss him and hug him, but she held back. Steve met the children and picked both of them up, one on each arm as he kissed them. The children kissed and hugged him back. Carrie went to join the group hug.

Steve glanced at Sandy's radiant, smiling face, and then his eyes lowered and stopped on her pregnant belly. Sandy waved at him, but she wasn't sure if he saw it. Steve carried Sheyenne and Taurea all the way into the house and took a seat on the sofa where he sat them on each of his legs.

Steve ignored Sandy when he and the children passed her by to enter the house. Sandy felt her heart being squeezed and wrung. She could barely breathe.

Before Carrie entered the house, she stopped to hug her. "I'm so sorry, Sandy..." Carrie hugged her tighter. "It breaks my heart to see you hurting like this. I love you."

"I love you, too, Carrie. Thank you. I appreciate you so much." She tried to fight the urge to cry when Carrie was hugging her, but her tears fell anyway. Sandy suggested for Carrie to go on inside the house.

As soon as Carrie went in, Sandy went to the backyard to cry some more. After a while, she settled down. She entered the back door and went into the guest bathroom to wash her face with some cold water. When finished, she went to the guest room where she would be sleeping from now on. She applied some compact powder on her face to cover the redness and puffiness. Then she went to the kitchen to finish cooking dinner.

While there was still fifteen minutes left until the lasagna was cooked, Sandy prepared some garden salad, along with some red grapes and freshly cut up apples in a separate bowl. She refrigerated the salad and the fruits when finished with them, and put some sliced garlic bread in the oven. Several minutes later, the lasagna was done, the garlic bread browned, and the fruits and salad were chilled. She set the table, and called everyone to eat.

At the table, Sandy gave Steve stolen glances. She noticed Steve doing the same thing. When her eyes happened to meet his several times, she smiled. But her smiles were tinged with sadness, for Steve didn't acknowledge her gesture.

If it weren't for the kids and Carrie making conversation with Steve, I'd feel the tension between us much more. Did he notice I cried, or that I was absent for at least twenty minutes since he arrived? Oh, how I missed him. I wonder if he missed me, too. Is he hurting inside the way I am?

"Thank you, Sandy. Dinner was delicious."

"You're welcome, honey." *Oops* … it was truly a slip on her part. She caught herself, but too late. Steve heard her loud and clear, she knew, but he didn't seem to mind.

Darkness had already descended when there was a knock on the door. Sandy saw Steve go to answer it. She watched him have a short, soft conversation with whoever was outside the door. Soon after she saw Col. Morrow come in, along with two military police officers.

Sandy was puzzled. "Hello Colonel Morrow," she said as she stood from where she was seating in the living room. "Is something the matter?"

"Hello, Sandy. Nothing's the matter. We're only here to pick some things up."

"Steve?" Her eyes were searching for his for validation.

"Everything's okay, Sandy. Would you please take the kids to their room?" Sandy wanted to be present and be in the loop to whatever was going on with Steve and the other men. She was reluctant to leave, but complied with his request, nevertheless.

While Sandy was herding the children to go to their rooms,

she glanced often toward the men. She saw Steve lead the men to the basement. I'm sure he's taking them to his man cave, Sandy thought.

It was already 8:00 p.m., so Sandy put Sheyenne and Taurea to bed. She read to them until they fell asleep—which didn't take more than five minutes. She went to her room and found Carrie in bed, reading a book. She told Carrie what had taken place while Carrie was in the bedroom.

After a while Carrie said, "I wonder what's going on in there? It sure is taking long, whatever it is."

"Don't know, either, but sure looks suspicious to me. I can hear them in Steve's office ... hm."

"Do you think Steve's in trouble?"

"He didn't seem worried when those guys showed up, so I really don't know." Sandy joggled her brains to come up with an explanation. "You know? I noticed two police cars parked across the street when we got home from school this afternoon." Sandy trotted to the living room and peeked outside through the curtains. When she returned, she said, "Guess what, Carrie, the two police cars are not across the street anymore, but there are two parked outside our driveway now. I wonder if they're the same ones."

Sandy could tell Carrie was just as baffled as she was. They tried to come up with theories to explain the suspicious activities taking place. Every theory was dismissed, however. After the two discussed and reasoned out each one, they gave up. Carrie resumed her reading while Sandy went to the living room to listen in. She sat on the part of the sofa closest to the basement entrance. She felt terrible about listening in on the men's private conversations, but she couldn't ignore her strong curiosity, either.

From where she sat, she could hear the four men having good conversations. From what she could gather, Col. Morrow and the two military policemen were taking inventory of Steve's weapons.

What the heck? Why are they taking stock of his guns? She

became even more curious at that point. Every so often she heard the men erupt into laughter. She could tell the atmosphere downstairs was friendly and relaxed. Every now and then, she'd hear the men say, "*Wow.*" When asked about a particular gun, she heard Steve tell a story or history about it. She concluded the other men were also hunters because they talked so much about hunting.

She heard a man say, "Major Richardson, we're done with our inventory now." *Finally*, Sandy thought. Next, she heard a man say, "We're leaving you a carbon copy of the inventory, along with legal documents that pertain to the storage of your weaponry."

"Thanks, guys. Thanks, Colonel Morrow," Sandy heard Steve say. As soon as she heard the men start to come up the stairs, she tiptoed to the opposite side of the sofa. She picked up a magazine and pretended to be reading it. She looked up at the clock on the wall. It showed 10:00 p.m. when the men emerged from the basement.

"Oh, hi, Sandy," said Col. Morrow. "Sorry, we kept you awake."

"No, worries, Colonel Morrow," she said with a smile. She couldn't help noticing the several hard-sided gun cases the three men carried. *Why are taking them away?*

Good night, Sandy ... Steve. We must be going now, so you'll be able to go to sleep."

"Good night Colonel Morrow," Sandy said. Steve opened the door for them. Sandy knew Steve didn't want to be talking to her, but her curiosity got the best of her. She had to ask.

"They think that you or I might do something stupid in the state we're in, so they want to store my guns away."

"Was that the reason why two police cars were parked across the street ever since you got home today? To be close by and be ready?"

"Yup."

Sandy cringed at the thought. It never occurred to her that Steve, or she, for that matter, would resort to violence in dealing with their situation. "So why did they have to wait 'til tonight to get your guns?"

"Colonel Morrow didn't want to attract attention."

"*Oh* … I'm so sorry, Steve, I didn't mean to cause all these problems."

Steve closed his eyes and gave out a huge sigh. He opened his lips and lifted his right hand, as if he was going to say something, but he retracted his moves and stayed mum.

Sandy still waited for a reply, but it never came. "Good night Steve, and welcome home," she said as she got up from the sofa to head to her bedroom. The sharp pang in her heart came back again. She had to fight the strong urge once again to go kiss and hug him.

"Thanks. Goodnight," Steve said.

In bed, Sandy thought about Steve. *Oh, how I want to go to him right now. I miss him so much. I wish he'd come to make love to me. But ooh, my pregnant belly. How can I be fantasizing about him in my condition? Surely, he's disgusted at the sight of me right now. My big belly is reminding him of my adultery. I can't fault him, of course.*

Carrie moved back to her dorm the day after Steve arrived, leaving Sandy feeling sad and empty. Sleeping in a separate bed from Steve felt so weird to her. She turned and tossed for a good part of the night the first week. She'd get up, pace back and forth, and then back to bed.

The second week was better; Sandy was back to work. At least she didn't think too much of Steve while sleeping in separate bedrooms at different times—Sandy sleeping during the day and evenings, and Steve sleeping during the night. The tossing and turning would happen again on the nights Sandy was off from work.

Sandy did everything she normally did at home, except not sleeping with Steve or giving Steve massages, hugs, or kisses. Dinner time was mostly occupied by Sheyenne and Taurea, which helped their uneasy situation. She was always careful of the way she acted around Steve. She wasn't sure whether to act happy when she was happy or stay subdued. Many times, she had to stop in a halt as she started to go toward Steve to give him some affection. She fantasized of giving him massages when he got home from work like she used to do.

She often wondered what he would do if she just walked into his bedroom while he was in bed and started massaging him. Will he turn down a massage and shove me away? Will he push me away if I join him in bed to cuddle with him? With the way Steve was not speaking to her and not even looking into her eyes, she concluded Steve would shove and push her away. So, she never ventured to find out. Besides, she didn't want to add more emotional pain to her already aching heart if Steve were to turn her away. And, worse, for Steve to tell her straight to her face that he didn't love her at all anymore.

Oh! How she hurt inside. She took long, deep breaths and exhaled big sighs to release her angst and pangs. *Does he even think of me the way I think of him? Does he want me the way I want him?*

* * *

Steve was hurting too. He also tossed and turned, punching his pillow every now and then. He fantasized of Sandy walking into his bedroom to join him in bed to make love to him. He knew he wouldn't turn her down, instead he would take her in to allow her to fulfill her womanly desires on him until he was fully aroused for her. Then he would return the favor by feasting on her and devouring her with his manly desires while she moaned in ecstasy over and over, begging him not to stop. He would make love to her until she begged him to stop, but not until he had his fill with her at the top of the summit as he unleashed his load. He just couldn't be the one to make the first move. No way!

Does she even think of me the way I do? Or does she think only of the other guy? Does she still love me, or is she still in love with the other man? Does she want me the way I want her? These feelings were tormenting him.

Steve didn't consult a lawyer right away. Instead, he talked to several people at work who had gone through a divorce. Each one had a different advice to give. Some were brutal with their counsel:

'Since she was the one who screwed you, I wouldn't give her a dime.'

'Deny her a shared custody of your kids because she's an unfit parent.'

'Throw her out on the streets; she's a whore.'

He still loved Sandy and cared for her a great deal, so he was hurt by those kinds of remarks.

How bad can it be to stay married if she still wants to and just accept the baby as my own like what my father-in-law had said? But his ego was in the way.

It had been a month and a half since Steve arrived in Minot. He finally took the plunge to consult and hire a divorce lawyer, after he was first counseled by a military Judge Advocate at the base legal office. His civilian lawyer let him know there would be a three-month waiting period before the divorce could become final. This, of course, after Sandy had signed the divorce paper and after it had been submitted at the courthouse. Perfect, he thought. It would be just about the time Sandy and the baby would be moving out of the house anyway.

✻ ✻ ✻

Sandy had kept up with her prenatal appointments. She had been buying baby things and putting them in her room. The preparation for this baby was not as exciting as it was with Sheyenne and Taurea, since Steve was not involved like he was with the other two.

But what do I expect? For Steve to jump happily in on a bandwagon that didn't belong to him? Duh. She had to remind herself that this time she was on her own. Rob didn't have any say or anything to do with the baby and neither did Steve.

Her mom and dad had bought furniture for the baby while they were there during Christmas time. Sandy's limited income on her own could not afford pricy merchandise. She didn't expect Steve to spend his money on another man's child.

Sandy had tried to prepare herself for this moment, but now that it had arrived, she was gripped with anxiety. She turned pale and her heart pounded furiously at the sight of the processor, who was handing her the divorce papers. It was heart-wrenching for her to read the document formally served to her by the court. Her hands felt clammy and shaky as she signed the papers. Tears streamed down her cheeks, and she started sobbing as soon as the processor left. She was relieved Steve and the children were not there to witness her falling apart. She started to get a terrible headache, so she took a couple Tylenol caplets and went to bed. She cried herself to sleep.

It was just a matter of waiting when she and her baby-on-the-way would be good enough to move out. She didn't want to contest Steve for wanting to be the custodial parent for Sheyenne and Taurea. She would have them every other weekend according to the divorce decree.

The hardest thing for Sandy was the children. They hadn't yet been informed of what was happening to their family. So far, when they had asked her why she had been sleeping in a separate room from their dad, she told them a lie.

"Mommy needs to sleep in the other bedroom because it has a higher bed. With my big belly, it's easier to get up and down on it than on the one in our bedroom, which is much lower." She figured the children were satisfied with her answer, for they didn't ask more questions. She was also glad they didn't ask why their Mommy and Daddy don't hug or kiss each other anymore.

CHAPTER 49

M om," Sandy said, jostling her sleeping mother. Her mother had been sleeping in Taurea's bedroom since her arrival five days ago, "I think it's time for me to go to the hospital. My contractions are getting closer together."

"Okay, Punkin'. What time is it?"

"Two o'clock. Both the girls are still asleep in Sheyenne's room." Sandy tried not to panic, but her contractions were now every two minutes apart. After she brushed her teeth, she put the bag she had gotten ready a week ago into the living room. She went to knock at Steve's door. The contractions were giving her fits. By the time Steve opened the door she was grimacing and squirming in pain. Steve's immediate reaction was to get ahold of her.

"What's the matter? Are you okay?" Steve was clearly overcome with concern as he led Sandy to sit on his bed.

She was panting, saying, "I'm having ... strong contractions, and ... I think I'm ready to ... deliver this baby."

"Okay, just have to get dressed and brush my teeth," Steve said without hesitation.

"Mom said she will take me there."

"Is that what you want?"

"Well, ah ... *ooh*." More panting, grimacing, and squirming. "No, but I thought you didn't want to get involved with this at all. Ooh!" Even in her pain, Sandy noticed Steve's nakedness, which made her feel uncomfortable—only because of their impending divorce, which was filed by the person who was talking to her at that moment.

"Well, we can't be arguing about it now when, clearly, you're in so much pain. Besides, I know exactly my way to the hospital and my way around there, so it makes more sense that I should be the one to take you," he said while he was throwing on his clothes. When he went to the bathroom, Sandy struggled to stand up from the bed. When she was able to, she went to see her mother to inform her that Steve decided to take her to the hospital instead. Her mother looked relieved. She said she totally agreed with Steve's decision.

"Okay then. I'll stay with the children."

"Let's go! Do you have a bag ready?" Steve said as he rushed out of the bedroom with keys in hand.

"I do. It's in the living room." Steve went to the living room to fetch it.

"Good luck, Punkin'. I'll be praying for a speedy and safe delivery." Both Steve and Sandy thanked her and said goodbye in a hurried way.

It was the first time Sandy had been in Steve's new truck. She admired it silently in between her moaning, panting, and squirming.

Steve turned the key, and the truck responded. Sandy was surprised at how quiet the engine was. Steve's left hand was on the steering wheel, and his right hand was on the back of her neck as he massaged it. She appreciated him massaging her. It helped soothe her labor pains. She noticed Steve was speeding. "Honey." *Oops.* She misspoke again.

"Yes?"

Sandy didn't notice Steve being upset by it. "I know you want to get me to the hospital quickly, but we don't want us et stopped by a security police, either."

"Well, if I get ticketed, so be it. With the way you're squirming in pain, I need to get you there right away. The security police can follow us all the way there." All the while he was driving, Steve kept one eye on the road and the other on her, Sandy observed. Sandy didn't feel Steve's anger toward her at that moment. Instead, she only felt his love, empathy, and support.

She was grateful for everything Steve was doing for her. *He may not have been there for me emotionally, most of the time, but I know I can count on him at times like this. It's admirable of him for letting go of any ill-feelings toward me in order to help me in my time of need. Oh! How I wish there's some way I could right the wrong.*

At the hospital, Sandy and Steve were rushed to the birthing room. Her contractions were now a minute apart. The head nurse asked another nurse to summon the on-call OB doctor. The nurse had Sandy change into a hospital gown and lay on the birthing bed. The nurse put two belt monitors around Sandy's belly—one to monitor the baby's heart, the other to monitor her contractions. The nurse also attached an oximeter and a vital sign monitor to Sandy. Another nurse came to attach an IV fluid. The nurse had a hard time inserting the needle into Sandy's vein on her wrist. After the third try, the nurse became frustrated.

"Misses Richardson, please try to relax," she said in a stern voice. "I can't put the needle in if you tighten up like this."

"But I'm not trying to tighten up. It's just happening without my control. I'm sorry!" Sandy was on the brink of crying. Frustrated too, since she was told not to push yet when, in fact, she was *so* ready to push. Sandy tried to focus on relaxing. After several attempts, she was able to relax her muscles, enabling the nurse to insert the IV needle. As that nurse was leaving, the head nurse was returning.

"Sandy, kindly scoot down lower, so I can measure your dilation."

"With the way you are huffing, panting, grimacing, and squirming with each contraction, Sandy, I can tell you're ready to deliver even before checking your cervix." She did so, as a matter of proper procedure. "It's nine centimeters. Like I expected. Is Doctor Morgan here yet?"

"Not yet, but he's on his way," the other nurse said.

"The doctor is not yet here, so try not to push yet, Sandy. Do your breathing techniques. Inhale deeply, and then blow. Hoo … hoo … hoo. Again. Breathe in. Then blow. Hoo … hoo … hoo …"

"I can't hold it anymore! Hmp! … whoh … whoh … whoh … I want to push now!"

"Not yet … *not yet*," the nurse pleaded in a panicked tone. Large beads of sweats formed on Sandy's face.

Steve, who was by her side, holding her hand, asked for some tissue paper. As soon as an aide handed him some, he dabbed the sweat off Sandy's face. Sandy tried to do the Lamaze breathing techniques along with the nurse, but the baby was definitely ready to be pushed out. After a while with the breathing technique, Sandy started to hyperventilate.

"I'll deliver the baby myself if I have to," Steve offered.

Dr. Morgan walked in.

"Am I so glad you're here now, Doctor Morgan," the head nurse said. Sandy was also relieved. It meant she could stop blowing and can start pushing.

"Hello, Doctor Richardson," Dr. Morgan said, "What a surprise to see *you* here."

"Brought my wife to deliver our number three."

"Our, number three"? Sandy wondered in appreciative disbelief.

"Yes, of course," Dr. Morgan said. With one look at the opening between Sandy's legs while putting on his gloves, he said it was time to deliver the baby. "The next time you feel the urge to push, I want you to push. And push hard."

Sandy was only too happy to obey. They were the words she was longing to hear since she set foot in the birthing room thirty minutes ago. It took only three hard pushes and the baby came out crying.

CHAPTER 50

"Oh, hi, Babe," exclaimed Clint when Makenna emerged from her home office. He was seated on the living room sofa reading a Hunting magazine.

"Hi, Babe. Didn't know you're back. You snuck up on me."

"Didn't want to disturb your writing. Chloe will be at the birthday party for hours."

She went to kiss him and then snuggled next to him on the sofa. "I think I'm done writing for today. The chapter I've just written wore me out."

"Why?"

Makenna laid her head on Clint's lap and then looked up at him while he looked down at her. "Well … you know how I haven't been able to experience the joys of pregnancy and delivering a baby?"

Clint started caressing her face. "Uhuh? I remembered you not wanting children right away because of your new career at CNN. Then you got shot and almost died. Long recovery ensued. After recovery and quitting your job at CNN, instead of starting a family, you wanted to divorce me.

Makenna pinched him.

"Ouch! What's that for?"

"You know what's for."

"Oh. Now, you made me lose my train of thought."

Makenna took over. "I decided to stay with you and was looking forward to getting pregnant. Alas, I was then diagnosed with endometriosis. The doctor informed us that I might not be able to conceive because of it. I was pretty devastated then and still am. And again, now with my recent bout with cancer and chemo treatments. I'm now one hundred percent sure not having a chance of getting pregnant. And, don't want to anyway. Who knows what effects those chemo treatments have on babies? Don't want to gamble." She sighed. As an afterthought, she said, "It was ironic that I was diagnosed with endometriosis a few months after we brought Chloe home."

Even though Clint wasn't talking, Makenna appreciated the sympathetic and understanding expressions his eyes and facial expressions were showing her. She was also appreciative of the way he was allowing her to have her monologue. She took his right hand and kissed it.

Clint continued to caress her face, including her neck and shoulder. "I felt pretty dejected, too, Makenna. Me, being an only child and with both my parents gone, I was hoping for us to have five kids …" He took Makenna's left hand and kissed it.

"Five kids? Why five?"

"Don't know why. Five sounds like good a number to me." He flashed her his handsome grin.

"Oh, Clint, I'm so sorry. I've never known 'til now what you've been feeling all this time." She gave him a morose face, then lifted herself and gave him a kiss. "Thank you for giving us Chloe." She kissed him again before laying herself back on his lap.

"You're welcome."

"I think God is punishing me for having put my career ahead of family," Makenna said.

"Oh, Baby, don't say that. Things happen in our lives, which we can't have control over. Look, if you didn't follow your dream of being a field reporter for CNN and have babies instead, you'd be wondering 'what could've been' all your life. You'd be miserable and be blaming me for it."

She raised an eyebrow to him. "Well, are you blaming me then for us not having five kids?"

"No, Darlin', I do not. My inner feeling tells me that God had created the different circumstances in our lives to keep us from having five kids." He snapped his fingers with a puzzled look. "So, you still didn't tell me why the chapter you wrote wore you out."

"Oh, yeah, well … so, anyway, when I was writing the labor and delivery scenes, I felt and experienced my character's emotional upheavals … labor pains … her thoughts. When her baby was born, I felt her relief and tremendous tiredness after that. It was bizarre. That's why I said the chapter wore me out."

"Ah … I see. If you, the writer, was affected, your readers will surely be." He picked up his iced tea drink from the end table to his right. "Would you like some?"

"No, thanks. I think I'm going to get myself some hot cappuccino, instead. Yes, it's my hope for my readers to feel my writing as well." She got up to go to the kitchen. When she returned, she sat on the other end of the sofa with her back against the armrest with her legs stretched out. She held her mug and sipped her cappuccino every so often.

"Just dawned on me, Baby. How were you able to write all the labor and delivery scenes? Did you watch YouTube videos?"

She laughed. "Nope, but I suppose I could have. When I was in my senior year of high school, one of my friends asked me if I could be her Lamaze partner, and if I'd accompany her when she delivered her baby."

"Why?"

"She and her boyfriend broke up when she was three months pregnant. Her boyfriend wanted her to abort the baby, but she wanted to keep it. Her mother was supposed to be her Lamaze and birthing buddy after that." Sandy took another sip.

"So, why didn't she?" His eyebrows wrinkled. He also drank some of his tea, and took a handful of cashews from a plastic jar.

Sandy sipped more cappuccino before she spoke. "Unfortunately, Honey, her mom died suddenly in a car accident when she was five months pregnant. She then asked me. I felt deeply honored that it was me she asked and not her other friends. From what I'd witnessed, along with the info I got from Mom on pregnancy, labor and delivery, I was able to write about them in my novel...with confidence."

CHAPTER 51

It had been three months since Makenna resumed her writing. It was sluggish the first two months, for she tired easily. Eventually, though, she regained her appetite, and soon started gaining some weight. When she reached her ideal weight, she also regained her full energy.

Makenna was getting antsy about finishing her novel, so she started writing as soon as Clint and Chloe left the house. She got her mug filled with some hot water, dropped a bag of green tea in, and then stirred in a teaspoonful of honey before sitting herself in front of her computer.

✻ ✻ ✻

Sandy had just disembarked her plane and was following the other passengers to the terminal. When she emerged, she saw a petite woman with silver hair holding up a sign with Sandy's name written on it. Sandy waved her hand and went toward the woman.

"Hi, I'm Nancy. Rob's secretary," the woman said.

"Nice to meet you, Nancy. Thank you for coming to meet me here."

"You're welcome. Do you have other bags?"

"No. I only brought this carry-on along with my handbag." They started walking.

"Would you like to go to Rob's house first or to the hospital first?"

She stopped walking. Nancy stopped also. "I had hoped that, by now, he'd be home recuperating. How is he doing?"

"Well, not great. He turned for the worse three days ago."

"What do you mean?" Sandy started tearing up. Nancy put her arm around her to comfort her. "I'm sorry for being emotional. Kindly take me to the hospital first?"

"Sure." They walked again, got in the elevator and got off on the third floor of the airport's parking garage.

During their drive to the hospital, they made conversations. "Were you the one who wrote the letter I received in the mail," Sandy asked.

"Yes. He wasn't able to write, so he dictated what he wanted me to write."

"Is he married now?"

"Oh, no. He often talked about a woman he loved in North Dakota. I didn't know until recently that you're that woman."

Sandy was touched. "What else did he say about me?"

"I asked him why he didn't marry you if he loved you that much. He said he couldn't marry you because you were already married."

"I bet you're pretty disappointed in me?"

"It's not my place, Sandy, but I hated seeing him hurting inside over you."

"I didn't know he loved me. Do you know what he said the last time we spoke? He said that I should refrain from calling or contacting him because he didn't want to get involved with anyone else, especially with me. He said that *he didn't love me.*"

Sandy started weeping. Painful memories of Rob's words had finally diminished over time. But now the heartache had come back to haunt her. A dagger—stabbing her in the heart once again.

"Do you know what his words did to me?" Sandy blurted out, "They hurt me terribly and scarred me for life!" Sandy continued to cry.

"I'm so sorry, Sandy. But he really loves you, you know?"

"Well, he sure had a strange way of showing it," Sandy said with a snort.

Nancy was silent for a few minutes, but then said, "By the way, he kept up with what was going on in your life and your daughter's. He has you and your daughter in his will. You'll find out all about it through his lawyer."

"He did? So, he knows he has a daughter, yet he chose to be an absent father?" Anger sprang from her voice and panic swept over her. "And, why are you talking about a Will and a lawyer? Is he that bad—about to die?"

Nancy was crying now also. "Two weeks ago, we thought he was finally out of the woods. That was when he had me write you a letter. He also had his lawyer re-write his Will that day. He said he wanted those two things done just in case.... That's the hospital where he's at," Nancy said as they exited the highway and went toward the hospital's parking lot.

Sandy looked out and read 'Flagstaff Medical Center' on the side of the three-story high building. When Nancy parked her car, Sandy checked herself in the mirror. "Oh, my gosh, I look horrible. May I apply some fresh powder before we go?"

"Oh, sure. Actually, I need to do the same."

They soon exited the car and walked in silence. Nancy took Sandy to Rob's room after first checking in at the nurse's station. Sandy was shocked and saddened at the sight of him. She couldn't bear to see him in his condition. She turned away and put both her hands in her face as she cried. Nancy went to hug her.

"I'm sorry for crying again."

"Shh ... It's okay," Nancy said, as she placed a consoling hand on Sandy's shoulder.

"Is he comatose?" she said in between sniffles.

Nancy pulled her in with both arms, patted her back. "Yes, but it's medically drug-induced."

Sandy jerked her head back to look Nancy in the eyes. "Why and what does that even mean?"

Nancy released her. "Let's have a seat there," she said,

motioning toward the cushioned bench by the window. In a soft voice, she said, "Well, the way it was explained to us three days ago, was that Rob's brain became very swollen. Rob was in excruciating pain from the swelling, so they had to put him into a coma until the swelling subsides. The doctor explained further that, by doing so, it lessens the stress to Rob's body while waiting for the swelling to go down."

"Oh, *wow* … so, I guess he'll never know that I even came to visit him."

"Well, when I came to visit him this morning, Doctor Dugan was doing his rounds. He informed me that the swelling is gone, so he plans on having Rob's ventilator removed sometime today. But before he can do that, he said Rob needs to be weaned off of the propofol medicine for at least six hours."

"What's a propofol medicine?" Even though Sandy was in the medical field, she was not familiar with it.

"That's the medicine they're giving him to induce coma."

"I see. No wonder I've never heard of it. It's not a drug we test in the lab where I work. It's not a drug I'd studied at school either." Sandy sniffled and shifted in her seat.

"Doctor Dugan also said that he was happy with Rob's improvements overall, considering …"

"Considering?"

"Considering all the different surgeries Rob had to undergo. Aside from the emergency trauma team who worked on him initially, there was also a team of surgeons in the O.R. who worked on him, too. They worked on his head, heart, lungs, liver, kidney, face, and all of his broken bones. It seems like they did a total overhaul on him. Poor man. He was a *mangled mess*."

"I'm overwhelmed just by hearing about it. It's amazing he survived it all. I wish I could give him a big hug right now to comfort him and to let him know how much I care."

"I know," Nancy said, an endearing look on her face.

"Do you know what time they started weaning him off the drug?"

"No, I sure don't, but I can go ask his nurse."

"Sure, if you don't mind asking. Do you think he'll recognize me and know that I'm here when he wakes up?"

"I hope so."

That statement saddened Sandy to tears. She *hopes* so? Hardly encouraging. Sandy took some tissue paper from her purse and wiped her eyes. She forced herself to face Rob's condition.

A nurse came into Rob's room. "Elayna, good thing you're here," Nancy said.

"Why?"

"Well, Doctor Dugan told me this morning that Rob is going to be off the ventilator sometime today."

"Yes, that's right. He wanted him off the ventilator at two p.m. Doctor Dugan's instruction is to start weaning him off the propofol six hours before two, which I started doing five hours ago."

"I've noticed that all the IV fluids are hardly flowing. Are they supposed to be that way?" Sandy said.

"Yep. I adjusted the flow for each to decrease the amount of fluids he's receiving in preparation for his extubation."

"Why?" Sandy and Nancy said at the same time.

"It's important that he's not overly hydrated before extubation. We don't want him end up with too much fluid in his lungs, which might cause him to choke as we remove the ventilator."

Sandy was satisfied with her explanation. She didn't ask any more questions after that and neither did Nancy. While the nurse was busy checking Rob and taking notes of his vital signs, Sandy was busy observing. She noticed the many monitors and machines attached to Rob. Their numbers were always changing, lights blinking, along with their beeping sounds. Sandy couldn't help noticing the multiple types and sizes of IV fluid bags hanging on four different poles. Two on each side of his bed. Rob's both arms had IV lines where fluids were going into. His respirator hissed at steady intervals.

Sandy noticed that Rob's chest and head were all wrapped

with white wraps. She wondered if he was missing his lower limbs, but Rob's feet twitching under the blanket every now and then put her mind at ease. It disturbed her, though, to see both his wrists tied down to the sides.

When Elayna left, Nancy said, "Sandy, I'm going to the waiting room while you visit with Rob."

"Thank you."

Both railings on Rob's bed were up and Rob's right wrist had an IV line also. So, Sandy put the left railing down before sitting on a chair next to the bed, facing him. Sandy held Rob's left hand between hers, caressing the top part of it.

"Rob, I'm here. Can you hear me? I'm so sad to see you like this. If you can hear me, kindly squeeze my hand?"

No response.

No matter, she continued giving Rob's hand a gentle massage and continued making small talk, all the while watching his face for any movements.

"I'm told that you already know about our daughter. Her name is Kenya, and she's absolutely adorable. She has a lot of you in her. She may not be the boy you might have wanted, but she sure is a fighter. Gosh, at age one she went through a major heart surgery to repair a large hole in her heart. She's now a healthy, rambunctious and intelligent six-year-old. You'd be very proud of her."

She felt a slight squeeze on her hand. She also noticed Rob's eyelids move. "Rob? Can you hear me?" Rob squeezed her hand, this time tighter.

"Have you heard everything I've said?"

Again, he squeezed. Sandy was ecstatic. She shed tears of joy. She kissed his hand. "I'm so glad you know I'm here and that you've heard everything I've said."

Rob squeezed her hand again. Instantly, he started gagging and coughing in a violent way. The monitors started beeping. Sandy panicked. She started out straightaway to the nurses' station, but Elayna was already on her way.

"What happened?" Elayna asked while rushing to attend to

Rob. She suctioned Rob's saliva.

"Well, I was seated on that chair holding his hand and was talking to him, even though he was still out of it. When he was coming to, he started gagging and coughing violently like that. He tried to reach for his ventilator. I'm glad his hands are tied down," Sandy said. *Now I understand why his hands are tied down.*

Scott, a male nurse, rushed in. "Hi Rob, buddy, try to relax," he said. "We're going to take your breathing tube out today."

Dr. Dugan arrived in the room soon after. After a quick evaluation, he said, "Have you given him some morphine yet?"

"Not yet," Elayna said, "I was to give it to him thirty minutes before two p.m. like you've prescribed. Unfortunately, he's waking up an hour before that."

"Yes, yes, of course. Kindly give him ten milligrams through his IV right now." Elayna did what was requested, while Scott was still trying to soothe and hold down Rob. Dr. Dugan wrote notes on Rob's chart before putting on a pair of gloves. After 20 minutes, Rob calmed down to an acceptable level.

"Feeling better, Rob?" Dr. Dugan asked. Rob nodded his head ever so slightly. "Are you ready for us to remove your ventilator tube?" Rob nodded again; eyes still closed.

Sandy was standing away from the foot of the bed, giving the others room to move around. Elayna suctioned more saliva Rob's mouth.

"Rob, I'm going to deflate the balloon of your respirator. While I'm pulling the tube out, I want you to keep coughing hard, so you won't choke, okay?" Dr. Dugan pulled out the tube. As soon as it was removed, Elayna suctioned more saliva. Rob still coughed after the tube was out, but not as bad as earlier. Sandy was certain the morphine helped minimized the irritation and the pain.

CHAPTER 52

After Rob was stabilized, Dr. Dugan checked him over, listening to his heart, lungs, and abdomen. He also checked his wounds and feet. "Kindly wiggle your left big toe." Rob wiggled it. "Now the right big toe." Rob wiggled it. "That's good. Based from numbers one to ten, how do you rate your overall pain right now?"

Rob thought for a minute. "Four or five," he whispered.

"How about your head?"

He thought a minute again before he spoke. "Two."

"*Wonderful.* Your wounds are continuing to heal well. This is probably not what you want to hear right now, but we still have to take you back to surgery next week to repair your hips. We weren't able to completely fix your hips before because the damage was less serious than the others at the time of your initial surgeries. But now, it has to be addressed."

"I don't … think I can … take another … surgery, doc."

"But if we don't repair your hips, you won't be able to walk properly, and you'll be in constant pain."

Rob wheezed in dismay.

"We'll discuss it more later, Rob. For now, just relax." Rob nodded even though his face revealed he was not happy about the news.

After the three left, Sandy came closer to Rob. His eyes were opened. Sandy went to fetch the chair she was sitting on earlier and placed it beside Rob's bed again.

"Sorry ... you had to witness ... all that," Rob said.

"Don't apologize, Rob. I'm okay with it. Just don't like seeing you this way. I'm so sorry about what happened to you."

"Thank you ... thank you also ... for visiting me."

Sandy took Rob's hand to hers before she spoke. "You're welcome."

Rob gave Sandy's hand a gentle squeeze. "How are you?" With a faint smile on his still groggy face, he looked lovingly and longingly into Sandy's eyes. "Really good ... to see ... you." He took laborious breaths in between syllables, followed with pauses.

"I'm good, Rob. Really good to see you, too." She kissed his hand as her tears started to flow.

"Sorry ... you caught me ... at my worst."

"No worries, Rob, really. Just sad to see you suffering like this. I want you to be mentally strong, so you'll get better soon, okay?"

"Okay," he mouthed and then squeezed her hand. "You ... look ... stunning ... as ever. I'm glad ... you came ... I wasn't sure ... if you'd come. I thought, perhaps ... you were mad ... at me ... that you'd ... ignore ... my request." Rob was too exhausted to talk after that.

Unable to say anything further, Sandy looked at him with sadness and sympathy as tears cascaded down her cheeks. Her throat felt painful and constricted that no words came. Instead, she cried more. *What the hell am I doing here? It could have been much easier if I'd just brushed him off completely.*

Sandy coughed to clear the huge and painful lump in her throat, restricting her speech. "To be honest with you, I had agonized for days what to do after receiving your letter ten days ago."

Sandy recalled the letter in her mind:

September 15, 2006

Hello Sandy,

As I lie in this hospital bed all mangled, wired, bandaged, tied up and down, with IV lines on both arms, and unable to move, I can see my past and present life being projected on the ceiling above me. It's like watching myself in a movie, and I don't like what I see. I realize that I haven't been very nice to some people, especially to you.

You've been the kindest, sweetest, and the most sensitive person I've ever encountered in my life. What I'd said over the phone seven years ago was all untrue. In reality, my heart and soul told me that I loved you and still do. You have a wonderful family, and I didn't want to be the cause of a family problem or a family break up, so I had to be the bad guy. I want you to know that I never stopped thinking about you and never stopped loving you. I hope you can find it in your heart to forgive me.

I would like very much if you could visit me here in Arizona. In case I don't survive this tragedy, at least I can die in peace by making amends to the person I care most deeply about.

Loving You Always,
Rob

"I understand," Rob said, jarring Sandy out of her memories. She shook her head clear.

"I thought seriously about denying your request. But how could I, in good conscience, ignore your poignant and conciliatory letter?"

Rob became emotional. "Thank you, Sandy. And, please ... forgive me ... for having hurt you ... in any way." He took a deep breath.

Sandy was crying more now, kissing Rob's hand and putting it against her cheeks often. "Even though I've suffered tremendously through the years from your hurtful words and from your years of silence, I want you to know that I've forgiven you."

Rob's eyes moistened more. "Thank you. It means ... so much to me. I love you, Sandy."

She cherished his words. "I love you, too, Rob."

"I now can ... die in peace."

"Please don't talk that way. I don't want you to die."

"My body is ... pretty beat up, Sandy. I don't think ... it can take ... more surgeries. I've been in ... this hospital for over ... a month now, I'm told. Had lots of surgeries ... to repair this or that. You've heard ... the doctor ... tell me to have ... another surgery. I've struggled ... to hang in here ... until you arrived. I wanted ... to see you ... one last time ... in order to ask ... for your forgiveness, so ... I hung in."

Sandy kept on sobbing as she listened to Rob. "Please stop talking about dying, Rob. If you're going to die now, you're going to break my heart again." Sandy's tears were gushing. "You're going to get well, so you'll be able to meet your daughter. I'm begging you, please." She kissed his hand again.

Rob was now crying too. Tears running down the sides of his eyes. "Oh, Sandy, I can't ... can't bear to ... see you crying so, sweetheart. I won't talk ... about dying ... anymore." He wheezed. "Promise."

"Thank you." Sandy took some tissue from her purse and wiped her tears. She took some fresh ones out and then dabbed Rob's eyes and face.

CHAPTER 53

Seeing that Rob was breathless and exhausted, Sandy decided to give him a break. "Rob, I'll let you rest for now. We'll visit more later." Rob's eyes were closed as he nodded. Sandy got up and gave him a peck on the cheek.

"Thank you," he said. He managed to blow her a kiss, now that his wrists were not tied down anymore. Sandy blew him back a kiss before she left to join Nancy in the waiting room.

"How did it go," Nancy asked. She made a pouty face. "Aww, you've been crying."

"It went well, but it was very emotional. He knows I'm here. We had a good talk. We made up. I assured him I've forgiven him. I could tell he's pretty worn out just by talking, so I left him to rest for a while."

"*Wonderful.* And, I'm glad you made up and had a good talk. I'd like to talk to him, too, but I'll wait till after we get a bite. Ready for dinner? I'm famished."

"Yeah, I'm ready. Funny, I didn't feel hungry until now. But, may I use the restroom first?"

"Sure, the restroom is over there." Nancy jabbed a finger in the direction.

"Thanks." Sandy went and later emerged from the restroom all refreshed. No more red and shiny face.

"Hope you don't mind us eating in the hospital cafeteria, instead of going somewhere. Don't think I can wait long enough to go drive to some restaurant."

"Oh, no, it's fine. I love hospital food."

"Good. Shall we go?"

In the cafeteria, they enjoyed their food. They talked some more. "What does your husband think of you coming to see Rob?"

"He's not happy, of course, but he allowed me nonetheless."

"Your husband seems like a good man."

"Yes, he is."

"I suppose Rob had no chance."

"Rob and I would have had a chance if only he gave us a chance."

"Oh, yeah?"

"Yeah," Sandy said, bobbing her head. "Steve served me divorce papers before I delivered Kenya. But he promised my dad that he would allow me and my new baby to stay with him until I was strong enough to be on my own. However, things changed after Kenya was born. Kenya was born with VSD. My prenatal ultrasound didn't catch the defect prior to delivery, unfortunately. So, the doctor and I were shocked to find out about Kenya having VSD when she was born."

"VSD? What's that?" Nancy stabbed at her food and put it in her mouth.

"Oh, sorry. It stands for Ventricular Septal Defect, a form of congenital heart defect. If you've heard people talking about a 'hole in the heart,' that's what she had. There are many congenital heart defects. But there are two kinds most commonly seen—Atrial Septal Defect, or ASD, and Ventricular Septal Defect or VSD. Hers was the VSD kind. It was a large hole that had to be surgically repaired when she was only a year old."

"Oh, my. How is she now?" Nancy said before she drank some of her water.

"She's good and healthy now. But, for a while there, she was a sickly baby. She was so skinny and way underweight. Steve stepped up to the plate in helping me care for her. He became quite attached to Kenya. He also saw that I needed his help in our situation, to the point where he retracted his divorce petition. He even gave Kenya his last name from the start, and then began raising her as his own. He is the only father Kenya knows."

"That's so noble of your husband to do all that."

"Indeed. I'm forever grateful to him." Sandy took a bite of her mushroom burger with Swiss. "Hmmm...," she said, while chewing. She swallowed and then followed it with her lemonade. "Have to say, Nancy, this burger is very tasty."

Nancy grinned. "Glad you like it. I should try that next time. Going back to you and Rob, you're saying that if Rob was around during that time, that Steve would have gone through with the divorce?"

"I'm sure of it," Sandy said. "I truly made a huge mistake in my life. But I'll never regret loving Rob. I only regretted loving him because of how he treated me when I reached out to him. I risked everything for him, but he mistreated me in return."

Sandy started to tear up again, head lowered, tapping a forefinger on the table. She stopped a forming tear from emerging with her finger and looked back up at Nancy.

Nancy put her elbows on the table and rested her chin on her clasped hands, her head in tiny sway. "I'm so sorry, Sandy. I don't know what to say. All I know is that Rob really loved you and still does."

"Well, I sure haven't felt his love since that one night we spent time together. I wish that he had shown it all these years."

"The times that Rob and I would get to talking about things, the subject of you would often come up. He said that a few days after he left North Dakota, he almost went back to ask you to leave your husband and marry him. For days, weeks, and months, he struggled with those thoughts. It took a lot of will power and a lot of convincing by his buddy, Jason, to keep him from pursuing you."

"Is that so?" Sandy said before she took another drink.

"Apparently, Jason kept on reminding him that he'd be tearing your family apart. Then he'd be riddled with guilt in the end. 'Not a happy ending for everyone involved,' Jason admonished him. He also relayed to me the pain he went through when his wife ran off with a surgeon. He didn't wish it on anyone, including your husband. He said that if you had chosen to leave your husband on your own accord, then it would have been fine with him. But he wasn't going to break up your family."

Sandy was having a hard time fighting back tears. The information being divulged to her was tearing her apart. It seems like all I've done during this trip was cry, she thought. She hated herself for it.

"How would he expect me to leave my husband for him when he told me he didn't love me? Didn't want me calling him? Didn't want to get involved with me?" She wiped off her tears, then took another bite of her burger while still sniffling.

"He also said that many times he wanted to answer your calls and emails and beg you to go to him, but he held off. He said he set aside his wants and gave up his chance for happiness with you. It utterly broke his heart when he spoke to you so harshly, unkindly, and rudely when he finally answered your last phone call."

Sandy rocked back in her chair, threw her hands up and wide, then plopped them back on her thighs with a flustered flap of her lips. "*Geez.* I wish I knew all of this much sooner. All these years, I thought of him as cruel and heartless." Sandy winced and shut her eyes tight to prevent more tears from escaping.

"It's better late than never, right?"

"I guess."

"If for some reason Rob were to ask you to marry him, would you leave your husband for him?"

Sandy thought for a minute. She noticed Nancy observing her closely for her reaction, while waiting for her answer. Sandy put her hands on her lap and, simultaneously, looked upward as she inhaled deep and long. She lowered her eyes to Nancy, exhaling long and slow before she spoke.

"As much as I still love Rob, I can't leave my husband for him. Not after what my husband and I went through because of my infidelity. Through it all, my husband stood by me.

Sandy could sense Nancy's disappointment with the way

she was biting and pursing her lips.

"The love I feel for my husband has become much stronger because of what he's done and still continues to do for me and my children. He also has become much more loving and dedicated to me after we ironed out our issues and differences." Sandy drank some of her lemonade.

"I still would like to have a friendly relationship with Rob because of our daughter, Kenya," Sandy said.

"Code blue ICU4. Code blue ICU4," was announced overhead.

"Isn't that Rob's room?" Sandy said.

"Oh, my, yes. *Let's go.*"

They hurried to dump their trash and rushed to go up to ICU. When they arrived, Rob was surrounded by the Rapid Response Team. Flurries of activities were going on to resuscitate him. A doctor was applying the defibrillator on his chest. Another was waiting to intubate him. Sandy and Nancy were stopped from entering the room and requested to go wait in the waiting room.

"I have to call his brother, Tom," Nancy said. But when they arrived in the waiting room, Tom and his wife, Lily, were already there.

"I was about to call you, guys. Didn't know you're already here," Nancy said before introducing Sandy to them.

"Nice to finally meet you," Tom said, with Lily bobbing her head in agreement.

"Likewise, and thank you."

"What happened with Rob?" Nancy said.

"Well, we were visiting and talking with him for about fifteen minutes. Then he became very quiet. I thought he just fell asleep, until, all of a sudden, he gasped for air, maybe three times. After that, all the monitors started beeping and then his heart monitor beeped in a steady tone. That's when the nurses came and told us to wait out here."

"*Oh, my gosh,*" Sandy exclaimed. She put her left hand over her trembling lips as her tears started to form. Just then Dr.

Lemay, the doctor in charge of the Emergency Response Team, entered the waiting room.

"Are you Robert McCall's family?"

"Yes, I'm his bother," Tom said.

"May we sit?" The doctor looked solemn.

Sandy and the rest sat with worried looks on their faces, feeling anxious of hearing what the doctor had to say.

"It is with a heavy heart for me to inform you that Robert has expired. We've done everything we could."

"No!" Sandy cried. She went running toward Rob's room without asking permission from the doctor.

"Sandy!" Nancy called out to her. But nothing was stopping Sandy. Nancy and Lily followed her. Tom and Dr. Lemay followed as well.

"No, Rob!" Sandy said, sobbing while draping herself over Rob's lifeless body. "You *can't* die yet. You left me once already! Please don't leave me again!" She grabbed at her chest during a series of choked breaths. "Besides, you haven't even met your daughter yet." She was all-consumed in her despair, to where she didn't care about the scene she was displaying in front of everybody.

Nancy was also crying, but was trying to soothe Sandy. "Sandy, honey, he's already gone. It's time to let him go. He suffered enough. He's in a better place now."

"No! huh! huh! huh! ..." Sandy kept on sobbing while still hugging Rob's limp body.

Tom and Lily were in a tight embrace, trying to console each other as they cried together. Even the response team and the ICU nurses became teary-eyed at the sight of them, especially at the sight of Sandy.

CHAPTER 54

T he theater was full to capacity, Makenna observed. She, her mom, her dad, her sisters, Shay and Tori, were seated in the uppermost right-hand side of the theater. Makenna could see the other patrons crying and wiping their eyes. She and her entourage were also affected by the movie.

At the moment, the *big screen* was showing the scene where the Response Team and ICU nurses were leaving Sandy and the rest to grieve in private. As one of the nurses drew the curtains together and closed the door on her way out, the musical score started to play, signaling it was THE END of the movie. Soon, the credits started rolling.

Makenna and her company stayed behind after the other patrons left.

"Makenna," said her sister Tori, "I'm truly impressed with your story. So sad, so emotional, and *so intense*."

"So moving," said her sister, Shay.

"A truly heart-wrenching movie," her dad said.

"Thank you, *all*," Makenna said. Her pride soared from all the compliments received. "Mom and Dad, thanks for your inputs and for giving me the liberty to write this story in my own way, with my own spin."

"Mom, are you okay?" Makenna asked when she noticed her mom still crying.

"I'm okay, honey. I'm deeply touched. You've captured the real essence of my raw emotions. Even after all these years, I still hurt thinking about that segment of my life."

"I'm so sorry, Mom. I hope after this, we can all heal and move on for good. I hope I did you justice in my story."

"Yes, honey, you have. I feel your love and forgiveness."

"Mom, there's nothing to forgive. I'm thankful for your mistake. I wouldn't be here if it weren't for it. And, Dad, thank you for loving me and accepting me as your own. You're the greatest and the most wonderful dad, ever. I'm eternally grateful to you."

"Thank you, sweetie. I love you, too. You'll always be my baby daughter. I feel privileged to have been your father. Things happen for a reason. It must be fate." They came together in a loving embrace.

"Shay and Tori, thanks for being my sisters."

"You're welcome," they said together.

Richard moved toward his wife, took her in his arms and gave her a warm squeeze. "Cassie, honey, I'm so sorry for what you've been through, emotionally and mentally. I love you. You know? I kinda feel sad for the other guy. I feel guilty for keeping you all to myself."

Cassandra smiled at Richard's words. She looked up and gave him a kiss. "You shouldn't feel guilty, hon. I'm your wife; therefore, you have the right to keep me all to yourself. I love you, too. Thank you again for your love and forgiveness."

Makenna and her siblings looked on with love on their faces. They exchanged hugs with one another one more time, and left the theater with their hearts filled with gladness.

THE END

ABOUT THE AUTHOR

 Minda Budzinak is an American Veteran who served in the United States Air Force in the 1980s. After she left the military, she followed her husband wherever the military sent him. For more than thirty years, Minda has worked in the medical laboratory science field.

Minda is also a first-time Wyoming author of a new romance novel: *The Bigger Picture. The Bigger Picture* has been published on Amazon in both digital and paperback formats.

Drawing extensively from her considerable military and medical backgrounds, Minda was able to impart a high degree of realism into her novel. She says that her novel was inspired, partly, by real-life experiences of the many people she encountered in her life. Most of it, she says, was simply the product of her wild imagination.

During her spare time, Minda writes for her blog: "The Big Picture Blog" (https://loveandromance-tashabud.blogspot.com/). As a blogger, she has tackled fiction and non-fiction posts on various topics for more than 10 years.

Minda is a wife, a mother of two, and a grandmother of five. She loves singing as a hobby. She also loves to go on road trips, hiking and sightseeing, discovering all the natural wonders her home

State of Wyoming and neighboring States have to offer.

www.ingramcontent.com/pod-product-compliance
Lightning Source LLC
Chambersburg PA
CBHW020244150626
46552CB00020B/50